Carl Weber's Kingpins:
Cincinnati

Carl Weber's Kingpins: Cincinnati

Juliyette

www.urbanbooks.net

Urban Books, LLC
300 Farmingdale Road, N.Y.-Route 109
Farmingdale, NY 11735

Carl Weber's Kingpins: Cincinnati
Copyright © 2025 Juliyette

All rights reserved. No part of this book may be reproduced in any form or by any means without prior consent of the Publisher, except brief quotes used in reviews.

To the extent that the image or images on the cover of this book depict a person or persons, such person or persons are merely models, and are not intended to portray any character or characters featured in the book.

ISBN 13: 978-1-64556-689-2
EBOOK ISBN: 978-1-64556-765-3

First Trade Paperback Printing August 2025
Printed in the United States of America

10 9 8 7 6 5 4 3 2 1

This is a work of fiction. Any references or similarities to actual events, real people, living or dead, or to real locales are intended to give the novel a sense of reality. Any similarity in other names, characters, places, and incidents is entirely coincidental.

Distributed by Kensington Publishing Corp.
Submit Orders to:
Customer Service
400 Hahn Road
Westminster, MD 21157-4627
Phone: 1-800-733-3000
Fax: 1-800-659-2436

The authorized representative in the EU for product safety and compliance
Is eucomply OU, Parnu mnt 139b-14, Apt 123
Tallinn, Berlin 11317, hello@eucompliancepartner.com

Prologue

Ke'Lasia heard the knock at the door. Knowing it was the UPS mail carrier, she closed the top on her lotion, removed her shower cap, letting her hair fall down her back, tightened her robe, and went to answer the door. She had been waiting on her package all week and was happy it was finally there. She looked through the peephole on her tiptoes rather quickly before opening the door.

"Thank you so much," she gushed at the UPS mail carrier with a brilliant smile on her face.

"You are welcome. And very gorgeous might I add." The mail carrier smiled back a sparkling smile. It caught Ke'Lasia off guard. She had never seen a smile so damn attractive before. Most men had a nice smile, but this one on his face was practically panty-dropping sexy.

"Thank you." She blushed at his compliment.

"I hope I keep this route. Seeing you every day wouldn't bother me at all," he flirted further.

She winked at him and softly closed the door, not wanting to be rude or dismissive but not having time to feed into the flirting of the handsome man. Ke'Lasia wasn't currently involved with anyone, but she wasn't checking for anyone either. She didn't even have time in her life right now to be getting caught up and goofy over no dude.

She leaned against the door, clutching her rather small package to her chest. *That man is sexy as shit,* she thought before waving the thoughts of the good-looking man in the brown UPS shorts away. Then she proceeded into the kitchen to find something to open her package.

With the newly arrived package sitting neatly on the kitchen island, Ke'Lasia looked for her golden, engraved letter opener. It was a present she was allowed to have from her mother after her great grandmother passed away three years ago. It was the only thing she was allowed to have from her house the last day she visited it. It meant a lot to her, so she tried to keep it nearby all the time. She fumbled through her junk drawers, coming up with nothing. Remembering she may have left it upstairs in her library the last time she was in there, she decided finally on a knife instead.

The package sliced open without incident and she took out the shoebox she craved so much. A brand-new pair of Jimmy Choo stilettos were within her grasp. Her mouth slightly watered at the thought of slipping on her new shoes. She had to contain the excitement she felt inside so she could get them out of the properly protected wrapping. Bubble wrap adorned the entire box, so she had to use the knife again to slice through that, too. Almost slicing the top of the box made her stop. "Oh, shit!" she yelled at her mistake.

"No, no, no, no," she stammered over herself, trying to extract the box more carefully. She let out a breath of renewed joy, seeing she had saved the box. "Yes!" she screamed once the box was open.

The gold from the glittery, custom-made shoes sparkled bright. Gold glitter atop gold leather made the shoes look as though they were dripping gold from them. Jewels lined the stiletto heels, giving them more sparkle. Small gold spikes adorned the rim of the pumps, giving them the edge and uniqueness she desired. They were just like she pictured them. People told her an all-gold shoe would be too much, but she was instantly in love.

"Beautiful," she admired.

Rushing to the adjacent living room, she placed the box on the glass coffee table and propped herself at the edge of the white Corinthian leather couch her late husband purchased before his untimely demise to try her shoes on. As she leaned forward to strap the second stiletto shoe into place around her ankle, she felt hands around her waist and mouth. Startled, she tried to scream, but it was muffled by the strong hand covering her mouth now.

"Don't scream and don't fight. Just be still and this will go quick," the deep yet masculine voice whispered roughly in her ear. "You scream and I'll be forced to fuck up that pretty-ass face of yours," he threatened.

Ke'Lasia stayed as still as she could. His hand dropped from her mouth and found her breast. Ke'Lasia didn't scream. A tear ran from her eye and found its way to her chin. He wiped it away as though he cared. Then she heard his lips smack as though he was tasting something delicious. Going into survival mode, she relaxed. She allowed this stranger she still hadn't seen to push her legs apart from behind her. He eased her forward, pushing down on her lower back. She obeyed. Her hands found the glass coffee table and she rested there. To make sure he had no reason to harm her further, she put more space between her legs so that he had easy access. She heard him groan and it made her shudder.

Feeling his face press against her ass cheeks almost made her cringe, but she caught herself in enough time. She stayed relaxed and let the intruder take her in. He breathed her scent in over and over before he did anything else. Once he had his fill of her smell, he slid her silky bathrobe up over her hips. She could tell he was crouching, and she thought briefly that maybe she could knock him over enough to run. Then she remembered the Jimmy Choos that saddled her feet. She knew she would never make it to the door quick enough in them, so that plan was out. She was too far away from the knife she used to open her package, so using that was also out. The Jimmy Choo stiletto heel would make a stellar weapon but with them being on her feet, there was no way she would be able to use them unless he somehow ended up under her.

His hands found her ass cheeks and spread them apart. His grip was strong and determined. Her fight plan quickly left. She was trapped. There was nothing she could do but allow this man to take what he wanted and obviously, he wanted her. She felt his tongue find her skin. Warm and wet, he patted her asshole with his tongue in rapid succession before trailing her crack from top to bottom. He was really savoring her. Every touch, taste, and smell. He was enjoying this whole thing. She always thought that a rape would be brutal, harsh and life shattering, but this one was like making love to your mate. Only she didn't know who her mate was. The feelings confused her because although this was a stranger touching her body without permission, he was making her feel amazing. She could feel her pussy lubricating itself at every line of saliva that he left on, around, and in her ass. The shit he was doing felt good as fuck and she hated herself for thinking and feeling it, but she couldn't help it.

Another flick of his tongue and her nipples hardened. *Traitors!* She couldn't believe her body was accepting this stranger's assault and liking it! What kinda shit was this? She should be disgusted and outraged. Instead, she was turned on and horny as fuck.

His tongue moved from her ass to her pussy and her body responded by leaning more toward the coffee table, creating an even deeper dip in her back that arched her ass higher in the air. It gave him full access to her soaked pussy. He licked it and moaned. "Sweet. So sweet," he reveled. His comment didn't disgust her. It only turned her on more. *What the fuck is wrong with me?*

He flicked his tongue against her moisture, opening up her lips with only his tongue, and sucked up her feminine juices. He sucked as though he were dehydrated. Hard and quick, he sucked her hole and swallowed every drop of her. Moans escaped the lips on her face, and she was embarrassed. *Don't like this!* she yelled at herself in her head. *Hate it!* she instructed to no avail. Her juices just replenished, and he devoured those too. Finally, he lapped like a dog at her hardened clit that hung exposed. Shudders went through her body. He didn't relent until her body was weak with an orgasm. Two. Three. Four.

"Aaaaaaaaaaaaahhhhhhhhhhh!" Ke'Lasia screamed out in ecstasy.

"Ohhhhhhh. My. Gooooooooooood!" she screamed as the fifth orgasm escaped her body and she lost her footing. He caught her from his position on the floor and lowered her to his level. He laid her body out on her stomach, and she couldn't fight him. He pushed her robe out of the way and spread her legs again.

"Are you on birth control?" he asked her in his hushed tone that was barely above a whisper. She couldn't speak, so she just shook her head no.

She lay shuddering and quivering from her orgasmic high as he covered himself in a condom she heard him tear from its wrapper. Adjusting to her answer, he parted her ass cheeks and guided himself slowly into her asshole.

"No! No, please," Ke'Lasia begged. "I can't."

"You can. Relax," he demanded aggressively yet soothing.

Ke'Lasia did as she was told and tried her best to relax. The lubricated condom mixed with moisture from her own love juices made it easier for him to enter her in that area. Her hands gripped at the plush carpet she lay upon. "Oh, shit," slipped out of her throat as her eyes shut tighter and he filled her up inch by inch.

He was able to guide his whole dick into her asshole with ease, surprising her but making her feel a whole different level of gratification. He eased himself in and out of her until he felt the grip of her asshole loosen. He used his fingers to feel around and spread the juices she was creating from her to him as well. With the ease being created and enough lubrication to help, he picked up his pace. Ke'Lasia yelped at the new amazing feelings he was giving her. Strange but wonderful, she held her grip on the carpet as he devoured her hole. His moans turned to deep growls and her yelps turned to full blown screams. The faster he went, the wetter she got. The faster he went, the louder she got. His stroked turned deeper and harder, but his pace didn't break.

"Gotdammit! The fuck! Bitch! Shit!" Ke'Lasia yelled as her body once again reached climax.

He too released himself at the same time, letting out a loud, throaty growl that resembled a wild grizzly bear in its territorial stance. The growl elicited more excitement from Ke'Lasia and yet another orgasm released itself from her hold, sounded through the two-bedroom condo, and bounced off the walls. She felt as though the ground literally shook. Her face tingled and felt numb. She couldn't feel her nose or lips and her head pounded in painful joy. She hadn't released her breath yet from her last climax and she didn't know if she would.

His strokes, still full, slowed down to almost none as she finally found the breath to let out and the last of her climactic orgasm eased away, making room for the high she immediately felt. Before she could get her thought process back, she realized that the strange intruder had gone, and she was alone. Not able to process, she laid her head back down and let the high take over. In not even five minutes, she was fast asleep where she lay.

Chapter 1

A Week Later

"Girl, where the hell have you been? I've been calling and messaging you for a week. I thought you were dead," September exaggeratedly overdramatized her actual concern once Ke'Lasia answered the phone.

"It's just been a lot going on. I needed to take some time for myself."

"Time for yourself? Honey, we do not have that luxury. Did you forget we had Winterfest coming up? If I can't take a 'me break,' then you can't either."

"I'm sorry, September. You're right. I'm back now though. What I miss?" Ke'Lasia's thoughts drifted off as she filled her in on everything that she had skipped in the last week. She cared but couldn't focus.

Ke'Lasia's thoughts kept going back to a week ago and the stranger who found his way into her house and gave her the best sex of her life without permission. She had been so fucked up since the encounter. She felt like she was violated and should be in shambles, but the other part of her was extremely satisfied, relaxed, and wished she knew who the man was. A situation that was usually so messed up for so many people was intriguing to her. She couldn't stop thinking about it and wondering who the man could've been. Even how great the sex could've been had it been entirely consensual. One minute she felt bad for these thoughts, and the next, she was turned on and hot. It was a mess.

"Yes, September. I heard you. Friday on top of Carew Tower. I got it. I'll be there," Ke'Lasia half-heartedly convinced her friend and coworker before hanging up. She had to get her head back in the game. They had a photoshoot coming up in two days and she couldn't miss it. She knew that she just couldn't care about that right now.

Ke'Lasia walked away from the mirror where she was looking at herself. She was going over every curve on her darkened body, thinking about the weight she could stand to lose in certain areas. Her ass sat up great, so there were no complaints there, but her stomach looked like it was starting to hang a bit lower. She had been slipping on gym time, and it was starting to show. Her triple D–cup titties didn't do all that great in masking the protrusion from her midsection, but they were nice to look at. Hell, nice to carry around without the best bras, but still nice to look at. Her damn waist was almost nonexistent as small as it was. But all that did was put a dip in her lower back that gave her ass the illusion that it hovered in the air all by itself. Her thick-ass thighs still touched each other but that was just something else she still had to work on. No bruises, bumps, or blemishes were on her skin thanks to the plastic surgeon she saw last year though. The scar she had on her side from appendicitis as a kid was basically invisible and the scar on her right hip she got from a fight with an old boyfriend at 16 was also pretty much missing. She lived with that scar for many years. She could still see it like it was fresh even though she knew no one else could. The memories behind it weren't as dim as the scar but the pain wasn't as prevalent anymore.

Being full-figured didn't weigh her down the way it once had. Especially now that she was a model, though that didn't stop her from working on changing things whenever she made it to the gym. At 284 pounds, she knew that carrying it was never truly easy for any woman, even those who learned to bear it with grace. The men who had come and gone in her life had bolstered her confidence, countering the hurtful words of an old boyfriend who, years ago, had tried to convince her that no one would ever love her "fat ass" but him. He had been so very wrong. The niggas couldn't get enough of her.

Ke'Lasia smirked at her reflection as she licked her full, thick lips and bounced her heavy tits up and down with her hands. "Suck on it, bitch," she teased at the fleeting memory of his face. She turned her juicy ass to the mirror and smacked it before walking into her room to sit down on her bed.

From where she sat, she had a clear line of vision directly into her closet to the shelf where her pair of heavenly gold Jimmy Choos sat. The sad part about it was what she was thinking now. She got up and went to the closet to retrieve the shoes, carrying them downstairs. She knew it might seem odd, but she repeated the exact same ritual she had performed a week ago. Placing the shoes on the coffee table, she leaned forward and carefully put on each shoe, one at a time, just as she had before. She even took her time strapping them up, savoring every moment. Deep down, she knew it was a little irrational, but she couldn't help hoping he might appear again. She had never experienced anything like that before, and the memory lingered, pulling her back into the moment.

Ke'Lasia knew she should be scared and checking all the doors and windows to make sure no one could get in. Instead, she was quietly leaving certain doors and windows opened in hopes that the stranger from last week would find his way in again. She knew it was crazy.

She just couldn't help it. She had, for the first time in all twenty-nine years of her life, finally found out what the term dope dick was 'cause Lord knows she was addicted. From an encounter that should've never even taken place, she was gone off that shit. She didn't even know who he was, but she still wanted him. That had to be some goofy-ass, stupid-ass, desperate bitch shit, but oh, fucking well. She was willing to send up the damn Bat-Signal if she had to just to bring the stranger back. She didn't care how the fuck it seemed, sounded, or even was.

  Ke'Lasia had been acting strangely for about a week. The last time they spoke, she had been just as enthusiastic about the photoshoot as her friend. But now, it seemed like she couldn't care less. She was distant and inattentive, and this came after disappearing for nearly an entire week. It was baffling, and her behavior didn't make any sense. She knew how important this gig was for them. It was their best shot at securing spots in Winterfest. Travis, their photographer, booking agent, and also a male model on their label, had been dropping hints that they'd be part of it. However, he remained tight-lipped about whether their spots were permanent. As two newer models, they knew they had to put in maximum effort to make this opportunity count. And yet, Ke'Lasia's behavior made it seem like she was losing focus at the worst possible time. They were already being played because not only were they full-figured, but they were also from the hood, so they already had two strikes against them.
  It was hard enough breaking into the world of dancing when you weren't exactly the "ideal" size, but modeling was a tad different. They didn't even know they had modeling agencies for big girls. When September told her

friends that she was going to be a model, they laughed at her. She was crushed, and like them, she started thinking it was all a joke. Like one of them schemes people pulled on unsuspecting, dumb-ass victims and get them for all their money.

She was only five seven. Most models were like six feet, five foot eleven at least. Here she was, short and fat, trying to be a damn model. *Please. This shit couldn't be real for me, right?* Don't get her wrong, she was cute. She had green eyes that no one believed were hers, thick, full lips, hips, and ass. Her tits were only a C-cup, but she knew how to give the illusion of banging-ass cleavage. Her face was round, and her stomach wasn't flat. It didn't hang over her pants or anything like that, but she was wide. She had to buy her shirts a size or two bigger so that the length could make up for the width. Her hair hung down her back, but no one believed she was mixed with Native American. Ho-Chunk tribe to be exact. Her mother's Ho-Chunk blood running through her mixed with Yoruba blood from her father made her cheekbones high, her nose slightly pointed at the tip with a slender bridge, and her chocolate skin with a reddish-brown tint to it. She looked like she had a shine to her all the time, so imagine what it was like putting on any kind of moisturizer. She kept running into people who would ask her, "So what are you?" like she was some kind of species of animal. She didn't mind her mixture. It made her look different than all the other girls. So, when her headshots slid across the desk of the top people at Pretty Plus Sized Inc., they couldn't resist her. Her brother Grave used to tell her that she was cute for a fat girl. He was right, 'cause here she was now, modeling for the biggest plus-sized agency in Cincinnati.

Looking at herself in the camera on her phone, trying to decide on what Snapchat filter to use, she was pretty confident that they had spots for Winterfest. She just needed to hear the words. They were the closest bitches the agency had. They pretty much built their company around them.

Although they hadn't been directly invited to Winterfest yet, they were extended an invite to attend the photoshoot at Carew Tower that week. They couldn't miss this.

"What's up, boo?" September greeted her man, Raheim, when she got to his car and leaned in the window. He was so damn fine to her even though he was average to everyone else. She thought it was the street in him that had her seeing Idris Elba when she looked at him and not Tracey Morgan. He was an average height of five six and had an average build. He only weighed about 145 pounds soaking wet. He had braids for as long as she could remember knowing him that he only got redone maybe once a month. His swag stayed on point though! He rocked all the latest fashion from the top of the line, and he was paid. He drove the nicest shit, so he only messed with the nicest chicks.

The main thing that kept girls around Raheim was his paper. He stayed laced and he made sure the lady on his arm did too. He kept her pussy wet, throwing that cash her way, and even though his seven-inch dick barely scratched the surface for her fat ass, it was still good. It wasn't back breaking, but it was okay. In her eyes, he was still everything. What he lacked in the bed and in looks, he made up for in money and street smarts. And that's why she fucked with him the heaviest. He stayed three steps ahead of all these street niggas, which was why he made the most money and why he was pushing a Benz while the other niggas were still getting Ubers and Lyfts. He was all right with her. Long as he kept his dick in his pants and his cash in her purse, she was one hundred.

"What's up?" he shot back with attitude, not even bothering to look up from his phone. September was thrown off. What the fuck was wrong with this nigga?

"Damn. You just gon' act like I ain't standing here?"

"I said what's up. What else you want me to say?" He was acting real aggy, and she wasn't feeling it.

"Never mind. I see some of my girls. I'ma go holla at them since you ain't pressed." September stood for a few seconds longer to see if he would stop her, but he didn't. He just responded with an a'ight, like he didn't even give a fuck either way.

September waved him off and walked up to some of her girls on the other side of the street, leaving him sitting in his damn car by himself talking to who-the-fuck-ever was on the other end of his messages or whatever. She knew it was probably a bitch, but she wasn't even about to trip off that bullshit. She ain't have time to fool with him today. She was in a good mood and wasn't gon' let his selfish ass fuck it up. Ke'Lasia was already zoning her out, and she wasn't gon' let him do it too. *Fuck him.*

"What's up, bitches?" She walked up on Amber, Monica, and Tatiana.

"Oh, look, it's Ms. Fuckin' Hollywood and shit," Tatiana said when she saw September. September was already hip to Tatiana's hating ass, but she was tripping off of her. Tatiana had been a hater since they met. Nobody paid her no fuckin' attention.

"Fuck you, bitch. I ain't Hollywood yet. You see I'm still slumming it wit' you hoes."

"Nah. You slummin' it wit' that dog-ass nigga Raheim," Amber said, putting all the laughter in the conversation. September was the butt of some fuckin' joke they had all of a sudden, and she wasn't feeling that li'l shit.

"What the fuck that li'l shit supposed to mean?" September questioned.

"That means he over there arguing wit' Keisha right now on his phone. You just missed the bitch. She was just right here all up in his face, bitchin' and complainin' about how he ain't left you alone yet. You pulled up too late or you would've seen her." Amber spilled all the fuckin' tea in 2.5 seconds. She ran it the fuck down! September was salty, but she decided to play that shit cool as fuck.

"Girl, fuck him. I just told his ass to get off my dick anyway. That's why I was at the car. He stopped me on my way over here, tryin'a question me and shit. I told that nigga to mind his fuckin' business and walked off," she lied.

September felt dumb as fuck. She couldn't believe Raheim was still out here fuckin' around on her after all they'd been through. She was gon' show his ass though. Travis had been hitting on her for a few months and she thought it was time to give him some play. Let that dry-ass Raheim know she wasn't trippin' off him no more. Two could play this li'l bullshit game he was playing. She was just gon' do it better.

"Oh, yeah?" September laughed at something Monica had said that she only half heard. Her mind was on how she was gon' get back at Raheim, so she wasn't really listening. She shook them thoughts off until later and tuned in to the girls and the tea she had been missing since she had been gone working.

See, September still stayed in the hood, unlike Ke'Lasia. She was keeping her li'l funky-ass apartment until she stacked some real bread. She wasn't ready to give up her subsidized apartment and the few bills she paid to go pay all of them high-ass bills and shit like she did. September would much rather stay in her run-down apartment and be able to spend her money how she wanted to and save until she started making some real coins. That's why she still hung with Amber and them, so that she could stay in the know while she was gone. These hoes heard and saw everything. They were real street bitches and that was never gon' change for them. She? She wanted more. Just not yet. For right now, she was cool with being a classy hood bitch. Unless Winterfest came through. Then it would be fuck all this hood shit and she would be Hollywood for real on they asses. She was gon' get real boujee on these bitches, while she gave 'em her ass to kiss all while flying out the hood like she was on fire. She would leave them hoes so far behind that they wouldn't see shit but her fat ole ass strolling away. Fuck they thought? Shit. She had plans. She wasn't gon' be just another hood chick forever.

"Eh! C'mere!" Raheim called to September from across the street.

"Nigga, who name eh? The fuck." She leaned back against the wrought iron fence that surrounded the park they stood in front of on Vine Street and folded her arms across her chest with mass attitude. She ain't know who the fuck he thought he was talking to.

"He talkin' to yo' ass!" a voice called out from a crowd of niggas nearby before laughter erupted.

"You better take yo' ass on, too!"

"Right now!" Other niggas joined in on the teasing convo, but September stayed put. Fuck him and them, her stance said, because he called out again.

"Eh! Quit playin' wit' me girl. Come the fuck here!"

"Nigga, I ain't," She defied him further.

"Don't make me come get you."

"Or what?" She made a production of acting like she was getting even more comfortable against the gate and going against his demands. He had had enough of her shit, 'cause he jumped out his cream-colored Benz truck and slammed the door behind him. He had never slammed any door to that damn Benz. He marched straight over to her and snatched her ass smooth the fuck up. Throwing her over his shoulder while she protested and her girls laughed, he ventured back across the street.

"That's what the fuck you get!" a male voice called out, the crowd getting weak at her current situation. It was funny as hell to September. She just acted mad because the shit was cute to her. She loved pissin' him off. Especially in front of people.

He threw her in his truck and closed the door behind her. Before he could get in on his side though, a car came screeching past him and knocked him to the ground. The crowd of people erupted into angry yells. The Keisha bitch leaned her head out the window of the offending vehicle.

"That should teach yo' ass to play with me, ho-ass nigga!" She screamed into the wind about what the driver of the vehicle she was in had just done.

One of Raheim's boys opened fire on the car the two were in and shot the tires out. The car went careening to the side of the road and hit a pole. That's when September jumped out of Raheim's Benz and ran over to the car Keisha was in that was now curbside. September popped the passenger door open and pulled Keisha out, letting her fall to the ground. A swift kick to the gut made her ball up.

"Get up, bitch!" September screamed in rage.

September grabbed a handful of Keisha's hair and started swinging. She was expecting less of a fight from someone who had just been in an accident, but she was mistaken. Keisha came up fighting like a madman. Although September had her hair, it meant nothing. Keisha connected blow after blow to September's stomach, almost causing her to throw up on her. September held her own and connected with Keisha's face again, but that just fueled the next punch Keisha threw to September's side. September hit her twice in her mouth back-to-back. Keisha immediately started leaking blood just like September's hand. September had hit her tooth and split her knuckle open. It didn't stop the fight in either of them though. September swung Keisha by her hair to make her lose her footing. She did and went down hard. September went down with her from the force of her pulling toward the ground. They ended up in a roll, tussling over who would end up on top.

"Let my hair go, bitch!" Keisha yelled. September ignored her and hit her on the top of her head. "Argh!" she screamed out, biting September's arm.

"Bitch!" September howled in pain.

September screeched obscenities with every punch she threw. Like a champ, she threw them right back, neither of them caring what they hit, just trying to hit something. Neither one of them stopped swinging until they were forced apart and pulled to their feet. In her rage, September assumed the niggas from the hood pulled them apart to stand them up so that they could continue the fight fair. No such luck. September swung again once she found her footing, only for her left-handed jab to land square dead in the jaw of the police officer who was trying to separate them.

It was in that moment that September realized she had fucked up.

Chapter 2

Ke'Lasia hadn't heard a thing from September in a few days. Winterfest was tomorrow and they hadn't met with a stylist yet. She called her cell phone, and it went straight to the voicemail. She hit the end button just to redial her number right back.

"Dammit!" Ke'Lasia spewed in frustration. *Where the fuck is she?* She decided against calling her again. She just left a voicemail telling her to call her when she charged her phone up. Ke'Lasia hated when September let her phone die. Especially when they had business to take care of.

Ke'Lasia hung up her number and called Travis. "What's up, pretty?" he answered on the third ring, catching it right before she hung up.

"What's up, Travis. I was tryin'a call September's ass to see what was up with the stylist or whatever, but she ain't answering, so I figured I'd call you."

"Yeah, she locked up still. I thought you knew. You supposed to be here at noon though to get your outfits for tomorrow. You know that part, right?"

"No, I didn't but cool. I'll be there." Ke'Lasia hung up before hearing anything else he had to say. They made her sick with this last-minute shit but fuck it. It was money on the line, so she brushed it off and started getting ready. Luckily for her, it was only 9:00 a.m., so she could take her time to get ready.

Ke'Lasia went into the bathroom and turned on the hot water. She couldn't help being pissed even though she tried hard not to be. September was fuckin' wit' their money being locked up and she was salty her ass hadn't even called her to bond her out. Ke'Lasia kept asking her ass to move the fuck out the hood, but did she listen? Of course not. *Hardheaded-ass girl. Ugh.* This shit was messy as fuck before Winterfest, and Ke'Lasia was sure it had every single thing to do with that nothing-ass nigga Raheim.

Ke'Lasia sighed hard. She was straight-up stressed. She hadn't had any dick since Mr. Stranger that day and she was tight as hell and backed up. He hadn't shown back up either and she was salty about that, too. She took a quick glance at the Jimmy Choos before going back into the bathroom to take her shower.

The water was good and hot just like she liked it. She stood under the water with her eyes closed for several minutes, just letting the water soothe her aching body. She was aching bad for some action and didn't know what to do. She hadn't had a boyfriend since she had broken up with Charles's ass. That had been six long months ago, and she was due. The stranger had her feening since the other day. She was fucked up. *Fuck it.*

She ran her hands down her body until one found her nipple and the other found her exposed clit. She slid her wet fingers over her nipple until it was hard and then twisted it hard. It almost hurt but the pain was nice. She had to feel something. The fingers on her clit flicked back and forth against her until she felt her pearl harden up. The sensation sent her head back against the shower wall. She felt great to herself, but it wasn't enough. It wasn't a dick or a tongue and that was pissing her off. She squeezed her clit until it hurt. Once she felt the pain, she released it, then washed up twice before lathering herself in a Bath & Body Works scent that she had just gotten with her loofah to exfoliate before ending her shower.

She dried off in front of her bed and discarded her towel on the floor. She reached to the nightstand and found the same matching scent in lotion as her bodywash to moisten her skin. She started from her arms and shoulders to work her way down to her stomach, ass, and legs. Once she got to her feet, there he was again. Behind her. Taking in her scent with his nose. She heard the sharp intake of air right behind her ear and felt his breath on the back of her neck as he let it out. She fought herself not to smile. His hands covered her eyes like a game of *Guess Who?*

Just like last time, he eased her forward with a nudge to her back. He didn't say a word after he let her eyes go, but she still did as she was told. She eased forward into the bed. She looked over her shoulder to see who this mystery man was, but he quickly covered her eyes with his hand again and turned her head back around before she could see anything except a glimpse of the green shirt he wore. She couldn't even tell what kind of shirt it was, just that it was dark green. Hunter green. Maybe forest green.

As soon as her head was turned and faced down on the bed, she heard the condom open. A few seconds later, she was filled with all of him. Straight in. He didn't waste any time.

"Aaahh," she breathed a breathy moan as she relaxed and felt her pussy expand around him.

He was no small guy in that area, which only made her wonder what the rest of him felt like. Her warm pussy moisture collided with the warmth of his dick, putting her on the verge of climaxing early. She felt the veins in his dick pulsate even with the rubber on. It was fantastic. She had thoughts of being able to feel that monster in the back of her throat, but she knew there was no chance that he would let her yet.

He slowly rocked his hips against her ass cheeks, and she took that as a sign to rock back. She was a tad salty she didn't have on the Jimmy Choos like last time. They would've given her a few more inches to leverage so she could show out on this dick this time. Yeah, she was living in a $2,000-a-month condo, sporting the latest fashion and labels now, but she hadn't forgotten where she'd come from or what she'd learned from growing up fuckin' wit hood niggas. Designer clothes or shoes didn't stop her from knowing how to work a dick, bet that.

She rocked to his beat, clenching and relaxing her pussy muscles on each slide. Relax on the slide in, clench on the slide out. Even with him pulling halfway out, it still felt like his whole dick was inside of her. She was in heaven, total bliss, rocking against him. Like a slow rhythmic love song, they collided. Her ass bounced off his pelvis as he thrust harder into her, still not picking up the pace. He moaned every time her ass came crashing back down on him. She decided to take the upper hand and stay in the air on the next thrust. Letting him slide out of her and expect her ass to fall back, she switched it up. She stayed in the air and instead of rocking back, she began to clap her cheeks together right on the head of his dick.

"Fuuuuck," escaped his throat and fought through his teeth.

While she clapped her ass, he grabbed her hips and slowly slid back inside of her, letting her have her moment. The sensuality of it almost made her weak in the knees, but she caught herself. She stopped her clap to trade it for a bounce. Once his dick was all the way back in, she bounced her ass cheeks one at a time against his abdomen.

"Hell yes," he whispered. His voice sounded strong and sexy, but he never spoke above a whisper, so she wasn't sure if she was right. She didn't care though. She was just glad she was doing her thing, and he was letting her know it.

The cycle continued. He would pick a rhythm, and she would find a trick to match. By this point, she was in a full Chinese split with her stomach pressed to the bed and her ass arched up. Thank God for yoga and stripping. She had never been fucked like this before, so she knew true to life this dope dick had her hooked. She had to keep getting this and the only way to ensure it was to show completely out every single time. After a fuck like this, she was sure he'd be back for more.

He smacked her ass, bringing her back to the here and now. He smacked it hard, too. The sting of his hand made her toes curl in and pushed a small yelp out of her. He smacked it again and again. She liked it. She used her huge thigh muscles to bounce her up and down on the bed, adding more velocity to their entwining. She was sure he hadn't had no bitch fuck back like her. She knew he had to be amazed, too. She could tell by how gently he handled her that he wasn't used to fuckin' big girls though. That didn't bother her a bit. She was gon' teach him something today! The sex she put on him would have him struggling to stay away from her big ass. Hell, maybe big girls, period! They say once you go fat, you can't do shit wit' a snack!

His strong hand found her small waist and pulled her in. He wasn't close enough because the other hand found her hair, grabbed a handful with its fingers, and yanked her head back, too. He still pushed for the dip in her back though, so there she was, pinned to her own mattress in a larger-than-life Chinese split, held down and snatched up at the same damn time by a fuckin' stranger, and loving every single fuckin' minute of it.

The shoving of his dick inside her swollen but still extremely wet cave began to pick up. The shit was getting more intense.

"Yes. Dammit. Yeah. Fuck. That. Shit. Just. Like. That. Fuck. Ssss. Fuck. Yes. Yeah. Hmmm." He seemed pleased at the show she was putting on. Theatrical but nothing fake about it. This man had her guts feeling better than anything she'd ever had before.

His rhythmic beat sped up. He pounded his flesh into hers relentlessly. Tears sprang into her eyes. Her body began to slide off the bed toward the floor. Instead of letting her slide, he picked her up into the air, her legs outstretched in front of her. Her heels tried to burrow into the bed for any kind of grip as he held her fast and pounded his orgasm to full blast behind her. Her eyes remained shut tight, but the tears spilled past her eyelids and rolled down her face. The noises erupting from the both of them could be mistaken for a wild jungle or a car auction. Loud. Soft. High-pitched. Low moaned. Mumbled. Yelled. Screeched. Almost even in tongues. The shit was wild. Her climax burst through her body and felt as though it would explode out of her head from behind her eyebrows. The sex juices exploding from her body and shooting forward did her comforter no mercy. Her body started to go slack at the same time his strong arms pulled a grip on her so tight and his body went rigid. His manly orgasm came out in a long breath behind her. His forehead dropped to the back of her neck as he lowered her to the soaking wet spot on the edge of her bed. His hold didn't loosen once she was safely placed down.

Ke'Lasia couldn't help wondering what his naked body would feel like pressed against hers. "You're mine," his whispered rumble filled her ear as his arms began releasing their hold on her.

"Can I open my eyes?"

"No."

She kept them closed but her head sank. It was weird but her feelings were hurt. She waited until she felt as though he was gone to let new tears flow freely.

She got to the meeting early even though she had such a nice morning. She would have rather been lying in her high after her stranger had gone, but she had coin to make.

Travis was already there setting up. His crew scurried around, putting last-minute touches on everything. It was 11:15 a.m., so she still had time before the stylist showed up. She found a chair to plop down in and took out her phone. Her legs were still weak from the hours before she arrived. Deciding she would call the jail while she had free time, she looked up the number to the county.

"Hamilton County Justice Center, how may I help you?"

"Hello. I called to ask about someone locked up."

"When did they come in?"

"I'm not sure. I was just told she was there."

"Name please."

"Her name is September Wilson."

"And what do you want to know?"

"Could you tell me her charges?"

"No, ma'am. Not unless you're her attorney. Then you would have to come to 1000 Sycamore Street and prove that."

"Okay. Can you tell me how long you're going to hold her for?"

"No, ma'am."

"Can you tell me her damn court date?"

"She went to court this morning."

"Are they keeping her?"

"Her bond is ten thousand dollars. If you need help, you can go to a bail bondsman." She rattled off the number of the closest bail bond place. She thanked her and hung up.

"What the hell is wrong with you?" Travis asked, walking up on her with worry on his face.

"I just got off the phone with the Justice Center, and they said September's ass is gon' need ten thousand dollars to get the fuck outta jail."

"Okay? So, what's the problem?"

"I don't got that kinda money for no fuckin' bond. Shit. This shit crazy."

"Chill, ma. It's only actually one thousand. You only gotta pay ten percent of the actual bond amount." He laughed. "You must ain't ever had to bond nobody out before."

"Nah, I haven't. I don't fuck wit' jailbirds." Ke'Lasia rolled her eyes at him, letting him know that his slick lines he was about to add wasn't gonna work.

"Damn, Ke. Why you actin' like that?"

"Because you think you slick. You stay tryin'a flirt and shit but when I ain't around, you stay in September's face though. You cool, but you ain't that cool. Over here tryin'a give me cute li'l nicknames and shit like we like that." She rolled her eyes, but she couldn't front, it was cute.

"Stay in September's face?" He looked appalled. "Who? Not me! I mean, don't get me wrong, September cool and all, she even cute as fuck, but she like a li'l sis. I ain't checkin' for her like that."

"So what? You checkin' for me, huh?" He just smiled at her and winked his eye real smooth before walking away. That shit instantly made her pussy jump.

Travis's ass did look good. Good as fuck. And that smile with them white-ass teeth solidified that. Yeah, he had a few that were crooked at the bottom, but it ain't take away from the smile that could even stop the heart of Greek goddess Aphrodite. He was taller than Ke'Lasia but not huge. His build was really nice. Nice-ass shoulders and arms but not too big. Nice stomach and pecks but not cut up like a washboard or nothing. His waves were always dippin' in a hard 360 degrees like he slept in a durag to keep his shit on point. He had a nice peanut butter complexion that had you almost tasting him damn near every time he took his shirt off. She didn't miss the way those Speedos looked like he would bust out of 'em in his summertime swimsuit shoot either. She just wasn't checking for him like that. Even though his eyes looked like he could see your soul and were outlined by the sexiest set of eyelashes on a man that she ever saw. Even the tattoos that littered his body but covered his arms in whole sleeves looked lickable. Honestly, Travis was sexy as fuck now that she was looking. But she still wasn't looking too hard because Travis's ass wasn't fooling nobody. He and September had been checking for each other for a minute even if they didn't wanna admit it.

 Ke'Lasia shook her head, getting the thoughts of Travis far away from her and focusing on her wardrobe that the stylist had arrived with. It was Winterfest so the whole rack was littered with winter clothes even though it still wasn't cold outside yet. It was only August, so it wouldn't be freezing. Although they would be wearing winter clothes, they would probably be burning the fuck up. Playing with Cincinnati weather, it wasn't no telling what it was gon' feel like outside.

 "What size are you, honey?" Lando, one of the stylists, asked Ke'Lasia.

 "A twenty-four, twenty-six."

 "Oh, baby! I got the flyest piece for you, bitch! I mean, girl," he said, covering his mouth quick. Ke'Lasia laughed and let him know it was cool and that she wasn't offended. "Girl, my bad. I be forgetting I'm at work. Gotta keep my stuff professional, you know."

"Trust me, I know. But we cool like that. Me and my girl September call each other bitches all the time. It ain't shit. We don't trip off li'l shit like that. Just keep it cute and don't be disrespectful." She gave him the eye.

He understood fully and relaxed a li'l bit. Ke'Lasia liked him a lot. She was hoping they worked with him more often because Judy, the other stylist there with him who they usually got stuck with, was no fun. All she did was walk around with her straight face and hand out clothes. She also acted like she had an attitude any time they ain't like some shit. But Lando was cool. He felt like one of them.

Ke'Lasia finished up picking out her outfits wit' Lando and Judy, let Travis know what she decided on, then said her goodbyes. It was about 4:30 p.m. and she had to be at the bail bondsman by 6:00 p.m. if she wanted September out today. She grabbed her purse and hauled ass.

Chapter 3

September was going fuckin' crazy in the jail. She had been there all damn week waiting for these muthafuckas to tell her what they had on her. The judge OR'ed her at the arraignment on Tuesday, yet she was still there. She was getting more pissed off by the second.

Bang! Bang! Bang!

She pounded in the thick ass glass on the heavy-duty reinforced door that was in between her and the guards on the other side.

"Don't bang on the damn glass!" a guard shouted.

"I need to talk to somebody!" she shouted back. The lazy-ass guard got up and waltzed her ass over to the glass.

"What?" the guard asked with an attitude.

"What am I down here for? Is somebody gon' tell me what's up or what? Damn."

"Sit down and chill out. They'll call yo' name in a minute."

"Yo' mouth sho' is fly, Becky," September sneered at the guard.

"I got yo' Becky, bitch." The guard rolled her eyes hard as hell and walked away.

"Girl, what you tripping for? They gon' call you in a minute. You probably getting released. They usually only call people down here when they going to court or getting released. They tell you that you got court when they brought you?"

"Nah. They ain't say shit. They just called my name, cuffed me, and walked me down here."

"Yeah, you probably gettin' out then." The white chick just sat back against the wall like what she said was definite. She didn't know if she believed her or not, but she did chill a li'l bit just to see.

"You that model chick, ain't you?" the white girl spoke up.

"What?"

"Ain't you a model? For that magazine, um, Cincinnati something? Something Cincinnati? Girl, I don't know."

"Yeah. That's me. What's up?"

"Girl, you be doing some cute shit. How you get in there?"

"In where? The magazine?"

"Girl, yeah. I'm tryin'a get in there too."

September looked at her like she was crazy. This bitch was sitting here lookin' dirty as fuck. Her flip-flops were clearly old, and her shorts were about two sizes too little. Her legs were visibly dirty, too. But looking at her face, she wasn't half bad. With a li'l makeup she could've been cute.

"Well, what's yo' name? You did some work before?"

"Me? Girl, hell nah," she laughed. "I was talking shit. Ain't nobody 'bout to hire my big ass to be no model." She tried to wave off the conversation.

"Why not? They hired me."

"Yeah, but you cute as hell."

"All you need is some fly-ass clothes and some makeup. Anybody can look the part." She ain't want to hurt her feelings by telling her she would need a lot of makeup but whatever.

"You really think so?" There was hope in her eyes and she couldn't bring herself to crush it.

"Yeah. I think so. I got hired through Pretty Plus Sized Inc. They only deal with plus-size girls like me and you."

"They work wit' white girls too?"

"For real, for real, I don't even know. I ain't ever seen one but I don't see why they wouldn't." She shrugged her shoulders. Shit, she figured it was worth a shot. At least she wouldn't think she was tryin'a play her. When she asked them and they shot her down, at least she'd know she was keepin' it one hundred.

"Waters!" The bitchy-ass guard called September's last name. "You September Waters?"

"I'm the one standing here, ain't I?"

"You must be trying to stay here with that smart-ass mouth."

"Bitch, you started wit' me!"

"You can have a seat. I don't have to do this with you."

"With me? Bitch, you came over here fuckin' wit' me!"

"Sit down, Waters." The guard walked right away like September wasn't even talking to her. September was salty.

"It took y'all long enough. Damn," September said as she sat down hard in Ke'Lasia's passenger seat.

"Y'all? Bitch, do you see anybody else in here besides me?" Ke'Lasia brandished her arm around her car.

"Well, you bitch, you took long enough."

"Girl, I came as soon as I could. I didn't even know yo' ass was in here until today when you called me, the fuck. Soon as I left the stylist, I flew over here to get you."

"The stylist! Fuuuuck! Did you get me something to wear?"

"You know I got you some fly-ass shit, girl, stop trippin'."

"Hell yeah. I knew you was gon' have me." Ke'Lasia and September high-fived with smiles. "You always got my back, bitch. That's why I fuck wit' you so heavy." September sat back and got comfortable for the ride.

"So then why yo' ass ain't call me when you got locked up?" She sounded hurt.

"Bitch 'cause you change yo' number every other day, the fuck! I couldn't remember yo' shit. I just figured Travis would tell you." September shrugged.

"Oh. But you remember his shit, huh, whore?" They laughed hard and got to gossiping. September told her all about what the hell had happened that led her to need to be bonded out and Ke'Lasia told September about some shit that was going on with the girls on the label.

"Them hoes always on some jealous shit."

"I know. I don't be on them though. Fuck 'em."

"Girl, quit sulking and toughen up. Fuck them hoes. We doin' Winterfest and they not. What the fuck you care about them for?" September was getting pissed.

"Girl, I know. I just be tired of all that shit."

"Well, then stop being so damn soft and stand up to them hoes. What, you scared or something?"

"Scared? Of who?"

"I'm just saying. If you don't speak up, them hoes gon' keep tryin'a play you."

Ke'Lasia pulled up to September's crib and she got out. "Thanks again for picking me up," September told Ke'Lasia through the window.

"Thanks, my ass! Bitch, you owe me a thousand dollars! Don't be tryin'a play like you forgot either!" They laughed and she pulled away from the curb.

September watched her drive off before she opened the door to her apartment and walked in. *A thousand dollars? She must be crazy.* No way in the world was she gonna give her a whole stack. She'd better wait until her court date and let the courts give it to her. Shit, she ain't have that kinda money to be giving away. Friend or not, Ke'Lasia wouldn't be getting a thousand dollars from her.

She kicked her shoes off by the door in her hallway and proceeded to the bathroom on the second floor of her decent-sized townhouse. Where she lived wasn't terribly bad. It just wasn't what she wanted. And it was smack dab in the middle of the hood. She stayed downtown on Republic Street. Who the fuck wanted to live downtown besides the hood-rat-ass chicks who grew up down there on those filthy-ass streets who thought it was cute for some reason? She shuddered and rolled her eyes just thinking about it. This shit was run-down, downtrodden, and depressing. There was no way anybody who wanted something out of life would choose to live this way on purpose.

Random gunshots rang loud outside all of a sudden. September shook her head at it. It was typical for this area. It was sad, but it was pretty much as regular as hearing a car with loud music playing from it ride down the street. Kids outside playing didn't even run or worry anymore. This neighborhood just made her sad all the way around. The people from the city were trying to fix it up little bit by little bit but it didn't change anything. The people were still the same and most of the housing and businesses were just dirty looking as fuck.

She didn't plan to live downtown forever. She just had to stack her coin. Right now, she paid $38 for her one-bedroom apartment in that raggedy-ass neighborhood. She didn't plan on giving that up until she knew she had found her dream house and that she could afford it. She had her bar set high on a nice-ass two-bedroom house. She wanted all the amenities in a nice neighborhood, two bathrooms, a spiral staircase, wooden floors, built-in bookshelves, and a banging-ass master bedroom with an en suite. Like, the shit she had in her brain for her house, you couldn't just find any ol' where. With that being said, she'd just be in that raggedy place until she found what she wanted and not a minute longer. Once she finally found her house, she was getting the fuck from down there and never looking back.

She turned the shower water on and stripped down right there. She waited until the water was steaming hot before she stepped in. Once the water hit her skin, all her stress melted away. The water would've scalded her skin had she not been used to it being so hot. The water cascading down her skin felt so damn good. In that moment, nothing else mattered. Any time she needed to relieve stress she got in the shower. It was like her sanctuary. Her church. Her safe haven.

She washed with Dove soap until she felt like all the grime and dirt from the county jail was off of her. Then she used some Dove bodywash with a cucumber and mint scent. Feeling fresh, she turned the water off and got out. Her room was the way she left it. A mess. She didn't have the energy to clean up right now, so she threw everything in the closet and smoothed her covers out. Picking up her phone, she sent Raheim a text to check on him since it didn't seem like he was checking for her at all.

September: Damn. What's up?

Raheim: Don't damn me. Where the fuck you been at?

September: Duh. In jail.

Raheim: You ain't been in jail this whole time. They OR'd yo' ass next day I guarantee.

September: Then they put a holder on me, tf!

Raheim: A holder for what though?

September: I still don't even fuckin' know. I gotta go back to court in a month though.

Raheim: That's cool. Wyd?

September: Chillin'. 'Bout to pass out. Tired.

Raheim: Good night then.

September looked at the clock and saw that it was only ten thirty. No way in the world this nigga was about to go to bed. All of a sudden, she was wide awake.

September: Good night then. (Dueces emoji)

Raheim: Love you, ma.

September: Love you too.

She rolled her eyes as she threw her phone down on the bed. Her mind was made up. She wasn't going to sleep as planned. With a brand-new surge of energy, she got up and got dressed. Throwing on some black tights, a black sports bra, and a black hoodie, she grabbed her keys and headed for her car.

She pulled up on Long Craft in Winton Terrace in about ten minutes. She did sixty-five mph the whole way. She knew something was up, and she was gon' find out what. She pulled up and double parked like fuck it. She wasn't worried about no ticket or nothing. She wouldn't be long. She looked around to see if she saw Raheim's Benz, and of course she did. She banged on the door like the Cincinnati Police Department. She knew he would be pissed, but she ain't give a fuck about that either.

"Who the fuck is it?" his deep voice growled at the door as it flung open. She stood there smiling the sweetest smile she could muster up.

"Hey, boo. What's up?" she sang sweet and innocently as she barged in the door like she lived there.

"What's up? Ain't you supposed to be at home asleep?"

"Yeah, I was, but I couldn't sleep once I lay down, so I decided to come see my boo." She smiled another sweet smile while she plopped down on the couch.

The girl on the loveseat was mortified. It was all over her face. Had Raheim not slammed the door after September barged in, she would probably be bolting toward it right now. You could see the fear in her eyes growing with each second. September was tickled.

"So, what we doing? Netflix or what?" September looked to both of them for an answer but neither of them answered.

"I'm sorry. I'm September. You are?" September turned to the shorty sitting nervously quiet with her legs bouncing furiously up and down. She extended her hand hung in the air, waiting for her to shake it.

"Uh, I'm uh, uh, um—"

"Yo, September. What's up?" Raheim interrupted to ask again.

"I thought we said that already. What's up, baby? I'm tryin'a talk to her."

"Nah. You tryin'a be funny."

"How? By asking her her name?"

"Come on, man. What's up for real?"

"Damn! I can't speak?"

"Come on, man. Get up outta here. You tryin'a be funny and ain't nobody on that shit at all."

"Oh, no, boo boo. I ain't going nowhere. Y'all was kickin' it, right?" September looked to the girl, who still hadn't said a word. "Right?" September nodded her head in a yes, waiting for her to at least do the same. Finally, she nodded back. "Right. So, we finna kick it then. Come sit down, boo." September motioned to Raheim, patting the cushion beside her. The smile plastered on September's face again. Sarcasm dripped from her and he knew it. He fuckin' knew it.

"Come on, September. I'll see you tomorrow. Ain't nobody doin' this with you. Go home. I'll holla at you tomorrow."

"Nigga, are you tryin'a put me out? 'Cause I'm sitting here being nice as fuck to you and yo' friend, who still ain't even told me her name, and I can't even stay and watch a movie? Are you fuckin' kiddin' me right now? I just got popped for you and I can't stay and watch a movie? You dead for real right now?"

"I ain't tryin'a argue with you. I'm just tryin'a chill, watch a movie, and rest my arm, man. I don't want no problems wit' you, man."

"So, in order for you to chill and rest yo' arm, I gotta leave? But Ms. Shuts-the-fuck-up can stay here?"

"I'm um, I'm not tryin'a uh—" She tripped over her words trying to speak up.

"Shut up, bitch," September demanded. "Is that what the fuck you sayin' right now?" September stood up, still fighting like hell to control her anger. "Is that what the fuck you tellin' me, Rah? Huh?" September walked up on him slowly. She knew he could see the hell in her eyes by this point. Now, she was beyond pissed. Now, she was ready to go right the fuck back to jail.

"Chill, ma. Just go home, a'ight?"

She slapped him smooth across his face.

"What the fuck?" he roared with anger. "Did you just put yo' fuckin' hands on me?"

"I'ma tell you like this, muthafucka. I'm done playin' these dumb-ass games with you. You want these hoes? You can have 'em. You on some bullshit, my nigga. Fuck you." September mugged him on the side of his head as she stormed past him. She flung the door to his funky-ass apartment open and left it that way. *Fuck him.* She hoped the hood niggas ran up in his shit and touched him and that bitch.

She jumped back in her Altima, happy as fuck the dickhead-ass cops in this area didn't come tow her shit. She cranked her engine and heard Raheim's door slam. Hot, angry tears stained her face as she put her foot to the gas pedal and sped off.

Chapter 4

"We did that shit, bitch!" Ke'Lasia and September slapped fives as they looked over the prints that Travis had given them from their photoshoot the day before.

"This means drinks. Shit!" September shouted.

"Barkeep! A round!" She yelled across the almost empty bar room. The girls had gathered at The Mad Frog, a bar in Clifton, where they sometimes went to blow off steam and catch up.

The server sauntered over to their booth with an attitude.

"What y'all need?" she asked them.

"First, for you to lose the attitude, damn. And then a round of Hennessy if you don't fuckin' mind." September rolled her eyes at the rude-ass server before she went back to talking. "Anyway," she said and waved the server off. "Like I was saying, we did that shit!" Her excitement returned. "Look at these fuckin' pictures! They are so bomb!"

"They are! Girl, we killed it for real. Ain't no way we ain't get a spot in Winterfest this year."

"Hell yeah, we fuckin' better! I know damn well we fucked this shit up!" The girls picked out their favorite pictures and admired them in silence for a second.

"What made you wanna model, Lasia? I never even asked you."

"Giiiirl. Honestly? I was just tired of that damn pole."

"Same here." September sat back with a faraway look in her eyes.

"What's up? Why you lookin' all sad?"

"Girl, I just be havin' shit on my mind."

"Like what, bitch, damn? I'm tryin'a be all open and chill here. Say somethin'."

"You silly. Girl, I just be thinkin' what my life would've been had I not moved out so early or gotten involved with Raheim's ass. Life just been crazy."

"I know what the fuck you mean. Sometimes I be salty I can't call Mom up and get a home-cooked meal or, shit, even move back into her place when I get tired of payin' damn bills."

"That damn part!" The girls high-fived again. The server finally came back with their drinks, so they took the opportunity to order wings and fries, too.

"Cheers!" the girls yelled, clinking their glasses together.

Travis pulled up to his baby mama's house for the third time that week. He took a deep breath, looked in the mirror for one last check, then got out the car.

"Who is it?" he heard his baby mama yell on the other side of the door.

"It's Travis!" he yelled through the thin, fake metal door of his baby mama's project apartment.

He looked around out of habit. Any time he was in this part of the hood, he felt like he had to watch his back. Travis was from another neighborhood close to the area. Cumminsville. But his baby mama lived in Moosewood. A hood-ass cul-de-sac going up toward Westwood. These niggas from around here didn't get along wit' niggas from Cumminsville but his hardhead-ass baby mama wouldn't listen and let him buy her and the kids an apartment in a better neighborhood. She insisted on not needing a nigga for nothing, so she relied on the government to help her pay her rent instead.

"Travis? Freight, keep that bullshit over there wit' yo' uppity-ass damn near white friends. Don't bring that bullshit over here. Yo' fuckin' name is Freight. Not no fuckin' Travis," his baby mama scolded after she had the door flung open all the way.

"Man, whatever, Keisha. Where my kids at?" he asked, pushing past her into the apartment.

"Yo' kids? You mean yo' son? The rest of them kids mine, nigga."

"Fuck you, Keisha." He traveled farther into the house and called for the kids.

"They not here wit' yo' dumb ass." She laughed at him like he had just told a joke. "I told you quit poppin' up over here. Maybe had you called, you'd know they wasn't here."

"If you answered the phone some fuckin' time, we wouldn't have this problem!" he spewed at her.

"Boy, fuck you. What you come over here for and you ain't bringing me no damn money?"

"Money? I just gave yo' ass some fuckin' money," he challenged, grabbing her hands and displaying her freshly shellacked nails. Keisha snatched her hand back and challenged his accusations.

"Nigga, don't accuse me of shit! Fuck. I get money. That li'l five hundred dollars you leave over here ain't shit. You think you do so much. I got four fuckin' kids. Nigga, five hundred funky-ass dollars ain't shit. Fuck you thought this was?"

"It's enough for you to not have to get no fuckin' job around here. Shit. You stay wit' ya freshly done hands out but always talkin' shit. Is my daughter's hands done? Huh? Or you gon' keep hittin' me wit' these kids ain't mine?"

"They not. Shit. You the one who only pop up every here and there since Omar been born like the rest of these kids don't matter. LaLa said she don't feel like you they daddy no more since Omar been born." She leaned against the door and crossed her arms over her chest like she had just said the best shit in the world.

"My baby ain't said that. I swear you a rude-ass bitch."

"Bitch?" She licked her lips like a cat in front of new pate. "You always wanna get to talkin' dirty like you can handle this pussy or somethin'." She eased over to him with what she thought was a sexy-ass stride. He stood there stone-faced, still watching her stalk toward him like she was irresistible.

"You talk shit like I can't tame that mouth."

"Oh, you can, can you?" She licked her lips again and played with his shirt in a flirtatious manner. "You sure? Huh, daddy?"

"Bitch, do what you do and stop playin' wit' me," he rudely checked her.

The way he spoke to Keisha didn't bother her at all. It did the opposite and turned her on. He hated that he had to give in to her and fuck her or let her suck his dick, but he did what he had to from time to time so that she'd let him see his kids. He hadn't seen them in two months since he wasn't making the money he used to. Keisha wasn't having that shit at all. He was either gonna pay her or fuck her, sometimes both. So, he did what he had to do.

Keisha slid to her knees in front of him and toyed with his jeans. "What the fuck you waitin' on? You know you want this dick."

Keisha smiled and cut the games. She tore through his pants to his boxer briefs, then pulled them apart from his body with her teeth. He stood rigid and watched her. She had been his baby mama for ten years. He had touched her multiple times over the years. Hell, he had four kids with her by this point. But she was nothing like she used to be, and now, he hated touching her. He hated her touching him. He hated he had to do this at all. He wished she'd just find a nigga to get caught up with so she would leave him the fuck alone wit' this shit. She ain't ever be on this unless she wasn't fuckin' some new nigga she found on the block like the rest of these dumb-ass niggas she involved herself with.

Travis found a way to keep his dick hard long enough to force a nut out. Keisha caught all of it in her mouth and gave Travis a show of playing with his jizz in her mouth, some shit he used to be turned on by.

"Swallow," he commanded. She did as she was told. She swallowed his nut down her throat with a satisfied smile. He hid his cringe under a hard jawline. "Where the kids at, Keish?"

"They'll be back in a couple days. They wit' my mama."

"I can't just go over there and see 'em?"

"You know my mama don't fuck wit' you like that," she reminded him through brush strokes of her teeth.

"Man, you can't talk to her? Ask her to let me come over? Come on, man."

"She ain't going for it, Freight. It's over." She finished her teeth and came back out the bathroom to finish the conversation.

"Why you wanna go over there so bad?"

"'Cause that's where my kids at, Keish. Come on with that."

"Yeah, well, they won't be home until Tuesday, so you gotta wait." She shrugged her shoulders like she ain't give a fuck about what he was saying. They finished their forced conversation at the door that Travis had come through initially. "Bye, Freight."

"Cut that shit out, Keish. My name is Travis."

He turned his back and stormed off. He hated when she called him that shit. He had left that shit behind him. He only just wished he could leave her ass in the past, too.

Travis pulled up the driveway that led him straight into his garage. Checking to make sure he had everything else, he grabbed his briefcase last and headed in the house. Where Travis stayed now was far from the hood. He had done his share of time there, and once he was out, he vowed that he would never go back unless it came down to it. But he had his mind made up that it would never, ever, ever come back down to that. Where he stayed now was a four-bedroom house in Forest Park. He had worked his ass off to get the house so that he could eventually get his kids away from Keisha. Travis was determined to get his kids out of that project apartment with that bitch they called a mother. It wasn't like he felt better than Keisha or nothing. It was just that the bitch didn't want shit else but the hood, and he ain't want that for his kids. It would've been whatever but since she had his kids attached to her, it was a problem for him that he needed to fix. It was a long time coming, but he was ready now. He had the house. He had the job. He was legit, and now it was time for him to step up.

Travis had hustled his ass off as a nigga named Freight in the hood for more than twenty years starting at age 12. His mama wasn't shit, running around with any nigga she could to make a quick buck to carry it back to her pimp Sweet Lick. Until he found out she was fuckin' his dad for feelings. Sweet Lick waited until she had Travis and killed her, forcing his dad to step up once the careless-ass pimp dropped Travis off on his doorstep when he wasn't even sure it was at the right address.

Travis's father had taught him everything he needed to know about the game as soon as he could speak. Once he turned 12 years old, his father (if that's what you could call him), gave him his first job. To kill Sweet Lick. Travis did that shit with no hesitation. That was the day he started his life as Freight. Quick, fast, and strong. That was the life he knew and lived until he had his first baby.

At 22 years old, he realized what it meant to give a fuck. And from that point on, he busted his ass to leave Freight in the wind and become Travis for his kid. He was finally able to do that. Now all he had to do was convince Keisha that if she let him get the kids, he'd still give her cash here and there. He knew the only thing keeping her from relinquishing custody was the cash she got from him and the government. He was in the position to keep her cash flowing to keep her ass off his back and let his kids go, but Kiesha was a stubborn-ass bitch. All she ever gave a fuck about was money. No matter what he did or how good he was to her and his kids, she bitched and complained, all the while demanding more money.

He had the right life now to be the right man for his kids. He just wished that he could make his ratchet-ass baby mama want the same.

"Yeah man, I remember. I'll be there," Travis said into the phone before hanging up.

He had a job to do in two hours, so he needed to shit, shave, and shower before he had to be there. He stripped his clothes off and stepped into the shower after doing everything else he needed to do. The bathroom was steamy just how he liked it, and the water was a wonderful hot temperature. He showered with all the eagerness of a 70-year-old man. He didn't rush at all.

"What's up, shorty duwhop? What you need?"
"Nothing. I was bored. What you doin'?"
"'Bout to go do this li'l gig."

"I wanna go."

"Why?"

"Didn't you just hear me say I was bored, nigga?" Travis heard the eye roll in September's voice.

"Eh. You can't talk shit to me and want something from me, nigga?" he teased her.

"You gon' come get me or not?" she whined.

"Nigga, you drive. Be over here in twenty minutes or I'm leavin' yo' ass, too."

They laughed and he hung up shaking his head. That girl wanted him bad and it tickled the shit out of him.

Chapter 5

This fool was easy as hell. September laughed to herself. Travis was fine as fuck and since she wasn't about to be fuckin' wit' Raheim's ass for a minute, she needed a nigga to keep her occupied. Travis's fine ass was gon' do the trick. He had been digging her for a minute now, probably longer than she had paid attention to, but she started picking up on it about a year ago. They were at a rinky-dink photoshoot that they agreed to do for a few quick dollars, and she caught him trying to look around the divider when she was getting changed. She knew he was a chubby chaser from the first night she met him in that club. It was only a matter of time before she let him get some of the pussy. She just ain't want the shit to get weird while they were at work, but by this point, they seemed cool enough to where she could fuck him and his ass not fall in love.

She hopped up and rushed to find something subtly sexy to put on. She couldn't look too thirsty, but she ain't wanna look like a homeboy either. She found some cute denim cutoffs and a tank top to throw on. She threw on some high-top Jordan 12's and grabbed her keys. She dashed to the car so she could get to him before he actually tried to leave a bitch behind. She did sixty-five mph in a forty mph zone and got there with five more minutes to spare. She smiled at the clock and called Travis back. She hung up the phone when she saw him walk out the house as the phone was ringing. She watched him look down at his phone after the beeping came through his ear in mid hello. She laughed to herself.

"What the hell?" he yelled at her window. She just laughed at him while she climbed in the front seat of his hunter green Dodge Charger.

"You mad as hell." She giggled.

"Shut up." He playfully punched her arm. She knew this nigga was digging her and tryin'a front like he wasn't. He turned his music up and she sat back and got settled. It felt good just to ride and think while she let the bass from his system rattle through her body and settle into her soul. He had to have twelves in the trunk. They were banging. She was in heaven.

"Come on, sleepyhead," he told her as they pulled up and parked outside of Findlay Market downtown.

"I wasn't asleep. I was chillin'."

"Yeah. Chillin' right into La La Land." He chuckled at his own li'l joke as he grabbed his equipment out the trunk of the Charger. He handed her a bag of spare items and a lighting pole.

She followed him into Findlay Market to a little boutique-like shop toward the end. They walked in and a white boy walked up to him all smiles. September stepped to the side and let them talk about whatever the hell it was they had to say. She bided her time by looking at the little trinkets they had in the store.

She paid for the Hello Kitty keychain and a tank top that had her new favorite rapper Cardi B on the front while the boys wrapped up their conversation. They slapped fives and she followed the white boy and Travis to the back of the store. The models were already there in their robes waiting on them—well, Travis, since this wasn't her gig—to set up. He gave her directions, and she followed them.

"What the fuck?" she yelled out. She had bent over to set a light in place and one of the male models smacked her ass.

"What?" He held up his hands like he was innocent. "You got a fat ass, ma."

"And apparently I got a sign on it that says 'touch here,' right?"

"Eh! Keep yo' fuckin' hands off my shit. You hear me? My lights, my equipment, my assistant. Don't touch nothin' that belongs to me unless you want this to go from sugar to shit real fast. Feel me?" Travis challenged the tall, lanky black dude who had touched September.

Travis would've kicked his ass with no problem, but he didn't. He just stared the guy down, daring him to bust a move. The lanky guy put his hands in the air again and walked off.

"That goes for all y'all. Hands off my shit." All men in attendance nodded in agreement. That's when September noticed there were quite a few dudes here. She counted and came up with seven. *Fuck*. They were gon' be here all damn day fuckin' wit' them. She knew she should've just called his ass later. It was seven dudes and two girls they had to get through before they left. She wasn't expecting to be here that damn long.

"Trav," she whispered. "You gotta shoot all them?" she asked in a hush voice once she got his attention.

"Yeah, why? What's the matter, shorty?"

"I wasn't tryin'a do this all night. I thought you and me were gon' kick it."

"We will. Chill out, temper tantrum. The market just closed, so now we can do our thing. It's gon' take about an hour, two tops. You good or you need my keys?"

"Nah, fuck it. I'm good. I should've got some food though." She stuck her lip out and put her hands on her hips.

"There you go," he lightly scolded. "Another damn temper tantrum. I'll feed you whatever you want when we leave. Deal?"

"Deal," she said, all smiles now.

September was smiling because he was gon' feed her, but even more so because of what she had planned to feed him. She batted her eyes at him real sexy, like she was giving him all the hints he needed. He just chuckled in return and shook his head, but she knew he understood her signals.

They got the lights and backdrops set up. Other cameras and video cameras were in place for different angles to be captured. Everything was running smoothly. September asked Travis to let her tag along with him just to be close to him and get him alone, but now, she was happy she came. She was having a good time and enjoying herself.

"Okay, people. We're ready for the first set. Let's get it!" Travis yelled loud enough to be heard by everyone.

September grabbed a snack from the table of refreshments provided, found a seat toward the back, and got comfortable. Hopefully this shoot wouldn't last too long. Seeing Travis at work and focused with so much attention to detail and care in what he was doing was making her hot for him more and more. From the way he moved about, making sure these people ended up with the best pictures possible, had her taking notice that his attention to detail would probably provide her with a great-ass fuck. At first, she just wanted to fuck him out of pure get backs toward Raheim, but now she was feeling like she may have made a great-ass decision. He was gonna fuck her crazy and she was gonna enjoy every fuckin' minute of it. She was so geeked for it to happen now. She pulled out her phone and shot Ke'Lasia a message.

September: Bitch! I ain't playin' wit' him no fuckin' more. I'm about to fuck the shit out this man. Stand by for details.

She slid her phone back in her pocket until she texted back and got prepared to watch the shoot.

Two black dudes and one white female model walked in and unrobed just outside the camera shot. They stepped in front of a backdrop and posed. The male models were blessed with enough to be proud to take pictures of. One of the men was stocky, not quite six foot and heavier than his male coworker. His shoulders and arms were huge, and he had a little weight around his midsection. It didn't keep September from looking at him though. Most girls were secretly chubby chasers and she was no different. The fact that he wasn't all skinny and lanky was a turn-on to her. Not to mention that he was packing, and his hands were big, too! His dick was bigger than his picture-taking compadres and that in and of itself added to her smile. He looked like he could stroke the cervical lining out a bitch if he wanted to. Her pussy muscles jumped at the excited thought of straddling him and hanging on for dear life as the ride got wild.

He kept her attention, but not more than the other male model who had nice abs and nice tattoos who was also blessed with a long, thick, chocolate rod that almost hung to his knees as well, but it did wander away from time to time. Although the second male model wasn't bad to look at, the first one with the weight was her type. Even his beard was wonderful. A big, full, black beard that only covered his chin and not his whole face. And he had no stupid sideburns taking up half his face either. The other guy had a nice face that you could appreciate looking at. Especially since he had no facial hair at all. She had never seen naked models taking pictures before, so she was hella interested.

She wondered if he was gon' take pictures of her pussy, too. The girl was a white chick, but she had a nice body. Her tits were a nice melon size like most people liked to have. Maybe about a D-cup. Her thighs were nice and slim, thick. She had a little waist and nice ass. It was a little one, but still nice. It was funny looking at her with her red hair and red pubes to match. It made her wonder if Travis had red hairs in his boxers to match the red on his head too. They were both natural redheads, but with Travis being black, it made his hair look orangish. A fleeting thought crossed her mind about all the wonderful things she would've done with these naked models had it been her photoshoot. She smiled to herself in thought. Then her smile grew even bigger as she watched the naked redheaded girl get down on her knees and take the smooth-faced black dude into her mouth. Travis was filming porn! September was so shocked. She didn't know what to do. It was happy shock but shock all the same.

The shit was sexy as hell! She watched the whole scene unfold in front of her. It was real different watching people have sex. Even though she knew it was all a part of the act, she could see for the first time the way people's bodies moved during different strokes and positions. The guys took turns filling her holes like the pros they were destined to be. They even paired up to take her at the same time, one on the top and one on the bottom to fill both her holes at the same time. Travis must've seen confusion on her face because he informed her that this move was called double penetration. It looked to her to be fuckin' heaven! She had never witnessed no shit like that but now all she could do was imagine Travis and Raheim sharing her at the same time. She had to know when Travis would be done with this shoot 'cause she had to change her panties by this point. The ones she was wearing were soaking damn wet. Now it was for certain—once she got Travis out of here, they were going straight back to her place. The positions she wanted him to put her body in would be right up his alley and fit for one of these kinds of movies. She was so thirsty her mouth was watering. Watching him get up close and personal on the group of sexually entwined people had her wishing him and her could join them. She had to step out and get a breather.

Ke'Lasia hadn't been chilling with September too often now seeing how she was caught up in her and Raheim's own shit and going back and forth to court. She got her bond money back, so that was an upside, but she was bored to death. She ain't mess with none of the old bitches from the neighborhood anymore after Kim's fake ass came over with Monica and Amber one night and stole $300 worth of shit from her. Not to mention the clothes them bitches stole that still had tags on them, so September was kind of the only friend she had right now. Except Travis, but they were just work friends. She wasn't about to be chilling and shit with him knowing that her homegirl was boning him and he was fake trying to flirt at the stylist meeting. That was snake shit, so she ain't want no parts of that. Now she was sitting here bored to fucking death with nothing to do.

"Bitch, roll out from under the dick and come on. I wanna get something to eat."

"What? What time is it?" a sleepy September asked when she answered the phone on the fourth ring.

"It's two o'clock. Get up. I'm booooored."

"Okay, dang. Give me a minute to get dressed."

"Well, tell Raheim's ass not to be tryin'a get a quickie in either. I don't feel like waiting another hour." Ke'Lasia rolled her eyes and giggled.

September and Raheim stayed going back and forth, making up only to break up again. But that making up she be telling Ke'Lasia about got her understanding why she couldn't leave his dog ass alone. Let her tell it, his sex was hellafied addictive and the head game on point, so Ke'Lasia saw why she kept going back. She'd been done fucking with Dragon's ass for about two hard-ass years now, so the only action she got was when her dope dick stranger came to creep. Even that was few and far between, not enough to even take the edge off, and a bitch was edgy. Ke'Lasia was tired of buying batteries at this point, too. Hearing September whisper in her sexy voice to Raheim in the background helped her make up her mind. She needed to get her a new dude. *Fuck it.*

"Girl, nobody is fuckin' wit' Raheim," she laughed. "That's some new shit. Chill out. I'll be there in a minute. We'll talk about it." They laughed and hung up.

Ke'Lasia was fake jealous that her friend had moved on that quick after Raheim, and here she was, dragging ass about an old nigga. She had to get her shit together fast. She couldn't keep staying cooped up in the house, waiting on a stranger to come by and screw her. She should be setting a trap to send his ass to jail, not longing for his damn visits like a desperate bitch. It was something obviously off about her in the first place that she was making it easy for this perv to creep into her house. But instead of feeling creeped out by even the thoughts of him, she was once again turned on. It was driving her mad. She longed for his touch. Yearned for it. Ached for it. Every single time she thought about this strange man, her breath caught, and her little miss danced a jig of her own. It wasn't just her brain that wanted him, she did too. Late nights, she had cravings for him. And when he didn't show up, she honestly felt stood up or some shit and she was more disappointed than she was. Like he was her man or something! He was sick, whoever he was. And there was something just as sick inside of her for her to be a willing participant in this hellish game. He could be anybody. Someone she hated. Some nasty-looking dude. Some registered sex offender who lived in the neighborhood and hid away from the public eye. Anybody. And she was letting this man into her home, into her bed. Giving him her body like he deserved it. Like it was owed to him. She knew she was sick for this, which was why she decided to seek help. She was sick and she was ashamed. So ashamed that she hadn't told anybody, not even September. Like she said, she was really the only friend she had. She couldn't even talk to her about this. She knew she wouldn't understand. How could she? Hell, she barely understood. This thing, whatever it was, was getting way out of hand, so hopefully, Dr. Sagent could help her fix it before she sat back and allowed something crazier to happen to her. Going on the path that she was on, that shit was easily possible.

Ke'Lasia ran to the door to answer the incessant knocking. "Bitch, how you gon' rush me over here and not even be dressed? You must be about to cook?" What September said wasn't really a question. "I'm tired anyway. Let's just stay here," she clarified, plopping down on the Corinthian leather couch.

"That's cool too. I got some steaks I just got from the grocery store. I could put them on."

"Beef. My favorite," she said, smiling a wicked smile and licking her lips suggestively.

"I bet it is, nasty." She rolled her eyes. "So, spill it. You said that wasn't Raheim with the deep voice in the background, so who was it?"

"Girl! So, let me start from the beginning. Yesterday I went with Travis to this photoshoot, right? Everything was smooth as hell, people were nice and shit, and it was chill. I helped him set up his li'l equipment so he could get started, and then I took a seat. The niggas he was shootin' was fine as fuck, might I add!"

Ke'Lasia was moving around the kitchen listening hard as hell to September's story. She almost tuned her out when she said she was with Travis. She knew she said she had been digging him, but Ke'Lasia didn't know they had started fucking. She wasn't mad or nothing, but damn, the nigga was just all in her face knowing he was fuckin' her friend. Then she was fucking him and hadn't even told her. That shit was lightweight rude. But when she got to the part about the fine-ass niggas, Ke'Lasia was all ears.

"Niggas? Girl, come in here so I can hear you better." She came into the kitchen and sat on the other side of the island while Ke'Lasia prepped the steaks.

"Girl, that shit look good already! You always could throw down in the kitchen just like your moms. What you need is a man up in here to eat some of that good-ass cooking." September eyed Ke'Lasia.

"Girl, get back to the story." Ke'Lasia waved her off.

"Oh, yeah! So anyway, the shoot was a nude one. Two dudes and a bitch. She was a white bitch, but she was all right, feel me? And the niggas she was shooting with? Bitch!"

"You already said they was fine, girl, damn." Ke'Lasia laughed and pulled out a flat griddle pan for the steak. September and Ke'Lasia both liked their steaks medium well, so they wouldn't take long to cook. Ke'Lasia decided to put some vegetables with them, too. She set the griddle on the stove, then pulled out the cutting board.

"That sounds odd though. Was he shooting all them together or one by one?"

"Together. Because it was really a fuckin' porn!"

Ke'Lasia's mouth dropped five feet to the floor.

"Bitch, you lyin'," she said barely above a whisper. The shock from her statement had just thrown her for a loop. A porn? A real-life porn? She had to be fucking with her. "You bullshittin'. Ain't no way."

"Bitch, if I'm lyin', God can strike me dead right now!" September sat up straight and raised her right hand in the air with the most serious face Ke'Lasia had ever seen. "Bitch, on God it was. And the dicks on them men! Baby! They had to be related to horses!" Then she used her hands and fingers to show her how big, long, and thick she remembered their penises being when she looked at them.

September told her the whole scenario, all the fucking and different positions. She made a big deal to tell her friend about the double penetration scene.

"Damn! She should be in the big leagues already!" Ke'Lasia said, jumping back in the convo with her friend.

"Who you tellin'! That shit was amazing to watch, girl. You should've been there! So anyway, I'm watchin', learning shit, and of course, getting hot and bothered, right? So, the shit over, we pack up, and everybody bounced. Travis had my pussy soaked right through the panties, you feel me!"

"That's why I don't even wear none. I don't got time for that shit."

"Bitch, right. So, since I know he on his way, I make a mad dash for the bathroom to freshen up real quick. You know how it is. Can't be giving no nigga the sweaty pussy." They high-fived on that 'cause she was sure right. "So, he get there and shit, and I'm tryin'a play it cool like my pussy ain't tryin'a jump in this nigga lap and shit. I then slid on the sexy see-through joint I got for Raheim a couple months ago that he never got to see."

"'Cause he stupid," Ke'Lasia said, jumping in and rolling her eyes, having her friend's back. She was never a huge fan of him and the way he did her girl anyway, so she rolled her eyes every chance she got.

"Anyway." She rolled her eyes back at Ke'Lasia. "We sittin' there making a li'l small talk until finally I couldn't take it no more, so I asked him was he gon' shoot or dribble. He stood up and took off his shirt, tryin'a flex and shit, so I stood up with him. I got to licking and kissing all on his chest and shit, and he playin' in my hair. I'm easing my way down to the good shit, right? Ready to get everything poppin', and he stop me."

"He stopped you?" Ke'Lasia looked up from cutting the peppers in confusion. "What you mean he stopped you? He ain't let you put that sloppy-ass head on him?"

"Bitch, no. He pushed me down on the coffee table, lifted my legs up, and went to town in this pussy! Bitch, I need to go back to that li'l store where we picked out that damn coffee table 'cause that bitch is built with the spirit of the angels! He locked me in his arms and held me down on that mu'fucka until I came like seven times all over his fuckin' beard. Bitch, I squirted all over his beard, his chest, the floor, all of it. Thank you, God, for hardwood floors!" September howled with laughter.

"Girl, say swear! Seven times?"

"Girl, seven. I ain't bullshittin'. That shit was live as fuck, too."

"It had to be if he was still there today."

"Had you not called me, we'd probably be going another round. Bitch, he been tagging my shit since last night. Every time I think we finished, and I shower or try to get some sleep, he's ready again. Bitch, I'm wore the fuck out!" September was smiling hard, and it made Ke'Lasia smile to see her happy. She hadn't smiled this hard in a long time.

Ke'Lasia finished cooking the food and set some plates out.

"So anyway, what's been up with you?" September asked Ke'Lasia after she blessed the food.

"Girl, nothing as wild as you, but I'm chillin'. I start seeing this therapist today. Set up a couple shoots to get my headshots updated. Girl, nothing really, I guess."

"This food is bomb, Ke! Thank you, girl. I hadn't had nothing since yesterday," she said through chews of her food. "Why you goin' to a therapist though? What's up with that? And why you ain't been hollerin' at me if you needed someone to talk to?"

"I just need to work out some shit." Ke'Lasia shrugged.

"You know therapy for white people, right?"

"Girl, no, it is not. Everybody needs help from time to time. It's just to get some stuff off my chest and learn better coping skills."

"You still having dreams about Ma?"

"All the time, for real," Ke'Lasia truthfully answered with her eyes down at her plate. She suddenly wasn't so hungry.

"I don't care, Ke'Lasia Ann! I need it, and if you don't get it for me, I'ma just get it myself!"

"Ma, you don't need it! It's killing you! Look at you! You're underweight and your eyes are sunken in. Ma, you're dying! Don't you care? Who the hell am I going to have when you die? Daddy? You know he don't care about me or you. Ma, please. Let's just go get you some help."

"I don't need no fuckin' help, girl! I need my medicine. Go get it, or so help me, you won't live in this house no more." She knew she meant what she said only because the drugs were talking. She didn't know what to do, but she knew she couldn't be the one to give her any more drugs. She'd had enough. She went to her room and packed her bags. When she came out, her mom was sitting on the couch rocking and talking to herself. Her

arms were wrapped around her thin body and her face was wet from crying and drooling.

"I love you, Ma, but I can't watch you kill yourself anymore." She kissed her forehead as she wrapped her arms around her for the first time in her life. She still didn't feel any comfort or warmth. All she felt was the shell of a woman who used to be her mother.

"Please help me, daughter. Please. September would do it." Struck to the heart by her words, as painful as they'd always been, she told her mother to take care of herself and left. That was the last time she saw her mother alive.

"You know that shit wasn't your fault, right?" September tried to soothe her friend for the millionth time.

"I know. I know." Ke'Lasia got up and took her plate to the sink to discard the now unwanted food. She dried her eyes on her sleeve and started cleaning up the kitchen.

"What brings you in today?" Dr. Sagent asked Ke'Lasia once they shook hands and were seated.

"Well, a lot I guess." Ke'Lasia fidgeted around in her seat, twirling her thumbs, not knowing what to do with herself.

"How about we start from most recent and work our way back if you choose to stay, okay? We have all the time you need. You're my last appointment of the day, so take your time. I'm here to listen." Dr. Sagent made Ke'Lasia feel comfortable, but she was second-guessing this decision. Did she really want to sit there and tell this man that she had been having sex with a stranger who set out to rape her? She felt judged already and she hadn't even told him yet.

"Maybe I should request a female doctor. I don't mean to be mean, but . . ." Ke'Lasia dropped her eyes in embarrassment.

"That's your choice. You can request someone different at any time. It's purely up to you. But I can assure you, Miss Tanner, I've heard it all. Excuse me for being so forward, but is what you want to talk about today sex related?"

Ke'Lasia shook her head yes, still not making eye contact with him.

"Yeah, I thought so. That's usually the problem. I'm gonna be blunt, Miss Tanner, is that okay?"

Again, Ke'Lasia chose to shake her head instead of speaking. She was nervous as shit and feeling dumb as hell sitting in front of this fine-ass man, ready to reveal to him that she was just another ho out here.

"I am a man. I have had lots of sex. I am in no position to judge you for anything you've done or want to do. Hell, I was in a porno when I was eighteen. We've all done things."

Ke'Lasia looked at him with hope in her eyes. "Seriously?" she asked, desperate to feel like she wasn't totally crazy.

"Seriously," he said.

So, she took a deep breath and spilled the whole thing in what seemed like one breath. When she was done, they sat there in a silence that felt like the heaviest thing in the world. Finally, the doctor spoke.

"So, you feel crazy because you liked the sex? Or because you don't know who he is?"

"Both, Dr. Sagent. Both. How do I—"

"Call me Justin," he interrupted.

"Justin? Is that really your first name?"

"Yes, it is." His eyebrows went up. "What's wrong with Justin?"

"Nothing." Ke'Lasia giggled. "You just looked more like a Marcus or Tyrone or something to me," she said, eyeing him.

"Well, that's because I got swag." His joke made her laugh and loosen up. This therapist was pretty cool.

"Well, Justin, how do I like the fact that some stranger creeps into my house and has sex with me? How is that not crazy?"

"Everyone likes sex."

"But he's a stranger! I don't even know him."

"So, you're turned on by the mystery of it. The anonymity of him. What's the crazy part in that?"

"He could have something!"

"But he uses protection. So, a lot of things you're probably protecting against, including pregnancy."

"But he's . . . I mean, I just . . ."

"Look, Miss Tanner—"

"Ke'Lasia."

"Excuse me, Ke'Lasia." He smiled. "I don't hear anything crazy. I hear a young woman who's turned on by some new and exciting things happening in her life and she might be a little afraid of things changing."

"But, Justin, he's a damn stranger. What if he kills me?"

"So, call the cops the next time he breaks in."

Ke'Lasia got quiet and looked at her hands.

"Why can't you call the police?" he asked her, noticing her demeanor had changed.

Ke'Lasia could feel his intriguing glare burrowing holes in the top of her head. She was so fuckin' embarrassed. Why the hell did she ever come here?

"He doesn't exactly break in, so to speak." Ke'Lasia's words were barely above a whisper. Justin asked her to repeat herself. "He, uh, he doesn't break in," she repeated as she lifted her head to meet his wondering stare. "I leave windows and sometimes the doors unlocked so he can get in." They stared at each other and Ke'Lasia felt her stomach sink lower and lower as each silent moment ticked by.

"Why?" the doctor asked her, breaking the unbearable silence.

"I told you. Because I like having sex with him." She lowered her gaze again. "I think, uh, I'ma go." She grabbed her purse and coat and hurried to leave. Once she got to the door, his voice stopped her.

"There's no need to run. I'm not here to judge."

"Thank you for your time, Dr. Sagent. Have a great day," she told him on her way out the door.

She made it to her car in a wild hurry, threw herself in, slammed the door, and let the tears flow free. What the fuck was she thinking? No one could know this. There would be no fixing her. She knew as soon as that stranger popped up again that she would once again let him have her. She was too far gone. She wanted this and nothing was going to change that.

Chapter 6

   Ke'Lasia woke up with her heart beating fast as hell. She had just dreamed that she was about to have sex with the still unseen stranger, face down on her queen-sized bed. Her nightshirt was pulled up, exposing her round ass, and he was just about to take her from behind when, all of a sudden, she started to drown. Nothing she did was stopping the water from filling up her lungs and she just knew she was about to die. For some reason, it was hot as fuck in her room. She was covered in sweat with her oversized nightshirt sticking to her. The comforter was nowhere to be found, and her sheet was wrapped around her legs in some weird-ass twist. She tried kicking it off of her, but it didn't work. She literally had to unravel herself out of it. She ain't know what was going on with her air conditioning. She remembered turning it down a few degrees before she got into bed that night. No one likes to be hot when they're trying to sleep, and she was no exception.

   Once free, she got up to drag herself to the thermostat for the central air to her place. She was really burning up now and it was pissing her off. She found her comforter on the floor under her feet and picked it up to put it back at the foot of her bed where it belonged.

   "Dammit!" she growled to herself after she stubbed her toe on her wooden bed frame in the dark.

   "Shit, shit, shit, shit, shit!" She hobbled around the bed, trying to walk off the pain.

"Let me kiss it for you." The bass from his heavy voice rumbled through the darkness and vibrated in her chest. She knew it was him although that was the first time she clearly heard his voice. Her pussy instantly started to dance.

"No." Her voice was so soft she almost didn't recognize it herself.

"Why not?" The confusion in his voice was evident.

"Because I don't know you and this is crazy."

"How?"

"You tried to rape me." The silence that followed her statement was stifling. She waited in the dark for him to respond. He didn't. The feelings she had were so mixed. She wanted to be angry with him, scared, even hurt. But she wasn't really. She was confused and drawn to him. A man she'd never even seen. A man whose plan was to break in her house and take advantage of her. She wasn't supposed to be okay with that. "You're a rapist. I can't have sex with a rapist. That's crazy."

"I didn't rape you."

"Well, what the fuck do you call it then?" Her voice raised in defensive agony.

Her body wanted him so bad. So bad that parts of her burned for his touch. She felt her clit harden just like her nipples did. Now hard, her nipples pressed against her nightshirt. She willed herself to stop moving because with every little movement, her nightshirt slid across her hard, sensitive nipples and turned her on more. She didn't want to be turned on. She didn't want to want him. She didn't want to be crazy anymore.

"We made love. I knew as soon as I touched you that you would be mine. I knew it. And you knew it too."

"I didn't know that some sick fuck would be creeping in my house and trying to take my pussy. You can bet your ass on that."

"But you let me. You gave yourself to me. You let me touch you. You dripped for me. You wanted me."

"I don't even know you."

"But our bodies know each other. You can't deny that."

"I don't belong to you. I don't belong to a rapist."

"Stop calling me that."

"That's what the fuck you are. A rapist. A sick fuckin' psycho rapist."

"Well, then why do you want me so bad?"

Her eyes had adjusted to the darkness, yet all she could make out was his massive silhouette. He was a big guy. She couldn't make out his exact build, but she knew he was big. She still couldn't see his face, but it didn't mean anything to her insides. He was right. She did want him. There was only one thing she wanted more than to go to him where he sat on her chaise, straddle him, and let him fill her up as she kissed his lips. One thing. And all that was, was to see him. To look at him. To be able to identify him on the street. To see the face of her would-be rapist.

"I don't," she lied as she walked over to him in her mind. She could feel his dick easing inside of her from the at least twenty steps that they had between them. She could feel the veins in his thick dick pulsate against her walls. Moisture ran down her thighs.

"You're lying."

"I'm not."

"You are. I can smell your pussy heating up from here. You want me and I want you."

"I don't want you." Her words caught in her throat and cracked as her eyes filled up. She hated that she wanted him. She hated it. But she wanted it. She always fantasized about being taken by someone she didn't know and giving in because it was so great. But she didn't really mean a real stranger. She thought it would be her boyfriend or something. Someone he wasn't. So, this was crazy and had to stop before she couldn't bring herself back to reality and he would have her for real.

"You're lying." She saw his silhouette raise from the chaise. Her heartbeat skipped a beat or two before going full throttle. He moved toward her in the dark room, and she couldn't move. She wanted to run to the other side of the bed to put more distance between them, but she couldn't move. She couldn't do anything but stand there, watching him move toward her in the dark, with her heart rate way up high. Her heart had to be beating at 10,000 beats a minute.

"I'm not lying."

"You are. You want me."

"I don't."

"You do. I can smell it. I can smell your pussy. I can feel it on me. I know it in me. You want me. I knew you wanted me, and I wanted you."

"I don't. I didn't," she stammered and lied.

"You do. You did. Just like now. I smelled you then too."

"It's true. I don't want you."

"Then why are you crying? Are you scared of me?"

"Yes," she whispered as his fingers touched the tears on her face. He wiped them with his fingertips, and then she heard him put them in his mouth. The room had gotten several degrees hotter when it already felt like eighty.

"Are you scared of me? Or us?" He kissed her wet right cheek in the same spot that he wiped the tears away from just as gentle. His lips felt like pillows on her face, only turning her on more. Then he kissed the other cheek and licked her salty tears from his soft lips. He then kissed her forehead. He dragged his lips across her face until he found her nose, and then he kissed the tip of it. He did the same thing, trailing his lips over her face until he reached her lips.

Ke'Lasia closed her eyes. The intensity of the moment was too much for her to bear. She wanted to pull away or make him stop, but she was frozen in front of him. She was frozen in place. She willed her body to move but it couldn't. She couldn't move without the chance of sending her body into his. He placed quiet, calming, soft kisses on her lips until she inhaled from sexual wanting. He was right. She wanted him bad.

"I . . . I . . ." He kissed her between words, not allowing her to get them out.

"You? You want me? You want me inside of you? Say you do," he challenged her with his mouth against hers, allowing her to taste his lips for the very first time. She tasted him and wanted more. The hunger for him grew inside of her like the virile urges of a vampire to blood. She now had a thirst for the taste of this man.

"Say that you belong to me and I to you. Say what we know. That this was meant for us."

"Well then, why can't I see your face?"

His body went rigid. The air around them turned cooler. All his movements stopped, leaving his lips hanging centimeters away from her lips. She could feel his breath caress her as it seeped out of his nose. She wanted him, but she didn't want him. She wanted him so bad it literally hurt. Her stomach dropped when he didn't continue his kisses, and her mouth tightened around her scream when she felt his presence pull away. *Don't go!* She wanted to scream after him, but she didn't. She stood there in the dark, basically having a whole meltdown. She sank to the ground where she stood and with knees to her face. She bawled like a newborn child. Him leaving and her knowing that he would never come back just broke her heart into pieces. She couldn't control her sobs, and she didn't even bother to try. She lay on the floor beside her bed and cried herself to sleep.

***

"He's never coming back, Justin. I just know it. I know he's not," Ke'Lasia cried to her therapist. She couldn't take it any longer. Weeks had passed and she'd not had one visit from the stranger. She had no one to talk to about it, so she called Dr. Sagent's office and made an emergency appointment. Her actual appointment wasn't for a few more days, but she couldn't wait that long. "He doesn't want me anymore," she howled with tears and snot pouring out of her face, looking like a plum fool like she had been since the night he left.

"How do you know he'll never come back?"

"It was just . . . different. The last time he was there, it was different. We didn't have sex. He didn't touch me in those ways. And after I asked him why I couldn't see him, he left. I can just tell he's not coming back. I fucked up and I knew it before I even asked. What the fuck is wrong with me? I knew he wasn't gonna go for that shit and I pushed anyway." Ke'Lasia cried more as silence fell over the room. She looked up to see why Dr. Sagent wasn't saying anything. "Why aren't you talking? Why aren't you fixing me, Doc?" She pleaded with him through her tears almost angrily. She couldn't fix her, so he had to. On second thought, maybe it wasn't anger. Maybe it was desperation. She was desperate to find a cure for the ache her heart felt.

"Well, because there's steps we have to take here, Ke'Lasia. Number one, you have to be ready to admit some stuff to yourself. I'm not entirely sure what all that entails yet, but I do know that you care about this man. Even though you don't exactly know him, you care about him."

She looked at this almost handsome doctor and wanted to punch him in his damn face.

"Yes, I care about him, Doc! Of course I do, or I wouldn't be sitting here crying my eyes out over a fuckin' stranger."

"Do you love him?" he asked her.

"How can I love a fuckin' stranger, Justin? I don't know shit about him. He could actually be a rapist for all I know! Hell! He could be a damn serial killer. He could be the fuckin' president of the United fuckin' States and I'd be none the wiser." She threw her hands up in frustration, still clutching the tissues she held on to for dear life. She couldn't understand why he was asking her such silly questions. The tissues were her comfort at the moment.

"Because he's technically a stranger doesn't mean that emotionally you don't love him," Justin continued, unfazed by her small outburst.

"I don't know."

"Healing or understanding can't be fixed until we are honest with ourselves."

"I don't know," she repeated.

"I think you do."

"But I don't . . ." The look on the doctor's face let her know that he wasn't buying it, so she took a deep breath and took a moment to think. *Do I love him? Could I love him? Is this what love feels like?* "Could I be in love with a stranger, Doc? Is that even possible?"

"Anything is possible, Ke'Lasia. Anything."

"But he's a rapist."

"Did he rape you? Did he do anything you didn't want done? Did he hurt you? Mentally? Physically? Emotionally? Do you feel abused or raped?"

"No. I guess not." She looked at her hands twisting roughly around in circles in her lap, feeling like a fool under the doctor's gaze. "No, I don't feel raped. I don't feel abused."

"What do you feel?"

"I feel empty and hungry when he's not there. I feel completed and full when he leaves. That's how I feel."

"Explain hungry." He leaned in closer to make sure he heard her answer. He seemed real interested in what she had to say.

"I feel like I could have something. Like, I want something. Like an unidentified craving you can't put your finger on until you have it. I just need him. I just want him so much that I can feel him inside of me when he's in the room. He doesn't even have to touch me. I can feel him."

"Do you connect these feelings to feelings of love?"

She looked at him with her head cocked to the side as she thought about it. "Honestly, Doc, I couldn't tell you."

"Why is that? What feelings do you associate with love?"

"I don't know. Honestly, I don't."

Justin took a deep breath before his next question. "Have you ever been in love, Ke'Lasia?"

"No, Doc," she answered truthfully. "I haven't."

"So, what did it feel like loving your mother? Or father? How did you and your siblings show love to one another? What did that feel like?"

Her eyes watered as she answered his questions as honest and open as she could. "I don't know, Justin. The only sister I really have is September. My mom took her in when she was about eight. Then she eventually adopted her. She was about fourteen when that happened. Once my mom got September, it was like I was replaced all over again. My brothers were always her favorite. She treated them like gold, but me? I was just there. My brothers are so much older than me that I never even got the chance to get to know them. They all got old enough and moved on. I never see or hear from them. My father came around for a while. But once September came, he left. He said my mom would rather have September than him. He kissed me goodbye and I haven't seen him since either. The only other sister I had died when she was four.

I woke up one day and the ambulance was taking her out the house. That was the end. My mom never talked about it. All I ever heard was that I made my brothers leave and that I didn't deserve a sister, so I should've been grateful to have September. My mom never showed love or affection to me. The only time I remember my mom putting her arms around me was the day she died." Tears seeped quietly from her eyes, but her outside shell remained poised. She didn't want to break down in front of Justin even though her complete tears would have only been for the three brothers she never knew and the father she missed out on. The silent tears she let show on her face were only for herself and for the realization that love never lived in her life.

"Ke'Lasia, that's hard to hear. It sounds to me like you don't even know what love is. Maybe that's why you're scared of it with your new admirer. Because it's foreign to you."

"Or maybe because he's sick, Doc. The man intended to break into my house and rape me."

"So, why did you let it happen? That's what you told me, right? That you liked it and wanted it and even wanted him to come back? Want him to come back still?"

He was right. She did like it. She did want it. She'd told several people about that being one of her fantasies. She always wanted it. And when she got it, she loved it. Why did she want to convince herself so bad that something she wanted was so wrong? She did not know. The doc and Ke'Lasia looked at each other full on while she realized that she was only fooling herself. The stranger wasn't a rapist. He was her fantasy and she loved him.

September knew that Ke'Lasia was going through something, and it was fuckin' hurtful that whatever it was, was something that she felt like she couldn't tell her.

They had been cool for years, basically like sisters. They told each other everything. September had been perpin' like she was fucking Travis and everything, but she wasn't ready to tell Ke'Lasia it was the porn dude yet. She ain't know how she was gon' take it and she didn't want to be judged.

September knew Slash fucked other women for money for a living, but it wasn't like they mattered to him. Those girls didn't mean shit to him, and she knew what she was getting into when she got with him. That li'l shit didn't bother her at all. But everybody ain't as open as her. Ke'Lasia definitely ain't. She acted like the only niggas she ever fucked was for love and September wasn't finna live like that. Slash had a big-ass dick, and he fucked her in hella different ways that she'd never experienced before in her life! She wasn't in love with him at all, but she was sure in love with that dick!

He was a cool dude. He listened to her when they talked about shit, unlike other niggas who just bobbed their heads when a bitch was talking. He opened doors and pulled out chairs when they went out, and they went out often. He took her everywhere all the time. It was way different than fucking with Raheim's dog ass. It felt good to not have to fight and argue with another bitch every other day.

She didn't even mean to get into no relationship with Slash. It just kinda happened. That first night they hooked up after the photoshoot was mind-blowing as fuck! And from then on, they had spent every night and day together. It had been two months, and they were still going strong. He fucked her like it was the first time every time and she was definitely lovin' it. All of it. From the back shots to the way he made her feel like her soul left her body every time he sucked her pussy. All of it was the bomb and it was all the time. Day, night, middle of the afternoon.

He even fucked her between sets one time. He wasn't up yet. He was just taking pictures first. He had come to the back to get "fluffed" as they call it and she handled that for him. They fucked until he was about to cum and then stopped six times. By the time he was ready to go on and do his scene, he was at full attention and ready to fuck the girl's brains out. That was the realest scene of porn she had ever seen! He fucked that bitch hard, angry, and fast like he was mad at the world and took it out on her pussy and asshole. He pounded into her like he would never get another piece of pussy as long as he lived! Once he was finally able to release his load for real, he jerked her head back and forth so fast, cramming it into his pelvis by her ponytail until he let go and put all his baby-making juices all over her face. Then he flung her backward onto the mattress they used for the scene and jacked off the rest of the hot, sticky liquid until it trailed from her face to her humongous titties. She watched the whole thing and couldn't be more turned on by it.

Things were going great with Slash and her, and even though they were technically seeing each other, September didn't have to do none of the relationship shit people usually required. It was fuckin' awesome! Just the type of shit she needed in her life.

"What's up, li'l mama? What you thinkin' about?"

"How good you feel to me." She smiled at him and he winked back at her. His little smirk made her panties wet as fuck. She wanted to jump on him at all times. Almost everything he did turned her on. The shit was crazy.

"You know you got that wet shit, ma. Keep a nigga tryin'a swim in that shit all day." He laughed at her as he bit into an apple.

"Boy, shut the fuck up and go to work before you be missing another day." He slapped her on the ass and winked again as he left. "Don't fuck them hoes too good," she teased.

"Ain't nobody got pussy like you, shorty."

The door closed behind him and she fell against it. She was feeling euphoric. Nothing in the world could bring her down from the high she was on. Fucking Slash two ways from Tuesday almost every day was giving her life. A new pep in her step and everything. Life was looking up. She never knew people who did porn still liked sex so much.

September hopped on the phone and called Travis up. She needed to check on the status of the photoshoot Travis had set up for Ke'Lasia and her. They were supposed to be shooting a Land of Candy theme for some adult candy company. Their company sold adult-like candies in the shape of sexual items, body parts, and also edibles. The shoot was supposed to be surrounded in candy but sexy at the same time, and she was excited about it.

"Yeah, Travis. What's the details I need?" she asked once he answered the phone. He filled her in on what all the shoot would entail, where she needed to be, and when. They were about to hang up when she heard a familiar voice in the background.

"Is that Ke'Lasia I hear in the back?"

"Yeah, that's her," he confirmed.

"Oh, yeah? What y'all up to? I ain't know y'all was together." A twinge of jealousy hit her hard. *How they gon' just be out kicking it and not invite me?*

"Oh, we just grabbin' something to eat. What's up with you? What you doin'?"

"Oh, I'm just sitting here by myself. Why y'all ain't invite me?"

"You ain't been nowhere to be found lately. You know I always like having lunch wit' you, ma. I ain't heard no funny-ass jokes in a long time, wit' yo' silly ass. We only see each other for work now. When we gon' hook up?"

She felt better now hearing that he was still showing interest in her. Even though she was fuckin' wit' Slash, she still held out hope that she was gon' be able to see what was up wit' Travis one of these days. She was still kinda salty at herself that she met up with Slash after the porn shoot that day instead of Travis. She always thought that Travis was the kind of man she could settle down with, but she wasn't ready to give up the fast life yet. She didn't want him to stop digging her either though. She liked knowing that Travis was an option. She was also feeling a little guilty that she led Ke'Lasia to believe it was Travis that she was messing with, too, but she had to make sure that she didn't move in on her spot. She knew Ke'Lasia, which meant that she knew she would never fuck with nobody she was fucking with or digging. She knew it was kinda mean. She never even asked her how she felt about the man either, and she was the one of them who hadn't had a man in a minute. Honestly, Travis would've probably been a great match for her girl, but she couldn't risk them fucking around and never getting a chance to fuck with him. Knowing she was doing it for a good reason helped her feel better about it. And since he was on her line still flirting and shit, she guessed his interest in her justified her behavior. He obviously wanted her, so what was she really doing wrong? She literally shrugged off the ill feelings she had about the situation and carried on. She wasn't doing nothing that another bitch wouldn't do in her situation. *A girl's gotta keep her options open, right?*

"Shit, you let me know. I'm free when you free," she flirted back.

"All right. I'ma hit you up tomorrow. Remember the shoot details. We'll talk later."

She wondered what him and Ke'Lasia had been up to and how long they had been kicking it without her, but she wasn't finna trip. They were grown, and she knew Ke'Lasia ain't finna fuck with nobody she thought she was fucking, so it was nothing to worry about really. She shrugged it off and turned on Netflix to find something good to watch.

Chapter 7

She pulled up at Smokies, a little restaurant on the west side of town. It was off of Montana and convenient for her since she was already out that way.

"Damn. What's up wit' you? You lookin' good today." She greeted Travis after she found him in a booth by the front door of the place when she came in.

"I look good every day, shit," he said, modeling like he was in a photoshoot.

They laughed and hugged before they sat down. He nestled back into his side of the booth while she ordered something to drink and an appetizer from the waitress who showed up to greet her.

"This a cool li'l place though. What's good here?"

"Girl, you ain't ever been here?"

"Nope. I don't really be over on this side too much. Never even heard of this place."

"Well, it's a barbeque joint, so they got ribs." They giggled as the waitress came back with her drink and appetizer. She asked if she could take their order and Travis ordered for the both of them.

"So, I guess I don't need to look at the menu then, huh?"

"Nah, shorty, I got yo' back." Travis winked and smiled at her.

She always looked forward to his amazing smile. Slash had a nice smile too, even though he had a chipped tooth in the front, but it was nothing like Travis. His smile could stop a bitch's heart from beating. Slash looked better with his mouth closed. That beard he wore did all the work for him.

They made small talk while they waited for their food to arrive. They caught up on some stuff and shared some laughs.

"Okay. We got—" The waitress was interrupted by screams from other patrons. She turned to see what was going on as she tried to see around her to be nosy too. That's when she saw the man in all black fire his first round right into the waitress standing at their table.

"Listen up! Don't nobody move and this will be quick!" the assailant shouted from his post in between them and the front door.

One of the other two men with him jumped behind the counter, smacking the male cashier with his gun. He started to raid the cash registers, and she couldn't do anything but watch in horror. The third man began scouring the place, taking all valuable possessions and cash from all the dine-in customers. Their waitress sat on the floor holding her stomach where she had been shot. Barbeque and dishes were everywhere. She was frozen solid in her seat, eyes wide with fear. She couldn't find the words in her throat to speak.

"September, don't trip, shorty. We gon' be good, okay? Don't panic," Travis assured her as the masked man headed toward their table.

"Sit down!" he roared angrily at Travis when he saw him trying to stand.

"Hold on, man." Travis held his hands up. "I'm just trying to help the lady. She shot. She bleeding to death, man. This about to turn from a robbery to a murder real quick. That's what you wanna do?" Travis eased his body in between September and the masked man as he spoke.

Kneeling down slightly toward the bleeding woman, he threw off the assailant's attention enough to charge him and get his gun. Expertly, he shot the man one time in the head, spun, shot the first guy who still stood by the door, and stepped over him to shoot again as he lay there bleeding out. He then pulled his cell phone from his pocket and called the police. The whole thing was over. People started to let out cries of relief, happy that they had escaped the bad situation with their lives.

"September, help her apply pressure to the wound to slow down the bleeding. Hurry up or she won't make it. Use your shirt."

September snatched her shirt from her body in a frantic attempt to hurry up. She scrambled to the floor to help the lady. Landing on a piece of broken plate, she yelled out in pain.

"Dammit, September! Be careful! I'm not tryin'a have you die in here!"

"I slipped. It's just a cut though. I'm cool."

Checking first to make sure, Travis then ran to the door to see if he could find the cops, or at least an ambulance. The waitress lady was bleeding out fast. She couldn't help September apply the pressure to her stomach anymore because she was too weak at this point. September coaxed her to keep her eyes open like she had seen in the movies. She even sang to her. Anything she could do to keep her awake and hopefully alive.

Travis rushed back in, yelling to everyone to stay seated because the police were on their way in. People cried everywhere.

"Can she stand?" the paramedic asked once he arrived and saw them sitting on the floor.

"I don't think so. She's lost too much blood." She didn't even recognize her own voice from the terror it contained. The paramedic then left but quickly returned with another paramedic and a stretcher.

"We're going to move her," the guy paramedic told her, signaling for her to clear the way.

She started to stand, but it was a struggle. She almost toppled back over. "Ma'am? Are you okay?" the lady paramedic asked her.

She looked down to see herself covered in blood and her knee, where she was cut by the broken plate, swollen to three times its normal size. "Somebody get her. She's bleeding." More paramedics rushed in to help. Officers questioned people and paramedics went to work on her and the shot waitress.

"We're going to walk you out now, okay? There's not enough room to bring another stretcher in. You have to walk for us, okay?" she instructed September. She shook her head to let her know she had heard her.

With their assistance, September got to her feet. She hobbled on one leg as they guided her as easily as possible toward the door. The next thing she heard was a loud bang, then people screaming. It wasn't until right at that moment that she heard the sirens for the first time.

"September!" She saw Travis running toward the same doors that she was headed to. Then everything went black.

The paramedics rushed September and the waitress through the doors of the University of Cincinnati emergency room, one behind the other. September was second through the doors, and Travis was right behind her. Nurses and doctors ran to meet the medical team at the door and immediately started firing questions about both girls. Travis couldn't do anything but look back and forth around the huge crowd of people gathered around the girls and try to catch anything he could that they said. He heard the paramedic tell the nurses that they were both gunshot victims and his heart dropped into his stomach. Tears threatened to spill over. He tried his best to keep it together so that he could listen as close as possible to anything that he could understand. They rushed them both on the stretchers through another set of double doors where he was abruptly stopped by a nurse.

"Sir, you can't go back there. You have to wait in the emergency waiting room for someone to come talk to you."

"Can you at least tell me what happened?" Travis pleaded with him.

"All I can tell you is that the medics said they were both shot. I don't know anything else, sir," he explained to Travis. "But right now, I need you to go sit in the waiting room while we work to save your friends."

Travis walked back down the hallway toward the way he just came until he found signs for the waiting room. Travis found an empty seat, sat down, and pulled his phone out again. He looked at it for a second, just staring at the smeared blood that covered it. He went to find something to clean his phone with, and then he called Ke'Lasia to let her know what happened. She didn't answer, so he sent her a text letting her know she needed to call as soon as possible. Then he called the company and let them know that September had been shot and was in the emergency department. After all the phone calls were made, he was left to his own thoughts in the mostly quiet waiting room. He held his head in his hands, trying to figure out what went wrong. He silently prayed for both girls to pull through and live. The waitress had lost a lot of blood, and he didn't even know where September had been hit or how she'd even been shot. Then he remembered he had killed both assailants. The realization set in that eventually he would have to talk to the police. He sat back in the hard plastic chair and tried to get as comfortable as he could. It was about to be a long night.

Ke'Lasia barely even heard the phone ringing between the cries of ecstasy being released in the room. She was splayed out on her dining room table with her ankles tied to the matching chairs. Her left ankle tied to a chair on the left side, and the right ankle tied to another chair that sat to the right side. Both, at the end of the table. For the first time since purchasing the table and chair set, she was salty at herself for not getting the lighter chairs. She had let the salesperson talk her into the heavier chairs and now it was backfiring. She couldn't free her legs from the restraints they struggled against. All she could do was lie there and squirm, clawing at his bald head while screaming as he devoured her like she was his last meal and he was on death row. She couldn't escape the assault. He licked her clit, sending chills and sputters through her body that she couldn't control. Her muscles clenched again as she screamed out. She held one hand to the back of his head, holding his lips in place, suctioned to her clit as her other hand held on to his ear like a handlebar as he rode the orgasm to an end.

"Please! Please! I can't! I can't cum anymore!" She cried happy tears. The tears escaped her clenched eyes and ran down the sides of her face. Her body shook violently as another orgasm took over her body.

"Pleeeeeeaaasssssssseeeeeee!" she begged as the release was too forceful to hold back. "Stop. Please," whispered out of her mouth. She barely heard herself.

Euphoric sleep found her, and she could barely keep her eyes open. She felt his eyes staring at her in the darkened dining room. She didn't dare open her eyes to see if she was right. She was way too tired anyway. Her body started to relax so deep. She felt herself sink against the table. The cherry-oak wood was cool against her skin. It felt amazing.

"Aaaahhh!" she moaned out as she felt his massive manhood begin to stretch her pussy open to allow him to slide in. "Yes, baby. That feel so good," she cooed to him still with closed eyes. She could already feel another nut building up inside of her, waiting for him to reach the right spot that would allow her to explode all over him. "Yes, baby! Yes! There! Right there! Don't stop!" she urged.

His strokes sped up as she encouraged him. She grabbed his lower back as much as she could and tried to pull him farther inside of her. Her ankles still attached to the chairs kept her from trying to wrap her thick legs around his hefty body. He felt so good. His skin was smooth, growing moist from building sweat. He felt strong and soft at the same time. Her eyes threatened to open, but she wouldn't let them. She was not finished with him, and she didn't want him to leave yet. It had been months since this stranger had visited her, and she wasn't about to let him leave before she milked him for every ounce of energy he had. He owed it to her, and she was going to take it. She showered him with her sweetness once again. She didn't know how she was going to keep going, but he felt so good that she couldn't stop.

"I wanna get on top," she told him between shudders and moans. "Let me get on top, baby. Come on."

She felt him ease out of her and she knew he would oblige her request. He unleashed her ankles and grabbed for her. She let him guide her to where he was. She slid off the edge of the table down to his lap on top of his waiting, hard dick. He positioned her in the right spot for her to just ease right down on him. She felt an instantaneous feeling of fullness. Exactly what she told Dr. Sagent about. She was full and she loved it. She lay against him and put her head over his shoulder. His shoulders were hard and strong. She bit down on his right shoulder until he growled in pleasurable pain.

"Shit," he growled. She bit him again in a spot right next to the first bite mark she left behind. "Ummm. Shit." Another growl. She was excited. She swirled her hips in a circle and felt his hands tighten around her small waist. She reached back and spread her heavy ass cheeks to allow every single inch of him room to enter her completely. "Fuuuuck," he whispered.

She swirled her hips faster, pushed his head backward, exposing his throat, and found his Adam's apple with her teeth. She grazed across him, threatening to bite down. She trailed down his skin, smelling him, taking him in, committing to memory what his love sweat smelled like.

Finding his left shoulder, she swirled her hips harder on his lap before biting down on the shoulder that hadn't yet received her mark. He growled and pushed her hips back and forth, letting her know he wanted more. She kept the same pace, ignoring his invitations to speed up. Continuing in circles, she used her pussy muscles to clench against him. She could feel the thump in his veins that excited her. She bit down again and when he opened his mouth to speak out, she lifted her hips and dropped them on him.

"Shit! Shit. Shit. Shit, girl." His mumbles vibrated against her chest as she used her legs, mainly her calf muscles, to stand and drop herself on his lap over and over until he let her know that he was about to cum. He matched her rhythm in his last minutes, using her waist to slam her down into him over and over until he snatched out of her and held her still while he removed the thin condom and exploded on her stomach. She lay back against the edge of the table with her face up toward the ceiling until he was drained and his breathing evened back out.

"Fuckin' shit," she said as her body relaxed, understanding the end of the session. "I can't even move," she said, not expecting a response.

He still tried his best to not let her hear much of what his voice actually sounded like, so they still didn't have much conversation. He picked her up and carried her upstairs to the bed. she felt his biceps flexing against her skin. He laid her on her back and stood up. After a few minutes of silence, she spoke.

"The bathroom is over there." She pointed to the left of the room. "Second door. The rags are on the shelf. Help yourself."

She felt him leave the room and assumed he found the bathroom. She heard the water start, and in minutes, he was back, and a warm, soapy cloth wiped her stomach clean of his man juices. He came back again and washed her whole lower region, and then she felt a towel drop on her. She dried herself as she heard the shower turn on. She listened with her eyes still closed to the sounds of the water hitting him and then the shower floor. She felt herself drifting to sleep but tried to fight to stay awake so that she could tell him goodbye when he left. When she felt him slide into the bed and under the covers, she couldn't fight it anymore. Wrapped in his arms she gave in to the sleep that was trying so hard to consume her.

She woke up rested but alone. She wasn't as sad as she had been before. This time felt different. She knew he was gone, but she knew he'd be back. She got up and opened the curtains to let some sunshine in the room before getting into the shower. She got out the shower and took the time to apply hair product and blow dry her hair before trying to find something to wear. She had the feeling she was supposed to be doing something today, but she couldn't remember what it was. She was feeling too good today. She didn't really care much what it was she was forgetting or had already forgotten. It felt later in the day than when she usually woke up but had no idea what time it actually was. She walked out of the closet in search of her phone to check the time. She couldn't find her phone anywhere. Then it dawned on her that it was still downstairs on the couch where she left it before the encounter with the stranger. She smiled, reminiscing about the time they spent together yesterday. She headed downstairs to get the phone.

She snatched it off the couch and noticed the light blinking, letting her know she had unchecked messages. She opened her phone to see it was one o'clock in the afternoon. "Well damn. I guess I needed that sleep," she chuckled out loud. She opened the phone and checked the missed calls. Six from Travis and four from the company. What the hell was going on? She wondered.

She checked the messages to see Travis asking her to call him back as soon as possible. She stopped looking, deciding to call Travis back first before she checked the other messages and got her day started. Maybe he could tell her what she was forgetting today.

"What's up, Travis?" she practically sang into the phone.

"Ke'Lasia, I been tryin'a call you. I can't believe you wasn't answering the damn phone."

"Travis, I'm grown. I don't have to—"

"September is in the hospital. She only been out of surgery an hour. I'm waiting to hear more. Get here."

"What the fuck you mean surgery? What happened, Travis? Where are you?" she snapped. She felt her heart catch in her throat and tears well up in her eyes.

"We at University. Come on, shorty. Get here. I'll fill you in on what I know when you get here."

She hung up on Travis and dashed to find something to throw on.

"God, please let her be okay!" she cried as she snatched a sweat outfit out the closet and threw it on. She threw her hair in a sloppy bun with no time to worry about what it looked like. She grabbed her keys, phone, and purse, then ran out the door.

She rushed up to the desk in the emergency room and asked the nurse for the room number to where September was. The nurse clicked around on her computer and let her know that September couldn't have visitors yet.

"What do you mean she can't have visitors? I need to see her! I need to know what's going on!"

"Well, ma'am, you can have a seat in the waiting area with her fiancé. I'm sure he'll fill you in."

"Fiancé?"

She looked around for a familiar face, lost as fuck. September didn't have a fiancé she knew about, and she was damn sure this lady wasn't talking about Raheim's ass. If he was up in here, she planned to kick his ass on sight. His grimy ass was probably the reason she was up in here anyway knowing him. She found a seat and dropped her stuff. She unlocked the phone to call Travis.

"What's up, Travis? I'm here. Where are you?"

"I just came downstairs to the vending machine. Here I come now." They hung up.

The phones were breaking up anyway due to the terrible reception in the hospital. She wrapped her arms around herself and waited for Travis. Her leg bounced out of control, but it was soothing at the moment. She was going crazy, racking her brain trying to figure out what could've happened to her girl and who could've possibly wanted to harm her. Maybe it was them weak, snake-ass bitches from the hood, Monica and Amber? She ain't know but after she found out what was up with her and how she was, she was damn sure gonna find out. She pulled out her phone again and shot off a quick text.

Ke'Lasia: Raheim, I swear to God if I found out you are the reason my friend is laid up in the hospital, I swear on my life you gon' be sorry.

She looked at the phone, wondering if she should send something else. Her thoughts of Raheim were interrupted by Travis's voice.

"I'm sorry, Ke'Lasia. I been tryin'a call you since yesterday to tell you what happened, but you weren't answering. Well, the part I know anyway."

"What you mean the part you know? Weren't you wit' her?"

"Yeah, at first. Then everything just got worse real quick. I thought I had everything under control. The police were there and everything. Next thing you know, they got her on a stretcher and we're here, and they're talking about she's a gunshot victim. I don't know, man. I don't know what the fuck happened."

Travis dropped his head to control himself. She could tell he was trying to keep from crying because his voice was cracking the whole time. Ke'Lasia asked him a few more questions and he told her everything that had taken place the day before. She was horrified. Someone had shot up the place they were in, and apparently, September was just an innocent victim like the lady she came in with. That shit made her even more mad because now, she had no idea where to start trying to figure out who played a part in this. She was relieved to hear Travis had taken care of two of the guys but sad to hear that there was a third one who managed to still have his life.

"So, where is he?"

"I don't know, Ke'Lasia. I killed the other two dudes. I don't think the police just gon' readily tell me where the boy is."

"So, is he locked up?"

"He was shot too, so I'm not sure if he's in jail already or at the hospital himself. I don't know how severe he was or wasn't."

"So, who the hell is this fiancé they're saying September has?" Travis hung his head before responding. Her eyebrows furrowed. "Who, Travis? Raheim?"

"Nah. Me."

"You?" She was shocked as hell. Her mouth hung open. She was surprised as hell to hear that Travis and September were engaged. Nobody told her nothing and her feelings were super hurt by it.

"Yeah, man. It's me. Don't say nothing, okay?"

"Who else would I tell? I'm just surprised y'all ain't tell me out of all people. I just had lunch with you a few days ago. Why you ain't tell me then?"

"What? Tell you what?"

"That y'all was getting married, Travis, duh."

"No, Ke'Lasia." He looked around like someone was following him. He looked so serious that she looked around too. "We're not engaged for real. I just told them that so that they would tell me what's going on with her."

Ke'Lasia was so relieved she let out a huge breath. She never even knew she was holding it in. She felt so much better to hear that it wasn't real. She didn't know why exactly. She just was.

"Damn, you sound happy."

"Huh?"

"You sound real relieved that we're not actually getting married."

She stayed quiet and looked at him, only blinking. She just didn't want to say the wrong thing to him and possibly hurt his feelings. It wasn't him. She just knew that the kind of guy she assumed he was would never match the kind of girl she knew September to be. Not that he was that great of a guy because he was just all in her face not too long ago just to end up fucking her friend anyway after he made it seem like they were just cool. So maybe they did go good together. September liked her men messy and that would be a messy situation Ke'Lasia wanted no parts of had she known what she did. Yeah, she was gonna keep her mouth shut and her feelings to herself. She was just happy they weren't really getting married.

"I don't know what I'm supposed to say about that. My best friend and who I thought was a close friend of mine getting married and didn't tell me? Would that make you happy if it was you?"

"Nah. I guess it wouldn't. Y'all are best friends, huh? I keep forgetting that." He said that last part more to himself than her before he looked away again. She could tell something was on his mind that he wasn't saying. She just didn't know what. Maybe he was embarrassed to tell her he actually did want to end up married to September.

"If you actually wanna marry her though, go 'head. Nothing's wrong with that. Don't let me or anyone else keep you from what you want."

"What?" He chuckled and shook his head. "I never said I wanted to marry September. I just keep forgetting that y'all are really best friends in real life."

"But you said that to say what though?" she asked him, silently trying to pry his personal thoughts from his head.

"I'm just thinking that me trying to fuck wit' you and we all work together would probably mess up a good thing is all."

"Fuck with me?" Now she was really surprised. "What you mean fuck with me?"

"Come on, Ke'Lasia. You mean to tell me that you haven't noticed that I'm feeling you?"

"You got a funny way of showing it." She crossed her arms with attitude, now in a funk.

"Why you say that?"

"'Cause how you diggin' me but fuckin' my best friend? I ain't ever seen a nigga show interest like that. That's some new shit to me." She rolled her eyes hard. Who the hell did this nigga think he was playing? Wasn't no way in the world she was about to be fucking with him in no capacity and his ass was fucking her friend. She may have been fat and sweet, but never the fuck had she ever been dumb. He was tripping and it was pissing her off.

Travis burst out laughing. Like, laughing hard. He was trying to cover his mouth to muffle the noise, but he wasn't doing a good job of it. She was horrified. This nigga had to be crazy. Her bestest fucking friend was laid up in the hospital fighting for her damn life and not only was he trying to fuck her behind her back, but he also thought it was funny. She was about to flip the fuck out on this nigga in here.

"How you figure I'm fuckin' her? 'Cause we had lunch a few times? So did you and I. When did going out to eat start meaning fuckin', Ke'Lasia?" He was weak, weak, like some shit was really funny. He was so busy laughing he didn't even notice that he had her fucked up.

"So, you really gon' sit here while my friend is up in this hospital and not only lie but think it's funny, too? For some pussy? I'm sitting up thinkin' you a good dude when you just as doggish as the rest of these niggas. Don't worry about shit though. I'll let her know yo' plans to get pussy out the both of us. You can go. She's finished and so am I." By this point, a few people in the waiting room were all in their mouths, but she didn't care. This nigga had her and her friend fucked up and ain't no way in hell she was letting him get away with it.

"Gettin' pussy? Lying? Fuckin' September?" Travis looked at her quizzically with a shocked look on his face like she had stuttered through his favorite song or something.

"Yeah, nigga. You been fuckin' her and now you trying to fuck me too. Not only am I no nigga's second weak-ass choice, but I'm—"

Travis held up his hand to stop her. "I would never consider you a second choice or just some pussy to get. That shit is first. Secondly," he said, lowering his voice to barely above a whisper that was filled with anger, "I don't know who the fuck you think I am, but I've never been a dog-ass nigga. I ain't ever fucked September. And if I had, I wouldn't have been in yo' face for months like a chump tryin'a figure out how to ask you out or tell you I like you. Had I been fuckin' yo' friend, I would have never looked your way. But I'm not. Nor have I ever wanted to or tried. September is a gorgeous girl. She's even built the way I like. But I have never been interested in her that way. She's just cool peoples. I've wanted you from the first day I laid eyes on you, but I could see that you were hurt and trying to heal, so I gave you that space. I don't know who told you I was fuckin' her, but they lied. That's the last time I'm going to tell you. Don't ever disrespect me like that ever again. You don't want me? Fine, say that.

Don't try to play me like I'm just these niggas y'all used to fuckin' wit' though."

Travis got up and walked away. Ke'Lasia was speechless. She didn't know what to say or do. She looked around the room to see who had heard and saw a guy sitting a couple chairs down shaking his head. Now, not only was she confused as hell, but she was embarrassed, too. She turned toward the direction of the TV that hung from the ceiling and acted as though she were watching intently.

"Excuse me, ma'am. Are you waiting to hear about Miss Waters?" A nurse nudged Ke'Lasia awake. She felt bad for even falling asleep at a time like this. She wiped her face and hurried to answer.

"Yes, ma'am. That's me. What's going on? Is everything okay?"

"It's just fine. She's doing great, in recovery, and has been moved to a private room. She can have visitors now but only for a few minutes because visiting hours are over for non-family members."

"I'm the closest thing she's got to family. Can I please stay with her?"

"What about her fiancé? Is he not here anymore?"

She kicked herself for forgetting Travis's story. "I mean, he can't stay though. I can. Can I just stay? If he tells you it's fine, can I stay?"

"If he agrees, that's fine. I won't argue with it. We'll just tell the nurse in attendance that you're her sister, okay." She winked at Ke'Lasia and led the way to the back.

"Oh, wait!" Ke'Lasia stopped her at the double doors leading to the ICU. "Can I call her fiancé so we can go back together? I don't want him to miss the time. He's been here since yesterday. I know he's around here somewhere."

"That's fine. Just be quick, okay? I'll be back in two minutes."

She felt a stab of anger calling Travis her fiancé after the way he acted earlier, but whatever. She wouldn't let him miss out on seeing September. She called him up and let the phone ring three times before she decided to hang up. She heard him answer right as she pushed the button to end the call. She waited a quick second for the phone to ring back.

"Where are you? You gotta get to the waiting area quick. They said September can have visitors for a few minutes. Come on. I'm by the water fountain on the other side of the waiting area by the double doors that got ICU on top of them." He confirmed he was on his way, and they hung up.

Ke'Lasia only had to wait thirty good seconds before she saw him bounding through the waiting area at full speed toward her. "Damn! Where were you? You got here quick. Thanks."

"No need to thank me. I was on the opposite side of you. I never left. I just sat on the other side of the wall. Just because I'm not fuckin' her don't mean I don't care about her."

Ke'Lasia felt so bad. She never meant to offend him. She only went off what September had told her. Now she didn't know what to believe. Until further notice though, she decided to believe her, so Travis would just have to be the fuck mad.

The nurse showed back up as they stood there in awkward silence and led them to a room among the many rooms in the back where their friend lay in a hospital bed with tubes running from her body to nearby machines.

"September," Ke'Lasia groaned in pain at the sight of her lying there as she gently fell across her feet. "What the hell happened to you, damn it?" She couldn't stop the tears. Travis handed her a box of tissues, and she wiped her face for nothing. New tears instantly moistened her cheeks again.

"I'll give you two a few minutes. Remember, only one of you can stay. I'll be back." The nurse quietly exited the room and left them to their friend and their sorrow.

Ke'Lasia couldn't believe what she was seeing. Her friend. Her sister. A shell of who she was. She lay there unconscious. She looked small and different. Not like she was used to her looking at all. She seemed so frail and fragile. So not September. It was disheartening. It was also sad to see. She felt helpless as hell. She just had to watch her lie there and do nothing. *Who could've done this to her and why?* Travis told her that it was just a robbery gone wrong at Smokies, but for some reason, she just couldn't believe it. She just couldn't come to grips with the fact that she was just in the wrong place at the wrong time. It just didn't make sense.

She was happy she was alive, but she was sad that she hadn't pulled through yet. The surgery was over, and they had gotten the bullet out. That was good news. Now they just had to wait until morning to see what else the doctors had to say.

Chapter 8

Travis's head was killing him, so he stopped at the corner store N&I in the neighborhood where he lived before finding his way home. He thanked God that Walnut Hills was one of the very few neighborhoods left that had a store that stayed open late. He popped the single package of headache medicine open and downed the two small blue pills with one swig of water. He pulled up at his house on Oak Street and jumped out quick. He needed to get in fast and lie down. He couldn't take one more second of being awake. His head hurt from all the thoughts of what went on at the restaurant. He couldn't understand how he had let one of them mu'fuckas live. Had he paid more attention, he would've remembered it was three of them niggas instead of just two. That last mu'fucka would've been just as dead as the other two.

He got close to his door and almost caught another body quick.

"Damn, Kiesh! What the fuck?"

"You act like I can't come over your house or something." She leaned against the front door and crossed her arms with an attitude. He tucked his gun back in his pants and shook his head.

"It's eleven o'clock, Keish. What the fuck you doin' here?"

"I came to see you. What you mean? Just open the fuckin' door, damn."

"Whatever. Where my kids at?"

"I told you where they were, damn."

She moved him out the way and barged in his house as soon as he got the door open. They walked in and Keisha found a seat on the couch while he went to the refrigerator and grabbed a beer. He didn't offer her one.

"Damn, I can't get a beer?"

"Ain't no more. What's up, Kiesh?"

"What you mean what's up?"

"It's damn near midnight and you at my house. Without my kids, might I add. You gotta want somethin'."

"I gotta want something? Why is that?" She started looking at him with that look that let him know he was gonna have to fight her off with everything he had left in him.

"Come on, Kiesh. Don't do that. I'm not in the mood for this. I had a long few days. Can I just holla at you tomorrow?"

"Nigga, please. You know you want this. You better quit playin' and run me that li'l shit before I change my damn mind."

"Well, change it then, Keisha, shit. I'm not on this shit tonight. I just wanna get some damn sleep." Kiesha ain't listen to nothing he said at all. At all. She just got up and got naked. He just shook his head. He really wasn't in the mood to deal with her right now, let alone fuck this girl. He just wanted some fuckin' sleep.

"Keisha, please. Not tonight, okay? We don't even get down like that."

She stood there in a sexy-ass panty and bra set. It was black and lace. It was even see-through. She was lookin' good as fuck. This the kinda shit that led to all of them damn kids they had.

He walked past her and headed to his bedroom. Attitude or no attitude, he was going to sleep. Keisha was just gon' have to be mad. He was worn out and had no more energy. Not for Keisha or no one else.

Travis got up early and jumped in the shower. His plan was to get back to the hospital to see what was up with September as soon as possible. He was still fucked up and feeling like September lying up in that hospital was his fault.

He got out the shower and found a red Adidas sweat suit to throw on. After putting on shoes, he grabbed his keys to head out the door. He got to the bottom of the steps and was halted by some sweet-ass aromas coming from the kitchen.

"What the fuck?" he mumbled. He walked in the kitchen to see Keisha in that sexy-ass underwear set and wearing one of his button-down shirts. It was open and showing all her assets. She was looking good as fuck and cooking something that smelled delicious. "I thought you left last night."

"No. I stayed here. I could tell you were going through some stuff and I figured you would need some breakfast."

"You don't even cook though."

He was confused as shit honestly. Kiesha hadn't cooked a real meal in years. Not for him, their kids, or nobody else. Her cooking was foreign as hell to him. He knew she had to be up to something.

"What's going on, Keish? Why you doin' all this?"

"I just wanted to do something nice for you, damn. What's wrong with that?"

"You don't do nice shit. Somethin' gotta be up. Just tell me what it is 'cause I gotta bounce."

"You gotta bounce? Where you going? I made all this food."

"I appreciate it, I really do. But a friend of mine in the hospital and I gotta go. Just leave it for me. I'll eat it when I get back. I'll talk to you later. Just lock up when you leave, okay?"

"Oh. Tell that bitch I said hi then." Keisha threw the spatula down and turned off the stove.

He looked back over his shoulder one last time before walking out the door. Kiesha was pissed and he knew it, but there was nothing he could do about that right now.

"Is there any new information on her condition?" Ke'Lasia inquired.

"Honestly, we're just waiting on her to wake up. She'll have some pain, but she won't feel much. She'll be under heavy pain medication for a while, but she'll be fine. The bullet missed all the important stuff. She suffered a little internal bleeding, but we got it under control. Right now, we're just waiting to see how well she comes off the drugs from the surgery. No allergic reactions or serious to no side effects is what we're hoping for. Everything else now is up to September. She's great. Your sister did fine." The doctor patted her hand before leaving the room, leaving her to her tears.

Ke'Lasia was so fucking happy to hear that she would make it. She wouldn't lose her friend.

Chapter 9

Six Months Later

September woke up with only a little pain that morning. "Baby, can you pass me my medicine please?"

"You still taking this shit? You ain't off of this yet?"

"Don't start that shit, Slash. Just give me my medicine, damn." She grabbed the bottle from him and rolled back over to the glass of now lukewarm water she had sitting on her nightstand. She swallowed two of the white pills quick and lay back to let them kick in.

"For real, ma, the doctor said you should've been off that shit months ago."

"Months though?" She rolled her eyes. It was just a couple of Percocet. She didn't know why he was making such a big deal about it.

"Yeah, months. Three to be exact." His sarcasm was irritating the fuck outta her. Like, why couldn't he just leave her the fuck alone about this?

"Well, is it my fault that the shit still hurt? I got fuckin' shot, Slash, damn. Why we keep going through this? My fuckin' chest and shoulder hurt every fuckin' day. What the hell you want me to do about it? Just sit here in pain and let it hurt? Damn. I don't understand why you always on my ass about the same shit."

"I want you to stop takin' this shit!" She knew he was mad as hell, but it wasn't shit she could do about it. She couldn't tell him that the pills just made her feel nice and she didn't want to stop taking them. He'd start talking that addicted shit again, and she wasn't trying to hear none of that. She was fine and he needed to stop tripping. She wasn't addicted. She just liked feeling better.

"Listen, baby. I appreciate everything you've done for me. Helping me get back well and all that. That shit was clutch. But I got it now. I'm okay. I promise," she told him, trying to soothe his anger. She didn't feel like fighting with him. The good feelings from the pain meds were kicking in and she wasn't trying to waste her good feelings arguing. Instead, she decided to switch gears.

She pulled the covers over her head and slid down the side of his body until his head was eye-level with his penis. "Come on, ma. What you doin' down there?" he asked her, looking under the covers to see her every move.

"I'm lightening the mood." She smiled up at him as seductively as she could, trying to keep his mind off of the conversation. Then she grabbed his soft member in her hand, beginning to stroke gently. "Why? Want me to stop?" She smiled again, hoping like hell that his answer was no.

"We gotta talk about this, ma."

"No, we don't." She took him into her mouth and gave him small suckles.

She felt him growing inside her jaws. She kept watch on him until his head fell back against the pillow and he let the covers drop back down. Then she went to work. She gave him the best blow job she had ever given before in her life. Her head swirled and her mouth tightened as she watched his toes curl. His moans filled the room like a low-budget concert. The TV in the background just made up for the missing crowd. She was going to work. One hand gripped her head through the sheet and pushed her over and over again toward his pelvis bone and the other hand gripped the sheets, damn near pulling them off the bed. She moaned wildly, getting turned on by the sounds he made. By the way his body moved, he loved what she was doing, and she loved doing it. She damn sure would have rather been sucking his dick than talking about her medicine.

"Hell yeah, baby. Suck that shit. Just like that. Hell. Fuckin'. Yeah!" His exaggerated moans coupled with the throbbing vein in his dick against her tongue let her know that he was on his way to explosion.

She decided to change the tempo. She sped up and used her hands. With each twist of her wrist and each flick of her tongue around his dick, and the fluttering on the inside of her warm, wet mouth, his excitement grew for her. His hunger for his nut warmed him. She teased his climax closer to the end with the combination of hand motions and prepared herself.

"Mmmm," she moaned.

"There it is, baby. Right there! Hell yeah!" He forced her head down as far as he could by the back of her head. She let him.

She opened her tonsils more and let his warm seed spill down her throat. She stroked his shaft softly with one hand, making sure every drop of liquid escaped him as she used the other to caress his balls. His toes, still curled tightly toward his feet, let her know that her job was done greatly.

After Slash got ready for work and left, she jumped in the shower after brushing her teeth. Thirty minutes later, she was standing in her closet looking for something to wear. She chose a hot pink Adidas tank top and pants with hot pink and white stripes to match. She strapped her phone to her arm, put in her headphones, slid into her Adidas runners, and walked toward the door to her apartment. As she reached for the doorknob, her hand shook. She snatched it back and let it hang by her side. She felt her heart rate accelerate. She hung her head as she turned toward the coffee table in the living room and picked up the pill bottle. With the even warmer water that had been sitting from the hours before, she swallowed two more pills. Putting the bottle back in its place on the table, she wiped the lone tear that escaped her eye and went back for the door.

"No, I'm good. You can come over. I'm just about to jump in the shower, so use yo' key." She hung up on Ke'Lasia and proceeded into the warm water awaiting her.

She washed off the sweat from her run. She got out the shower, dried off, and slipped into her robe. She stood in the mirror for a while just looking at herself. The robe she wore belonged to her mother. It was the only thing she left behind when she packed up and left in the middle of the night. She didn't know why she kept it. She just did.

"What's up, mama? How you feelin'?" Ke'Lasia asked once she got in the door.

"I'm doing all right. What's up with you? You was busy?"

"Nah. Just finished running."

"That's good. You back working out?"

"Trying to." She grabbed a bottle of water and sat down next to Ke'Lasia. She laid her head on her shoulder and they sat there in silence.

After a few minutes, she picked up the remote to turn on the TV while she ordered pizza. They got good and into the fourth season of *Orange Is the New Black* when someone knocked on the door.

"Who is it?"

"Me."

She opened the door for Slash and walked back to the couch. "What's up, baby?" she tossed at him, retaking her seat.

"Not shit. How you doin', Ms. Lady?"

"What's up. I'm Ke'Lasia since this rude-ass ho ain't gon' introduce us." She looked at September and rolled her eyes. A long conversation was ahead of her. She knew that Ke'Lasia was going to have so many questions about Slash since she hadn't filled her in, but she would deal with that when the timing was right. For now, she chose to ignore her sarcastic looks.

"Oh, yeah, I'm sorry. Babe, this my sister, Ke'Lasia. Bitch, that's Slash." He walked over and shook her hand. After grabbing a beer out of the fridge, he came and sat next to her on the couch to watch the show with them.

"Damn, what's this?"

"*Orange Is the New Black*," Ke'Lasia told him, smiling hard.

"This our shit. I can't believe she ain't tell you. This shit be wild."

They caught him up on who was who and he got right into it with them. She watched him out the side of her eye and realized in that moment that she was actually feeling him a lot. She was fake falling for this man and it was fucking with her.

Everything was going good with Keisha since Travis put her in her place a while back. She ain't stayed out of his pockets, but she was letting him see the kids more. That's all a nigga really wanted. He loved his kids and all he wanted in life was to make them happy. He was riddled with guilt having to leave his kids to go meet up with an old nigga he used to run with back in the day. They used to get heavy in the streets back in the day and now he was going right back to what he tried so hard to run from all those years ago. But he had to do what he had to do.

Travis shook hands with G4. He was the go-to guy now for anyone who needed info on what went on in the hood. He wouldn't call him his nigga no more, but he was still cool people. They called him Skool because he was older than the other niggas who ran on the block now. He was older than all of them, but he was still on the block while a lot of the rest of them had moved on. Some to jail, some to the grave, and others legit. A few niggas had even moved up to being connects. G4, though, stayed hitting blocks and chilling wit' the new, younger hustlers. The upside to G4's old ass was that he was nosy. He listened to everything and everyone. He was useful in the information department.

"What's up, Skool?"

"Not much, my nigga. What's up with you?"

"Shit, same shit, different day. You know how it go." They both chuckled. More so to themselves than each other. "You got that li'l information for me?"

"That shit was hard as hell to get, man, I tell you," G4 hinted.

"You know I got you, bra." Travis leaned next to him on the wall where he stood and passed him the joint he smoked. On the sly, Travis also slid him an envelope full of cash. G4 always requested money for his info, which was why only older niggas fucked with him. "So, what's up? What you got for me?"

"Shit, that shit wasn't no coincidence, li'l nigga." Travis gritted his teeth and continued listening. He hated when he was called that, but he dealt with it to get what he needed. "No other nigga would've been able to find out what I did, but I got that shit though." He hit the joint again before passing it back.

"So, who was it?"

"Some new niggas from over there in Price Hill. Ain't nobody even really know them. But shit, fuck 'em." He shrugged.

"Who sent 'em?"

"Some nigga named Vic. Old-school nigga like me. The plan was to make it look like a robbery gone bad, but the target was shorty. The one you was wit'."

"What? Why her?" The information hit Travis hard. He figured if it was personal, it would be from the lame-ass nigga Raheim she was fucking with. He never heard her talk about nobody named Vic.

"That part I don't know. All niggas know is that she was supposed to die that day. And since she didn't, somebody gon' be at her. In a minute, her body go'n go to the first taker so you need to get to her before one of these brazen-ass, hot-headed, young niggas who don't give a fuck do."

They stood there in silence, smoking the rest of the joint they passed back and forth. His mind went wild. Travis had to find out who the fuck Vic was before September was back in the hospital again. Or worse.

Chapter 10

Travis hadn't had any sleep again that night. His pillow was calling him, but every time he lay down, sleep evaded his brain. He was up all night racking his brain trying to figure out why the fuck this nigga Vic wanted September dead and who the fuck he even was. He had some young niggas he knew from the hood keeping their ears to the ground to see if they could come up on some information about the nigga. Travis hadn't asked September about him yet because there was no need to upset her. Especially if he didn't have to. He didn't know if she was beefin' with a nigga he ain't know about, or if she was targeted for some reason that even she ain't know about. All he knew was that it was some funny shit going on and bringing up that day just wasn't something he was prepared to do. He hated weird shit, and all this shit was weird. He still felt guilty as fuck for her getting shot.

I swear that shit was my fault, regardless of who said different. The thoughts and memories of that night played over and over again in his head every day and every night. Had he remembered the last lame-ass nigga behind the counter with the gun who came running in and shooting up shit, September or the waitress who got shot just like her would've never been in that situation. He convinced himself that there was more he could've done.

He couldn't help the waitress lady who sadly got hit before his friend. He wished he could've though. It was fucked up she was dead. He heard her people were from his hood though, so he went to the funeral to pay his respects like any real nigga would. He wouldn't be any different either. He even dropped some cash off to her family a couple times to help out. They were good people, and it was sad that they had to lose her like that. It's not to say that it had nothing to do with guilt because maybe it did somewhat. That still ain't mean that he, by any means, wanted to watch them struggle either way it went, guilt consuming him or not. It wasn't much money that he gave, but it was the least he could do.

That day still ate him up a lot. He was kind of sure it didn't bother him as much as it did the actual victims, but he was barely sleeping, so he knew it was still messing with them. The episodes of that day took a toll on everyone there in different capacities. He assumed more than just he was still dealing with it. It hadn't been that long since the shit happened.

September and Travis had spoken a couple of times over the last few months, and that girl was still in major pain. From what he'd heard, she was still taking the meds they gave her after the incident, even though she probably shouldn't. He even tried to talk to her about it, but she hung up in his face. He was salty at her for it, but he understood.

We all got demons to fight in our own way.

His phone started to ring, and he answered it.

"What's up, Kiesh?" he quizzed when he answered the phone.

"What's up, baby daddy? You busy?"

"Nah. I'm just chillin'."

"So, you saying you want some company then?"

He could hear the hinting in her voice. He wasn't opposed to female company. He just wished it didn't have to be Kiesha. She could never just get the dick without thinking that they were going to get back together, and that wasn't something he felt like dealing with. But turning down company didn't sound good either. He already couldn't sleep, so having somebody next to him at least would probably make that easier. He hadn't been that boo'd up with a chick since Kiesha all those years ago, and although he wasn't trying to boo up with his baby mama now, at least he wouldn't be alone. He mulled it over before he responded to her trick question.

"That's cool," he conceded. "I'll leave the door open." Travis hung up with Kiesha and got in the shower after going downstairs and unlocking the door for her to get in.

Halfway through his shower, he felt a cold breeze drift through the bathroom, signaling that the door had been opened. Hurriedly, he rinsed the soap off his body in case things were about to get freaky between the two of them, which he not only assumed but hoped, since she came into the bathroom knowing he was in the shower. He didn't see any other reason why she'd join him in the bathroom instead of just waiting for him in his room. It was cool, though. He'd much rather get straight to the point of her being there instead of making silly small talk and being awkward. It always worked better with them when they didn't do too much talking.

"Why you just standing out there like a creep? Bring yo' ass in here and quit playin'."

His dick was getting hard thinking about the pussy he was about to get. Honestly, he ain't wanna be back with his baby mama at all, but he couldn't deny the fact that her pussy was bomb as fuck. He missed the days that he could wake up with morning wood and roll over to her gushy shit. She never stopped him from feeling that shit straight up out his sleep, not once. He would lift her leg up and hold it in the air while he pushed his dick in her, listened to her moan awake, then enjoy the ride as she came to life and threw that ass all over the place for the sweet pleasure of the both of them. Kiesha was a good fuck. And her mouth was put to better use wrapped around his dick than talking his ear off about some bullshit. He could only imagine how good this shit was gon' be and he wanted her to hurry the fuck up. He had to push all the extra shit out of his brain. All of the reasons why he ever started hating her touch in the first place, because truth be told, it had been a minute for him and he really didn't have another offhand option. Keisha was good as fuck in bed, and that helped him decide to not hate her enough to bust this nut that she was offering him, but damn this was a thin-ass line to cross. Keisha was usually the one trying to get dick out of him, just like she was now. And he usually participated against his will. But tonight, his dick was hard, and he was lonely as fuck. He was going to regret this shit in the morning but fuck it. His dick was getting harder by the minute just thinking of the things that this girl was willing to do and let be done.

The curtain pulled back as he rinsed off for the second time. He always washed up at least twice, so he was happy to be able to get the second washing out the way before he was interrupted.

"It took you long enough. You scared or something?" he said over his shoulder to Kiesha once she finally got up the courage to get in with her.

"I am a li'l bit, honestly. I don't even know if I should be doing this."

Travis was shocked as hell. Turning around, his eyes locked with Ke'Lasia's and he was stuck. At a loss for words, he couldn't say shit. What the fuck was she doing here? He quickly searched his brain for a reason that he may have forgotten.

"Ke'Lasia? What you doin' here? How you get in?"

"The door was unlocked. I was knocking on it and it came open, so I came in to find you."

"And you just happened to come into my bathroom?" he questioned.

"This was where you were. I heard the water running, so I came in to talk. You invited me in here with you."

He watched as her eyes dropped down to his swollen manhood. He tried to play it off like she wasn't looking, but he had already seen her size him up. He didn't try to cover up either. He just stood there at full attention in front of her. He was so hard that his manhood almost reached out to touch her in the custom-made shower/bathtub combo. He smirked at the knowledge that she was curious about his parts. She wasn't alone in her curiosity though. Seeing that it was her and not his baby mama in the shower with all of her assets exposed made his dick harder than Chinese arithmetic.

"I didn't know it was you." He looked her up and down openly, letting his eyes trail slowly over her sexy-ass body.

He had only imagined what she would look like naked up until this point. He was happy as hell on the low that she was standing in front of him like this. All he could think about was wrapping her thick-ass thighs around his head and listening to her enjoying him sucking the life out of her pussy. He probably shouldn't even be thinking like this, but he was. He couldn't help it. He had been wanting her for so damn long that it was like a dream come true that she was standing there, basically offering herself to him. He could tell by the look in her eyes that she tried to hide from him, that she was intrigued by what he held in his possession. Hopefully, her excitement would allow him to explore her insides once and for all.

"I should've known that you were waiting on company. I'll go. I'm sorry." She started to pull the curtain back with a sad look on her face, but he stopped her.

"I didn't say you had to go."

"You actin' like you don't want me to stay. I ain't tryin'a step on no toes. I'm trippin'. That's my fault. I should've never come in here. I don't know what the hell I was thinkin'." Ke'Lasia backed up from the shower and left.

He stood there naked and rock hard. He rushed to turn the water off so he could jump out to follow her. He wasted no time trying to put a towel on. He caught up to her in his room, standing there still naked. She was looking around for something that she obviously had no clue how to find. He had no idea what she could've been searching for, He was just happy as hell she couldn't find it. Whatever it was, he hoped like hell that she'd never find it if it meant keeping her here with him.

"I thought you were gonna leave," he said once he could finally speak again. A sigh of relief washed over him in that moment. He was happy as hell and trying to contain his excitement. He realized then that he still had a chance to get her to stay.

"I was. I just couldn't find something. I don't think my clothes—"

Before she could finish, his mouth was on hers. "What are you doing?" she asked, breaking their kiss.

"Girl, I've been wanting you since the first time I saw you. I'm not playin' with you no more. I'm about to fuck the shit out of you and you about to let me." They held eye contact. He gave her a few seconds to stop him before he placed his mouth on hers again. Her kissing him back let him know that she was down for whatever it was that he had in store for her.

"This ain't right. You and September."

"Me and September what? I told you at the hospital there was nothin' goin' on with me and her. Nothin'. Never have. I fuck wit' September. I love her like a li'l sister or li'l cousin, but that's it. I never fucked her or fucked with her. What don't you get?"

"I don't get why she would tell me that if it wasn't true. I shouldn't have come here."

"I don't know why she told you that, but it ain't true. I'm not gon' keep sayin' it either. I never touched that girl like that. I've wanted you this whole time. From the beginning, it's always been you, Ke."

He politely stepped over her clothes that lay at her feet as he guided her backward to the bed. His lips found hers again and never left. He felt her grow hungrier for him, as their kiss got deeper. He wasn't upset about what she thought. He wasn't upset that September let her think it. All he wanted to focus on was her. He wanted her just as bad as it felt like she did him. He could feel her body giving in to him. That was the sign he needed to let him know that his dreams were finally about to come true.

Before he could comprehend what was happening, Ke'Lasia pulled away from him, slapping him across the face. Instincts kicked in and he let her go immediately. Stepping back, she fell to the bed. His dick instantly went soft. Now she was the one with a smirk on her face.

"What the fuck, Ke'Lasia? Why you hit me?"

"Stop actin' like you scared of this pussy and take it."

Travis stared her down as his face stung. He wasn't sure what the fuck to do. He was lightweight salty she hit him, but he wasn't technically mad. He was actually kind of turned on.

He had never been in this situation before. When Kiesha hit him back in the day, the only woman to ever put her hands on him, it was a different situation. She wanted to fight. But the look in Ke'Lasia's eyes wasn't one of anger or hatred, but of lust. He could tell that she wasn't playing. She had a smirk on her face that he now wanted to fuck right off. He watched her eyes as she watched his dick begin to grow back to full attention. He saw the lust dancing all over her. Her pretty nipples were hard. He silently thanked God she couldn't find whatever it was that she was looking for. She was so fucking gorgeous. Every plus-sized inch of her. She didn't even try to hide her hunger for him either.

She was baiting him, waiting for him to take some kind of action.

She knew Travis. She secretly knew all about him. She knew about his past in the streets and how, at one point, most of the niggas he knew in Cincinnati feared him. Even if they didn't know him personally, his reputation superseded him. Everyone knew that he was a force to be reckoned with. Yeah, she knew him. The real him. The him who was Freight. That was the man she wanted. The man she needed. And since he couldn't sneak up on her and give her what she actually craved, she would settle for some of that hood-ass thug loving that she heard he was good for giving out.

Even though she wasn't the one he was expecting to be here, Ke'Lasia ain't seem to give a fuck about none of that no more. She knew what she needed. Now that September was in a whole-ass relationship with the nigga Slash everyone was just now hearing about, and they never had anything between them anyway, he figured September wouldn't mind if Ke'Lasia dipped in the cookie jar just once. He hoped. He just needed to knock her proverbial socks off and get her back in the right mindset. Without someone to be with in this way for so long, he had been going fucking crazy. As long as he could give her some deep, hard-ass back shots with her neck choked and face slapped before she left here, he was pretty sure that she would be okay long enough to figure out what else to do about them. Because now he couldn't help but to think of them.

He slowly walked back to the bed and gently lifted her legs up to his waist level. Her feet were planted at the edge, and he nudged her knees apart. She resisted him. He nudged again but her legs remained closed. He looked at her confused and she looked at him right back. *What kinda game is she playing with me?* he questioned himself.

"I said take it. I'm guessin' you don't want it. You actin' scared. Let me get my clothes." She sat up with an attitude and pushed heavy to get past. The back-and-forth games were beginning to piss him off. The confusion of this situation was starting to get to him. Did she want him or not? He wanted her bad as hell, but he wasn't about to rape her or even feel like he was. He was becoming uncomfortable with this whole situation. The need for her to let him in was serious for him. But she was going to have to let him know what she wanted. He couldn't bring himself to make a move without her letting him know what she really wanted.

"I'm out here looking dumb as fuck," she scolded herself. He was no longer Freight, the nigga she heard was so rough, dangerous, and heavy in the streets back in the day. The nigga she heard was fucking the shit out of the baddest bitches and even had a special move called the helicopter. This nigga standing in front of her was far from that man now. This nigga right here was soft as fuck and she was salty that she was gonna miss out on all the wonderful stories, but he had a trick for that. He had been trying to get people to understand that he had changed his thuggish, street ways for a long time now. She should've just listened.

"Fuck!" she grumbled under her breath with a strong-ass attitude. She was full-fledged heated now. She couldn't believe she had wasted her time coming over here and looking stupid in front of him. Her eyes teared up again.

"Lay yo ass back." He nudged her backward toward the bed once more. "Why you think you lookin' dumb? This ain't what you wanna do?"

"Nigga, move. You scary," she said, not falling back as instructed. She was over it and ready to go.

"You playing games," he told her, growing tired of the shit she was on.

"And you actin' soft." She pushed past like he was a little nigga and grabbed her clothes up off the floor.

She had him fucked up. No way was he letting her leave. And now, he damn sure wasn't letting her leave after talking to him like that. He had something to prove to her after that. He wasn't those young boys he assumed she was used to playing with. He was a grown-ass man, and he was gonna show her. He was gonna show her why his name rang bells in these streets back in the day.

Picking up on what she needed from him, he readily, happily obliged. He reached out and grabbed her by her ponytail, bringing her backside into his body with some force. With her back pressed against his chest, his dick caressed against the top of her ass. He leaned into her ear with his grip still on her ponytail so that she couldn't move away from him, and whispered her instructions with his deep, baritone voice.

"Put that shit down and get the fuck in the bed," he instructed in a strong, determined voice. If she wanted him to take charge, that was exactly what the fuck he was going to do.

She dropped her clothes and tried turning toward him, but his grip held firm. She was alive now. Awakened by the senses that had heightened by the new energy that he'd brought to her. Now she was ready to let him fuck her brains out with absolutely no care or restraint. Ke'Lasia was ready to take him on an adventure of his damn life, and he was all but too ready to strap up and enjoy the ride!

"Or, what?" she challenged. Her voice was throaty, and he could tell she was trying not to moan. Her whole body was reacting to him, and he liked it. It was turning him on in a major way.

"Fuck it. Don't." He spun her around so that she faced him. Then he looked her dead in her eyes. She smirked, and that time, he smirked back, now understanding the rules of the game that she was playing. "You better not fuckin' move either. You wanna play? Then we gon' fuckin' play."

"What you—"

"Shut up and be still," he demanded against her lips as he shoved his tongue down her throat, shutting her up. She opened up for him and let him have her mouth. He played his tongue against her tongue, teeth, and lips. He let her feel his tongue play around in her mouth before telling her what was about to happen.

"You gon' stand here since yo' hardheaded ass don't wanna lie down. The thing I just did to your mouth"—he paused while he licked his tongue across her lips again—"is the same thing I'm gon' do to this pussy."

He slid his hand down her stomach until he found her pussy. With a handful of it and a firm hold, his fingers toyed with her pussy lips as his tongue darted in and out of her mouth again. He found her moisture and separated her lower lips to push his fingers into her moistened cave. His fingers, one at first, then two, then three, found the same rhythm in her opening that his tongue found in her mouth. Her moans finally escaped her throat, and it made him happy. He was about to fuck the shit outta her and it was going to be phenomenal.

"Where you about to go?" he asked Ke'Lasia when he woke up and saw her getting dressed even though he was still half asleep.

"I got some shit I gotta go do." Ke'Lasia never turned around to look at him in his face.

"Oh, yeah?" he asked, not believing her at all.

"Yeah."

"You coming back soon?"

"I'on know." Ke'Lasia shrugged her shoulders nonchalantly.

"What you mean you don't know?" He sat up confused and feeling played, looking at the back of her head like he meant nothing. "So, all this was just to get your nut off? You ain't even feelin' me for real, are you?" He watched the sides of Ke'Lasia's face as she continued to get dressed like no one was even talking to her. He was hurt and trying to keep it out of his voice. He really liked this girl and the realization that she ain't feel the same was a crushing blow. He thought he stood a chance. Especially since she'd let him fuck. Ke'Lasia never seemed to him to be one of those girls who just hooked up with a nigga to get her a nut, but apparently, he was mistaken. With a deep breath, she finally responded.

"Look, Travis, we're cool and I don't wanna mess that up. What we did was just fuck. That don't mean we together or none of that, so don't start actin' strange. We're friends and that's it."

The way Ke'Lasia snapped on him over her shoulder like he was some trick off–ass nigga let him know not to say anything else unless he was ready to argue. He heard the attitude all in her voice and although he wanted to say something about it, she had already shut him down and out with just those few words. He sat there salty, feeling played and used. *I can't believe this girl is really playin' me like this. What the fuck she means just friends?* He continued looking at the back of her head.

"So, that's it? You just out?" he asked again for clarity, just to make sure this wasn't all a joke while he silently hoped it was.

"That's it. I'm out." She shrugged.

"You weren't even gon' tell me you were leavin' either, were you?" Ke'Lasia kept quiet, letting him come to his own conclusions. She pulled on her pants, buttoned them, then looked around for her purse. Finding it, she threw it across her body and headed to the door.

"So, fuck me?" he asked with hurt in his voice that he didn't try to hide anymore. He thought he meant more to Ke'Lasia than he obviously did, and he wasn't ashamed that he was hurt by it. He thought they were better than something like this.

"Nah, not fuck you. It's never fuck you. This part is just over."

Ke'Lasia walked out of his bedroom without another word or even a glance his way. She never even looked back. Not once. She had gotten what she'd come for and it was over. Just like that.

As she walked out the door, he picked up the phone to check the time, only to realize that he had forgotten all about Keisha. Luckily, she had already hit him up to tell him that something came up. A new nigga was his guess, but that wasn't his business or concern. Besides, all he could care about now was how Ke'Lasia was playing him. He heard the door close softly as he just lay there in the silence and replayed the event in his mind, wondering what he could have done wrong, or if it was even him at all. *Maybe she really just needed to get her rocks off.* He wouldn't lie and say he wasn't salty. He sent a message to her phone and went back to lying down, waiting to see if she would respond.

Chapter 11

"Man, this girl must mean somethin' to you, young blood. She costin' you a pretty fuckin' penny wit' this li'l shit."

Travis rolled his eyes with a clenched jaw as he watched G4 count the new envelope of cash that Travis had just given him. He didn't feel as though what the old-school player had said needed a response, so he stood quietly, waiting for his information.

"Yeah, this bitch must be a real sweet piece the way you comin' off the dough. That's just you, or she up for playtime?"

Travis watched the toothpick swirl around the wet corners of this nigga's mouth and wished he could punch it down his throat. G4 used to be a cool cat back in the day. Even though he taught him a couple things. But now, he was just a nasty, thirsty, clout-chasing, old, washed-up player Travis hated having to do business with. This nigga was a full-out creep now and he didn't care who knew it. Looking at G4, Travis remembered the rumors from a couple years ago that he was even into young girls now. Young, young, like 15 and 16 young. Just being around him irritated Travis, but he had to do what he had to do. He couldn't let September down. Or Ashley, the waitress from that day. As much as he didn't want to, he had to deal with G4 until he no longer needed information, so right now, kicking his ass was out the question.

"That's somethin' like family you disrespectin', Skool. I'ma need you to chill with all that." G4 took the hint that Travis gave him and threw his hands up.

"No disrespek, young blood. No disrespek." He continued chewing on the ratty toothpick, waiting for Travis to ask his questions, still counting his money like the number would change.

"So, maybe not her, but you still into runnin' them bitches like you used to? Whew whee! You had some of the sweetest tail I'd ever seen out here. Them young bitches used to take all my gotdamn money." G4 smacked his lips, reminiscing. It made Travis cringe to hear him say that. The girls Travis had running around were of legal age. They were just young to this nigga because he was fifteen years older than the majority of them.

"I ain't into shit no more, Skool, I told you that. All I'm tryin'a do is get some information to help my peoples. What you got for me, man? I got shit to do." Travis fidgeted around where he stood, uncomfortable with his old friend and the entire situation.

"Damn, it's like dat?"

"Ain't like nothin', my nigga. I'm just tryin'a be out. It's hot as fuck right here." Travis lied to take the attention away from his mounting attitude. He didn't wanna blow his top and lose his temper on the old man before he found out what he needed to know.

"You right. You right," G4 agreed, lookin' around to make sure no one was close enough to hear their conversation. Finally, down to business, he spilled everything he knew to an impatiently waiting Travis. "Look here, young blood. The nigga you lookin' for think he low-key. He be over there in Lincoln Heights with the rest of them old niggas at the bar."

"The bar? It's a bar in Lincoln Heights still jumpin'?"

"Hell yeah! The Mint, young blood. You know it."

Travis took a second to think, quickly remembering the old bar they called The Peppermint that used to be all the hype around Lincoln Heights, Lockland, and some of the surrounding neighborhoods. People even came from farther out to go chill there back in the day. The

Peppermint nightclub took a lot of lives with it when it died. Or when Travis thought it had died anyway.

"The Peppermint?" he asked to make sure his thoughts were correct.

"That'll do it." G4 nodded his head like the bar was the best thing going.

"Them cats still hanging around there? I thought they been closed that down."

"Naw. The Mint still going strong. They closed it for a second but niggas wasn't gon' let it stay that way. They opened it back up and now all the old niggas with they low-hanging balls be in that muthafucka like they 'bout thurdy years old and shit!" Old Skool laughed at his own sneak diss like he didn't fit in that category. Travis couldn't help but to laugh. What G4 just said wasn't as funny to Travis as was G4 himself thinking he wasn't just the same as the older niggas he was bagging on. He was still out here trying to keep up with the times too like he wasn't old as fuck just like them.

"You crazy, Skool." Travis blew him off again. He was growing leery of this song and dance he had to put up with. "So, the nigga Vic be up in there?" Travis asked, getting the old-school dude back on track with the matter at hand.

"Yeah, he be up in there knockin' back them twelve dollar Henny shots wit' the rest of them niggas. Still fuckin' on them ol' worn-out hoes, too." G4 shook his head. "It's a shame how them hoes let themselves go. Them used to be some of the baddest bit—"

"So, he be there a lot?" Travis cut him off. He wasn't in the mood to walk down memory lane with this nigga. Whoever Vic was up there fucking or fucking with was none of Travis's concern. All he was concerned about was getting the information he needed.

"Oh. Oh, yeah. He be in there. Him and Cornell. I even heard he be wit' Ears."

"Ears! That nigga had life, I thought."

"Shit, young blood, me too. But what was told to me was that the nigga got out. Been out about ninety days now."

"Damn. How that nigga get out?" Travis literally scratched his head. The question was more so to himself than to G4. He was pretty sure that G4 wouldn't know what the fuck he was talking about any damn way. Travis was baffled. He couldn't understand how a nigga who was supposed to be in jail serving a double life sentence was at the bar throwing back Hennessy shots, let alone walking the streets a free man. *How the fuck he do that?*

"Yeah, they sayin' them niggas over there terrorizin' shit since Ears been home. They got the whole place on lock. Say they got some of the best dope flowin' in and outta there." He nodded his head in agreement like he wasn't the one telling the story.

"Okay. So, what Ears gotta do wit' the nigga Vic and what I need to know?"

"Well, way I hear it, the nigga Vic owed Ears some money since fo' he got popped. A lot of niggas did apparently. Folks say when he got outta jail, it scared niggas so much that it was easy for the nigga Ears to slide back in and take over again. The nigga Vic workin' for him now like a lot of other niggas that owed down. Ears and Vic made some type of deal when they were both up there at Lebanon that Vic would handle something for Ears in exchange for Vic's safe return home to the streets."

"Oh, yeah?" Travis coaxed.

"Oh, yeah. Say what he was supposed to do was hold up the restaurant and get Ears the money he owed. From what I hear, that li'l barbeque joint they was at is owned by Ears though."

"Ears?"

"Uh hmm." G4 leaned back on his borrowed car and gnawed his over-chewed toothpick like he was a shoo-in for the first draft pick in the NBA. The smugness of this cat was pissing Travis off. He was stalling him out and Travis didn't appreciate it at all. He wasn't as slick and cool as he thought he was. If the situation were different, Travis would've been fucked him up. It was too bad he couldn't.

"Why the fuck would his own goons hit his shit? That ain't making no sense, my nigga. Nah," Travis shook his head as he thought the information through. "Something ain't right about that."

"Bingo!" G4 pointed that nasty, wet toothpick at Travis to emphasize his point before flicking it away. He pulled a case that looked like it held cigarettes in it but was smaller out of his pocket and put another toothpick in his crusty but wet lips.

"You's absolutely right, young blood. Somethin' wasn't right."

"So, what they hit him for then? Explain that shit to me."

"They was supposed to be hittin' a joint up the road. The niggas went there and got a high off the hit. You know how that shit be. Niggas came up on thirty fuckin' grand from that one job."

"Damn! Thirty grand at a barbeque joint?"

"Well, it was a sandwich joint, but yeah. They hit the safe. Knew the combo, so it was easy. Another nigga Ears was locked up wit' told him everything he needed to know. Ears sent the niggas to go hit the joint and bring him back thirty grand."

"How was they gon' give him thirty if they only got thirty? Come on, man." Travis was beginning to not believe G4 at all. His story wasn't making sense.

"You listenin', slow young buck. They got the whole sixty. Supposed to had split it four ways after Ears got his cut. But the nigga whose spot it was bargained with the young cats. Told them about another lick they could hit in exchange for lettin' him keep his money."

"They ain't even know it was Ears's spot," Travis realized out loud.

"Hell nah, they didn't," G4 agreed, shaking his head.

"How much they get from Ears?"

"A whole hunnit thousand bucks."

"Swear to God!" Travis exclaimed with wide eyes. "I'm guessing Ears wasn't happy about that huh?"

"Nope. Sho' wasn't," G4 confirmed, answering a question that wasn't really a question at all.

"Damn. These niggas fuckin' wit' some big pockets. Everybody out here tryin'a eat. Shit crazy."

"Real crazy. Especially now since Ears's ass gotta figure out how to get that money back up. You know the boys took the whole shit." He referenced the police officers who took the money from the dead cadets to enter into evidence. Travis recalled the police carrying duffle bags out of the restaurant. He never even stopped to think what it could've been in those bags. He was so focused on the well-being of September that he ain't even pay the shit no mind. He just figured it was some kind of evidence.

"So, who was the other nigga that Vic and Ears got hit? I'm salty. This whole thing sounding like a whole bunch of jealous female shit. Meaning, my peoples got hit, and somebody else peoples died for fuckin' nothin'. Over some petty-ass hatin' shit." That realization made Travis the saltiest about the whole damn situation. "And did they let the nigga keep his money? 'Cause I know Ears wasn't feelin' that shit at all."

"The nigga who owned the sandwich spot was salty. With Ears out, he wasn't the man no mo'. They say the nigga was the one got Ears popped on some salty shit in the first place. And you know like I know, them young, hot-headed-ass niggas ain't den let that fool keep that loot. They had to give it to Ears if they wanted to live! Not to mention they had to cut Vic's grimy ass in too. Sheit." He spat a wad of yellow mucus from his throat onto the sidewalk and continued. "Them dummies wasn't even gon' get ten bands had they not hit the second spot. You know they wasn't gon' be satisfied with that when they would've had to give Ears's ass thirty of whatever they got from the other spot. Ain't no nigga that's tryin'a eat doin' that. They pistol whipped that nigga somethin' good and took his shit anyway."

"These niggas wildin' for real," Travis added. "What the fuck make a nigga salty enough to snitch on a nigga anyway? Man, these new niggas different. I guess ol' boy got what was comin' to him, shit." Travis had no remorse for the snitching sandwich shop owner. *The streets are an unsafe place and telling on niggas with that much clout don't make it safer.*

"Yeah, they is." G4 shook his head up and down. He knew all too well what Travis meant. He himself had been caught up two separate times because a jealous, hating-ass nigga snitched on him. His jaw flexed in anger at the too familiar saltiness.

"Some bitch shit, for sure. They say Ears was fuckin' the nigga Heim's girl. Ain't that about a bitch? All this over a broad." G4 huffed to himself at the thought of men wasting time beefing with each other over one female when there were so many more out in the world.

"Heim? Heim who?"

"His name Raheim but they call him Heim. Not too street but not too common I guess." G4 shrugged, not knowing the significance of what he had just revealed.

"Raheim? From down the way? From the lot?" Travis stood up from leaning on his car, eagerly leaning in to hear G4's next words. Downtown's small Tot Lot community was extremely known for holding a lot of street niggas. Especially a lot of dope boys and niggas who wanted to be dope boys. Everybody knew that Raheim, September's ex-dude, was one of the biggest dope boys from downtown and he had Tot Lot on lock. So, if there was a Heim from Tot Lot, it had to be the same one.

"One and the same," G4 told him. Travis's jaw dropped. He couldn't believe it. He already knew what G4 would confirm for him and yet it still fucked him up to hear it.

"What the fuck?"

"What the fuck is right. 'Parently, Ears had been fuckin' Heim's girl to get back at him for taking a lot of his clientele. So, Heim took the opportunity of the robbery to send the li'l niggas after a nigga he had beef wit' already. Two birds, one stone." He waved his hand like it wasn't shit to him and it made perfect sense that it wouldn't be. G4 didn't know any of these niggas personally, just from stories he had heard. So, he didn't give a fuck either way on what happened to any of them.

"Damn. Wrong place. Fuck."

"Wrong place? Nah, I told you to listen. You think them niggas just happened to be sent there that day? Nigga, not only was the money not picked up that day for the scheduled drop-off like every week at the same time, but his bitch was there wit' a whole 'nother nigga."

"What? What you mean?"

G4 looked at Travis and shook his head up and down again. He wanted Travis to know that the thoughts he had were true. Nobody needed to confirm them for him. What was understood already didn't need to be explained any further. G4 knew that Travis was picking up on what he said, he just didn't want to.

September got shot over jealousy. Raheim found out that she was at Ears's restaurant with Travis that day when the young boys came and robbed him after he had already found out she was supposedly involved romantically with Ears. So, all Raheim did was use them as patsies to go do his dirty work. It was Travis's fault why the waitress was dead and why September was almost killed. He had been the one who invited September out with him to that restaurant that day. Had he not, September would've never been shot, and the waitress would still be alive.

Chapter 12

"Shit!" Ke'Lasia yelled out as her little purple friend brought her to her third and last climax of that moment. She was jonesing like a crack addict for some loving that she just wasn't getting. Her vibrator had been keeping her from being bottled up since the day she left Travis, but it wasn't working anymore. She needed a fix. Bad. But she was trying everything she could to not have to call Travis for dick at all. After the way she played him the last time she saw him, Ke'Lasia was quite certain that Travis wouldn't even answer her phone call even if she did try calling.

"Shit!" she yelled again, hitting the sink. This time her curse words were for a different reason. Why did she have to play Travis like that? Now, she couldn't even call him up and get some of that bomb-ass thug passion that he gave her last time. Especially since that thug lovin' had her toes bent up damn near into fists and her stranger still hadn't come to her yet.

Ke'Lasia knew that the path she was venturing down was a bad one, but she couldn't help it. Even all the talking to Dr. Sagent she had been doing wasn't helping. Here she was, thirty minutes away from her weekly appointment with him, in the sparkly white, freshly cleaned bathroom of Doctor Sagent's vast, upscale office building, getting her nut off. She should've been ashamed of her damn self. She was losing the battle to any self-control that she may have had before. She didn't see herself getting it back either. The stranger that visited her had awakened a beast inside of her whose hunger she could not quell.

"I've tried, Justin, I really have. I've tried everything I could. I don't know what to do at this point." Ke'Lasia looked at her hands that she wrung together nervously in her lap.

"Have you tried what I suggested?" her therapist asked her, looking over the glasses he usually only wore to read. Ke'Lasia noticed, not for the first time, how handsome the doctor was. How his lips curled, and his tongue slightly licked his teeth and lips as he spoke. He didn't have a lisp or speech impediment of any kind. He just absentmindedly ran his tongue across his teeth from time to time after he finished sentences. Ke'Lasia liked it. It almost turned her on. Thinking about what he could possibly do with that same tongue turned her on even more though. She shook her head in despair, shaking off the thoughts.

"Tell me what you're thinking, Ke'Lasia." Doctor Sagent leaned in toward Ke'Lasia, ready to listen intently.

"I can't tell you what I was thinking," she admitted.

"You can. This is a safe space. You can tell me anything, you know that. We may need to explore those thoughts."

"I was thinking about your tongue." Her eyes dropped back down. She was so embarrassed that she wanted to crawl in a hole and hide for the rest of her life.

"My tongue?"

"Yes. Yours."

"What about my tongue?" He sat back and settled himself in his chair, preparing to listen to whatever Ke'Lasia said.

"How good it would feel on my pussy. How good it would feel in my mouth. How good it would feel pressed against my asshole. How good it would feel licking my lips after you've tasted me. You licking my teeth like you lick yours."

"I lick my teeth?" Dr. Sagent asked before absentmindedly licking his teeth again the way Ke'Lasia had just mentioned.

Her panties instantly got moist. The excitement built in her chest. The thoughts of the doctor and her touching each other made her squirm in her seat, even though she knew it wasn't right. Probably even more so because of that.

Justin Sagent watched Ke'Lasia squirm. Silently, he liked watching her. She was so interesting to him. He never had a patient before with a sex addiction. It was all new but intriguing just the same. He was hungry to hear her thoughts and her fantasies in her head even if they were about him. He knew that it was unethical to even let her tell him these stories, but they were too intriguing to him. Too enticing. He had to know. This was his most complex case to date, and he had no intention of giving her case to anyone else.

Justin cleared his throat and loosened his tie, then positioned himself in a more comfortable way to sit in his chair so that his growing erection was not detected. He poised his yellow legal pad on his knee and prepared to record her thoughts and stories in his own shorthand to go over again later.

"You do. You do it sometimes and I don't think you know you do it, but you do. And it's sexy. Sexy to me for some reason. I don't know why, it just is. I noticed it earlier on in our sessions and I tried to ignore it, but now I can't. Not while my appetite is growing. Not now that almost everything and everybody has something or does something that turns me on. Now everywhere I go and everything I do reminds me of how bad I want to have sex. I have a vibrator. It feels good, real good, but it's not enough. It's not doing what I need it to do. It's not scratching the itch."

"Scratching the itch?"

"Yes. It's like when you're itching really bad in a spot you almost can't reach. You can only reach it a little bit, but it's not enough to really get to the itch to scratch it good enough to make it stop itching. It's like that. My need is the itch and sex is the scratch. I'm itching, but I can't seem to scratch it." Ke'Lasia told the story without ever looking up at Justin.

All the while, Justin never took his eyes off of Ke'Lasia. His mouth watered at what else she could tell him. He decided to pick her brain more to see what she would tell him and what she wouldn't. *Why did I have to be her therapist?*

He wanted to ask her more questions to gather more details about the lurid act she'd been participating in. "Tell me about your vibrator."

"My vibrator?" Confusion settled over her face.

"Yes, your vibrator. You said you had one, but it wasn't"—he flipped his yellow pages looking for the words she already used—"scratching your itch. Tell me more about that."

"What's to tell? It's a vibrator." She shrugged.

"Tell me why your itch isn't being scratched."

"I don't know." She shrugged again. "It's just not. I keep using it. I've replaced the batteries four times this week already. Four times," she repeated. Justin looked over the glasses that he wore for reading that were still perched atop his nose and waited expectantly.

"Four times? Sounds like you need to buy better batteries." Justin chuckled slightly at his own remark.

"I bought Energizer."

"And you still needed more each time?" Justin scribbled again excitedly.

Ke'Lasia fidgeted some more. Telling him what she did by herself was making her uncomfortable. She didn't want him to know that she had just used her vibrator in a bathroom in his building or that she had used it in the parking garage in her car before she came up to see him. Or even that she'd used it in front of her window in her bedroom with her blinds open so that her neighbor who looked in her window every day at the same time could see her. She didn't want to tell him about all the filthy sex scenes she had put on for this same neighbor every day for the last month alone in her room. She didn't want to tell him that this was her third vibrator because the first two stopped working on her because of overuse.

"I just . . ." she started. "I just . . ."

"You just?" The two looked each other in the eyes and held the gaze.

Fuck it, she said to herself, shrugging the embarrassment off the best way she could. She spilled everything that had been going on, everything she had been thinking or doing . . . everything. She told Justin everything finally. He exhaled lowly while listening to her story.

"And right now, all I can think about is dropping to my knees in front of you, unbuckling your pants, and sucking your dick. All I can think about is letting you cum down my throat so I can see what you taste like finally."

Justin's eyes widened. He felt his new erection press against his slacks. He had to cross his legs to keep it completely concealed from the outside world, meaning Ke'Lasia. The images in his mind were of him ramming his dick down her throat over and over again until he did indeed spill his man seed down her throat. Instead, he cleared his throat and put the conversation back on topic.

"So, when you use your vibrator, how do you feel?"
"Horny."
"How else?"

Ke'Lasia thought for a minute. Then she said, "Empty. I feel empty and unwanted. I feel like no one wants me." Ke'Lasia put her face in her hands and cried like a baby.

Chapter 13

"You there yet?"

"No. I'm on my way though. You okay?"

"Yeah, I'm good. Just running late. Let me know when you get there." Travis hung up in Ke'Lasia's ear. She just looked at the phone in her hand. The traffic light she sat at turned green and she pulled off.

Travis stopped at the corner and discreetly looked around. Seeing no one close enough to be paying attention to him, he proceeded into the alley two feet away from where he once stood. Checking one more time to make sure no one was watching, Travis tightened the tarp with the bloodstained clothes it carried in a full knot before tossing it in the dumpster in front of him. Then he took a match and threw it in behind it. Once he saw the smoke, he used the bottle of vinegar he had and sprayed it all over the other bags of trash that were there and stood back to watch the flame ignite and spread. Before walking away, he lit the whole matchbook on fire and tossed it in too. The fire leaped around each bag and grew. It grew bigger and brighter as Travis disappeared around the same corner he came from.

Ke'Lasia: I'm here. What you need me to do?

Travis: Who all there? I'm 'bout to be there in like ten minutes.

Ke'Lasia: Just two of the other models and a couple people puttin' food out.

Travis: Bet. I'll be there.

Ke'Lasia put her phone back in her pocket and looked around. The setup was done really nice. The colors for the photoshoot that day were rainbow in honor of Pride Month. There were rainbows everywhere. Everything was littered in exploding colors. Ke'Lasia smiled then pulled out her phone to make a call.

"You don't gotta call me, bitch, I'm right here."

She looked up to see a smiling September decked out in Pride gear. She had on the cutest pair of rainbow-furred booties Ke'Lasia had ever seen.

"Biiiiitch! Where you get these?" she exclaimed, admiring the boots. "And why the fuck yo' ass ain't get me none? Why you ain't tell me you were goin' shopping? I would've gone wit' you." Ke'Lasia circled September, checking out the rest of her outfit while her friend posed like the camera was already clicking away.

"Girl, I ordered this shit online last month when they told us about the shoot. It's cute, ain't it?"

The girls laughed and talked about September's outfit from the metallic rainbow-colored fanny pack she carried to the rainbow stiletto nails she had on her fingers. Her leggings were pure white under her rainbow-colored miniskirt, and she had picked out her favorite color of the rainbow to wear as her matching shirt. The sheer see-through yellow hung against her caramel skin perfectly. The white bra that was under the thin fabric set the outfit off right. Her sunglasses had to be custom-made.

"Bitch, I know you ain't ordered these online," Ke'Lasia pointed out matter-of-factly, taking the frames from September's face and trying them on.

"Yes, I did. My man got me hip to a new website where you design your own glasses in any style and color you want. So, he helped me design those for my outfit." She posed again, extremely proud of herself and the outfit she had been able to pull together to warrant this much wanted attention even though she was embellishing. *Bitch won't get these,* September thought, making sure that she kept the secret to herself. Even though Ke'Lasia was like a sister to her, she ain't have time for no bitch to be jocking her swag. She was stunting hard and wasn't about to let nobody, not even Ke'Lasia, steal her shine or her thunder.

"Anyway, bitch, where's Travis?" September switched the subject to make sure Ke'Lasia didn't ask any more questions about her glasses or their website. She had no intention of telling her the truth. She didn't want anyone else to know about it so that she would be the main one in the circle of coworkers and colleagues to have the exclusive glasses that no one else could get. She didn't want to give up her source and she wasn't going to.

"He comin'. He just hit me up and said he'd be here in a minute."

"Oh, yeah? He hit you up?" September eyed Ke'Lasia suspiciously.

"Yeah, bitch. Why you say it like that?" September knew when Ke'Lasia was up to something. Her best friend was never able to hide anything from her. Ke'Lasia diverted her eyes, hoping that her friend didn't see the truth written all over her face.

"Girl, you pretty much my sister. Blood couldn't make us no closer, so spill it. You know I know when you're hiding somethin'." September rolled her eyes, waiting on an answer.

"Girl, ain't nobody hidin' nothin'." The embarrassed friend waved her hand in September's direction to keep her from digging further. She didn't think September would be mad, but she didn't want to take the chance on finding out while they were working either. When she told her, if she ever volunteered that information, it would be in a better place than this. Ke'Lasia was open to the conversation if it came up, but not if it affected her getting her coins. *Fuck that shit. That shit can wait.*

"You boning him?" September crossed her arms and tapped her foot, waiting on an answer.

"Shut up!" Ke'Lasia howled in laughter at September's unintended joke. "I am not boning no damn body, thank you." She skirted around the truth, blowing September off.

"Oh, you boning somebody, bitch. I see the glow all in your face and eyes. Somebody been making that ass clap!" September smirked, knowing the truth while Ke'Lasia rolled her eyes.

She hoped like hell that September couldn't tell her secrets in her eyes. She damn sure had been busting all kinds of nuts all over the place. Ashamed, she had just busted a few in her dressing room of the photoshoot. That's why she was there earlier than mostly everyone else. She was compelled to use her vibrator again. She was going to town too until one of the crewmen walked in on her with her legs kicked up on her mirrored desk and her thighs spread wide open. The movie lights that surrounded the three portrait mirrors illuminated her dripping pussy as she brought herself to another self-induced orgasm. He couldn't do anything but stand there, mouth gaping open in astonishment. His moan caught her attention as she heard it mix with hers. Jumping out of her pleasure, she saw him standing there. Her eyes caught his before they drifted down to the front of his denim jeans that now had what seemed like a humongous bulge protruding from them. She licked her lips and returned her stare to his eyes. They held eye contact with each other as he unbuckled his pants to unleash the bulge that was indeed the monster she assumed it to be. Although she watched him wrap his hand around his love toy, it meant nothing. He may as well have been holding it with just two fingers by the amount of it that was left exposed. She smiled seductively, then lay back to finish her nut with her eyes closed as he made the space between them smaller. A half-hour ride and about four amazing nuts later, she was standing there with September, trying not to let on that she was just in the back being hoeish.

"I told yo' ass ain't nobody boning nobody besides you and Slash nasty asses. I know you muthafuckas been doin' unspeakable things to each other!"

The girls high-fived and laughed through the rest of the conversation until they were notified that the shoot was starting.

"How are we starting a shoot and our cameraman ain't even here?" September asked the other models and the rest of Travis's crew.

"He is here, duh."

"Bitch, I'll slap the shit outta you! Who the fuck you think you talkin' to?" September walked a couple of steps closer to the smart-mouthed bitch she was addressing. Ke'Lasia pulled her by her arm quick to put a cap on the argument before it turned to something more or anything bigger.

"Come on, girl, don't even trip off that."

"Nah, fuck that. This bitch got the right one today. I'll fuck this ho up! She better ask a mu'fucka about me!"

"Girl, fuck her. She ain't nobody."

"Nobody that knows where Travis is while you hoes all askin' and whisperin' about him." She rolled her eyes at them both. "Silly-ass hoes." Shaking her head, the new model started walking away.

"Bitch, don't nobody need yo' raggedy ass to tell us shit about no fuckin' Travis," Ke'Lasia countered, getting in her feelings about what this girl was insinuating.

"Well, then why y'all don't know where the fuck he at, like I do?" She smiled a sarcastic smile before continuing. "Y'all salty but oh well. He here. Y'all can get off his dick now. He ain't worried about either one of y'all fat asses."

"Bitch, you said that shit like you a size two though. Bitch, please miss me with that shit. Go ahead wit' that dumb shit, okay, just 'cause you know he here." Ke'Lasia and September looked at each other and shrugged simultaneously. "What the fuck does that mean? Girl, you act like you fuckin' him or somethin'." Ke'Lasia waved the dumb-ass new girl off.

"Girl, she ain't fuckin' him," September interrupted. "And if she is, he ain't claiming that duck-ass bitch." September was loud enough for the girl to hear but Miss Lady wasn't having it.

"You fat hoes kill me walkin' around like y'all runnin' somethin' or somebody give a fuck about y'all because y'all was on a couple covers. Bitch, I couldn't care less about nan one of you hoes. Like I said, Travis is here, so you hoes can get up off his dick. Especially since that's the closest to his dick either of you hoes will ever get." The new girl looked at her friend and laughed. She knew she was irritating the hell out of Ke'Lasia and September, but since that was her plan, she was happy as fuck about it.

An all-out argument started between the girls. Travis finally appeared and interrupted right before either of them decided to take a swing. "Bitch! Keep that nasty-ass spit to yo'self! You probably got AIDS or some shit!" the new model yelled in Ke'lasia's face, spewing her own uncontrollable speckles of unintended spit.

"Shut the fuck up!" Travis roared over the gaggle of cackling women. All the girls stopped, looking at Travis like he was crazy. Travis had the bridge of his nose pinched between his forefinger and thumb, signaling that he was getting a headache.

"How you gon' come in here talkin' to us like that and these fat hoes the ones that started the shit?"

"Shut the fuck up, Kiesha, damn! Why is you even here starting shit? This is where I'm workin'. What the fuck are you on?" Travis tried pulling Kiesha to the side, but she wasn't going. She wasn't finished putting on her show.

"Don't grab me up like that, fool! You gon' try and show out in front of these hoes like I'm some stranger? Is that what we doin' now, baby daddy?"

"Baby daddy?" Both Ke'Lasia and September repeated at the same time in total shock. "That's yo' kid mama, Travis?" Ke'Lasia asked, unable to believe what she had just heard.

"Kiesha, get the fuck outta here. You blowin' the spot up like a mu'fucka. I gotta work here. Man, damn!"

"Travis? I know you heard my damn question." Ke'Lasia stepped back with her arms crossed, waiting for answers. He had her fucked up. Why would he even have this bitch up in here where she worked? She told him she ain't want these kinds of problems, which was one of the main reasons why she ain't wanna fuck with him outside of getting that bomb-ass dick. This was the same bitch she sidestepped the night she showed up at his door. That's why she never went back. She knew he was still fucking with her, and she wasn't ready to be lied to.

"Travis? You can't hear now?"

"Eh, yeah, this my baby mama. So what? I ain't invite her here and you ain't fuckin' wit' me anyway, so what difference it make?" His anger finally boiled over. He'd had enough of the both of these women. Ke'Lasia was playing with his feelings and Kiesha was just trying to make life hard for him.

Kiesha knew what she was doing, but she ain't care. *Fat bitch*. She smirked to herself. She knew one of these model chicks was the girl her baby daddy was fucking with. She just didn't know which one. Now that she did though, it was time to really show out. "She ain't fuckin' wi't you? So, you ain't tellin' yo' li'l hoes that you still fuckin' yo' baby mama? That's why she all in here questioning me about yo' whereabouts?" She lied through her devious smile. *I bet she won't be fuckin' wit' you no more,* Kiesha thought, satisfied. "Check yo'."

"Watch yo' fuckin' mouth, Kiesha, and she not my girl. She just my friend. You know I ain't got no girl, so you can take this bullshit on somewhere. I got work to do." Travis started to walk away but was stopped in his tracks by Ke'lasia's next words.

"Just yo' friend? So, you touch all yo' friends' guts? Or is that just the 'close friend' package?" Ke'Lasia stared Kiesha right in the eyes, reveling at the sight of her slack-jawed look as she let her words drip in sarcasm. She had hit the mark she intended.

"So, you are fuckin' somebody?"

Ke'Lasia turned wide-eyed toward a salty September.

She shook her head back and forth sadly. "And I thought we were sisters."

"September, I'm sorry. I am. I thought y'all li'l shit was over. Plus, Travis said—"

"So that was all it took? For a nigga to tell you somethin' different than I did and yo' panties just drop, huh? Did yo' nasty ass even have on panties? Tuh," September scoffed. "All this time. All this time I thought it was Monica and them that I needed to watch out for but here yo' ass go."

"He wasn't even yo' man, September!"

"I don't give a fuck!" she spat. "You knew I was tryin'a get wit' him! You knew I was feelin' him and this what you do? I can't believe this shit."

This shit better than I thought, Kiesha thought, settling in a chair not far from where all the drama she had caused was unfolding. She leaned over to her friend and whispered about how funny the shit was and the two girls fell out laughing.

"Wait a minute, September." Travis grabbed her by the arm to keep her from walking away from the conversation and what she had just said. "We were never fuckin' around, September. I ain't even know you was feeling me like that. I told Lasia we weren't fuckin' around because we wasn't. I pushed down on her basically. You can't be mad at her for what I did."

"Ain't that sweet?" Kiesha yelled from her spot in the corner, trying to add fuel to the fire.

"Shut up, Kiesha, damn! All this shit yo' damn fault."

"Meeee?" She feigned surprise with her hand to her chest, clutching her invisible pearls. "How dare you blame me? I ain't the one fuckin' three different women," she poked.

"I am not fuckin' three different women. I fucked Ke'Lasia, but it was once. She made it clear she ain't want me like I wanted her. And, September." He turned back to his friend and met the hurt in her eyes head-on. "I never meant to hurt you, my nigga. Never. I didn't even know you was feelin' me like that. I thought we were just homies. But I'm feelin' the fuck outta Lasia and I'm not gon' apologize for that ever."

September saw the sincerity in his face and heard it in his voice. She knew that what he said was real and she couldn't be salty. She never made no move and he never made one on her. That man was fair game, and she knew it.

"It ain't shit. Y'all cool. Y'all just could've told me." She tried keeping her calm and fixing her feelings. She honestly couldn't be salty. They weren't fucking around, plus, she was in a whole-ass relationship with Slash. The shit just had to be what it was. She sucked that shit up right then. "I'm really just tryin'a figure out why she even here though for real," she said, her head tilting toward Kiesha and her instigating-ass friend.

"I honestly don't know why the fuck she's here," Travis admitted.

"Yeah," Ke'Lasia retorted, turning back to the two unwanted hood rats. "Why are y'all here?" Everybody in the room stopped what they were doing so that they wouldn't miss the answers.

"Girl, fuck you! Ain't nobody gotta answer shit fa you! Like, who the fuck is you? Girl, bye." Kiesha's ratchet friend piped up loud and proud. "We here because my cousin's man asked us to be here, the fuck!" she snapped with her neck rolling just as much as her eyes were.

"Hold up. Who her man?" Travis interrupted.

"Don't stand in here actin' like you weren't just all in my cousin's face last night, nigga! And like yo' face wasn't other places, too, shit."

"That part, bitch!" The cousin slapped high fives with Kiesha, knowing that they were making Travis uncomfortable.

"Kiesha, take you and that female and get the fuck outta here before I have y'all thrown out. I'm sick of this shit. I'm not yo' man and I'm not fuckin' you either. Get the fuck out of here. Now, Kiesha!"

"Yeah, whatever. Fuck you and them lies you wanna tell," Kiesha told him, getting up to go. "But if you think I'm leavin' without my cash, you got the game fucked up." She walked up on Travis and held her hand out expectantly. They locked eyes. Travis looked like someone had just smacked his grandmother, but Kiesha looked like she had just won the lotto. Something was going to go down and everyone in the room was tuned in to catch every single second of it. Kiesha was under the impression that she had her baby daddy right where she wanted him.

She knew he'd rather just give her the money she asked for than to be further embarrassed.

"Kiesha, I just gave you four thousand dollars. What the fuck are you even talking about?" Once again, his hand flew to his face in exasperation, holding his eyes closed with his fingers. "I'm not giving you shit else. Can you just leave please? We already an hour and some change behind schedule because of this shit. You really buggin' right now. Go 'head on, man."

"Nigga, I said I'm not goin' no fuckin' where until you give me my fuckin' cash. What the fuck didn't you hear me say?"

"Bye, Kiesha!" he shouted in her face. She took a step back in surprise.

"Who the fuck you think you talkin' to, bitch-ass nigga?"

"Kiesha, don't disrespect me. Listen—"

"No, soft-ass nigga." She took two fingers and mugged him upside his head from the side by his left temple. "You listen. I'm not leavin' until you reach in yo' pocket and count them bills out." She clapped her hands together after every single word, reminding people that she was definitely from the hood and ready to go there with him. "My kids ain't about to starve 'cause they bitch-ass daddy wanna act crazy."

Travis took a few steps back and turned toward the wall. Everyone in the room could see that his patience was wearing super thin. *This girl gon' make me kill her,* Travis thought while he tried to take a few deep breaths to calm himself down.

"I'm not doin' this with you, Kiesh. I'm gon' ask you one more time to leave," he said, still turned toward the wall.

"We ain't goin' no fuckin' where." Everybody jumped back in surprise. September stood, frozen in the spot where she stood, wide-eyed and scared to death. Everyone else scrambled for a place to duck or hide from the chaos that was erupting rapidly in the room. Kiesha's cousin decided she would strong-arm what the girls wanted from Travis instead of continuing to ask. "My cousin said she wants the fuckin' money and you gon' give it to her or ain't nobody going nowhere period." She cocked the pistol she held in her hand, training it on the back of Travis's skull. "What the fuck is it gon' be, pussy?"

"Tavia! What the fuck are you doing? Put the damn gun up! You trippin' right now!" Even Kiesha was scared as hell and it was her cousin with the gun. *I gotta get her outta here before this goes bad.* Kiesha looked around, desperate to find a way out of there now.

"Kiesha, what kinda shit are you on? Why would you bring this bullshit in here?" Travis turned from the wall, only to see the messy bitch Kiesha brought with her holding a gun on him. His temper neared the boiling point. It was taking everything in him to not lose it. This was a female. He couldn't take the kinds of actions he normally would've had this been a male on the other end of the threat on his life. September standing there, frozen in her spot with terror riddling her face, only pushed him further toward snapping. He couldn't believe the situation Kiesha had him in. Especially about money that he definitely didn't owe.

"And you know I don't owe you shit. What I give you is out the kindness of my heart and this shit ain't makin' me feel too fuckin' kind." As Travis spoke, he had a severe case of déjà vu as he eased over in front of a frozen September who almost sent him into a tailspin of emotions. He saw that September couldn't move, and he totally got why. After just being shot and fighting for her life only six months ago, he was sure she wasn't expecting to be in this situation again anytime soon. The difference this time though was the fact that his baby mama's hothead-ass cousin was gon' have to kill him before he let September or anyone in this room today be shot. He couldn't let that happen to September again and he couldn't live with another death of an innocent person on his conscience. It came down to the only decision that could be made here. Someone was going to die. He looked into the eyes of Kiesha's cousin Tavia before looking down the barrel of her gun and decided that it wasn't going to be him.

Chapter 14

Ambulance, fire truck, and police sirens pierced the air. EMTs and law enforcement were everywhere. People scrambled around. There were screams that erupted here and there followed up with tears and wails of pain. No one knew what to think or how to feel about the situation at hand. Hearts tore and emotions ripped out of people's chests. Ke'Lasia was glued to the spot where she stood with her mouth hanging open. She didn't know what to do. All she could do was stand there in shock just looking. She couldn't bring herself to react in any kind of way.

"Miss Tanner? Miss Tanner! Miss Tanner, can you hear me? Can you speak? Miss Tanner?" The paramedic in his official deep blue uniform and his purple gloves stood in front of Ke'Lasia's face, shining a light in her eyes. She heard him. She heard every word he said and every question he asked. She just couldn't answer. She was stuck. Tears slid silently down her face and she could barely even blink. Fear and grief gripped her. Too scared to blink, Ke'Lasia's wide eyes took in the whole situation. Even though she wasn't able to process any of it, she saw it all. She saw everything unfold. And as she stood there with the EMT who was trying to determine if the blood splattered across her face was hers, the worst-case scenario played out in her mind over and over. She didn't know if Travis would live or die, and at this point, it wasn't looking good.

Travis hadn't moved since the sound of the gun firing quieted the entire room. She watched him go down in slow motion. After the bullet rang out, everything seemed to slow down for Ke'Lasia. The scream that escaped Kiesha's throat was inaudible and her fall to the ground didn't seem real. Picking herself back up, she could only assume that the single gunshot had hit Travis after he lunged toward Kiesha's cousin. Him lying there in a pool of blood didn't change her mind either. It only made the situation all that more real.

"Noooooooooo! Nooooo! Lord, please don't do this. Please! I'm so sorry! God, please don't take him!" Kiesha fell to her knees where Travis lay, begging and pleading with God to save the man she put in harm's way in the first place. It took three officers to get her away from what was now a crime scene. One officer on either side had her by the arms, pretty much dragging her back as she kicked and screamed for Travis to get up. The third officer acted as a shield between her and a bloody Travis to keep her from being able to contaminate anything on the floor if she was to break free. The blood splatter didn't skip her either. There was blood and what looked like hunks of chewed-up food that covered Kiesha as she wailed. The officers covered her in a plastic suit against her will. The pain that was heard in her cries made it that much harder for Ke'Lasia to compute what had just taken place.

September stood close against the back wall with tears streaming down her face. An almost whispered "I'm sorry" chanted from her lips over and over again. She spoke these words to no one in particular. Medics tended to her as well as other guests to make sure no one else was injured.

"My cousin. My peoples. Y'all gotta get my peoples. Please. Get her. Please. My cousin," Kiesha told the officers with her.

"Ma'am?" the female officer questioned in confusion. She looked to her counterparts to see if anybody understood what Kiesha meant. They all shrugged, just as confused. The short, long-haired lady officer walked back over to the other officers who were putting up barriers and crime scene tape around Travis's slain body far enough out so that no one was able to get close enough to mess anything up. She relayed Kiesha's confusing message only. They were also confused. No one knew what or whom she was speaking of.

"Her cousin."

"Excuse me?" The medic attending Ke'Lasia registered when she finally spoke. "Did you say something?" Again, he repeated the flashing of lights into Ke'Lasia's eyes along with the asking of already asked questions. "Ma'am?" he prompted.

"Her cousin."

"Her cousin? Whose cousin? I don't understand." He checked her vitals out of fear that she was slipping into a new level of shock. He figured she was incoherently rambling.

"Her cousin. Kiesha's cousin is under him."

"Under who, ma'am? Who is Kiesha's cousin?"

"She's under him. She's under Travis." Although Ke'Lasia's voice hadn't raised over a whisper, what she said had the young paramedic spooked. His eyes were just as wide as hers had been. He looked like he'd seen a ghost. Ke'Lasia, now back into a semblance of reality, tried to tell the fright-filled paramedic what Kiesha was trying to say.

"Kiesha's cousin is under Travis. He's on top of her." The medic was super handsome, Ke'Lasia noticed while staring in his large, almost golden eyes to get her point.

"Under him? Are you sure? He's covering her?"

Ke'Lasia nodded her head to confirm the fear that gripped all of their hearts.

Finally finding his legs and understanding the situation, the young, handsome medic walked across the room to notify the police of what Ke'Lasia had said. The group of attending officers and paramedics broke out into a frenzy. No one honestly knew what to do. The crime scene tape and dividers had been placed. The EMTs were concerned with the safety of the cousin they had just found out about while the officers were concerned with the preservation of their crime scene. They figured that, by this time, the cousin was also dead. And for that reason, their crime scene shouldn't be disturbed. The EMTs, on the other hand, were trained to try to save any life possible no matter how bleak the situation looked or seemed to anyone. They were determined to cross this tape to get to the victim who could possibly still be saved. The team of medics decided to ignore the pleadings of the police and proceeded to enter into the crime scene anyway. The officers protested more and more, but it meant nothing. The paramedics were already beyond the tape and nearing the body of almost everyone's slain friend to move him around to save someone else's life if possible. The life of the person who laid him there in the first place. The person whose fault this was. The person who took willing part in creating this whole mess. The paramedics were determined to do what they could to save her. None of this was a conventional situation. The police weren't doing what they usually did when there was a shooting given the circumstances.

The room they were all in was bigger than just a regular room. Usually the police would remove everyone from the room and tape off the entrance to the crime scene so that no one could get in except police officials. This time, because there were so many people covered in blood and so many witnesses, the police had left the people in the room and only tried to tape off the bodies and surrounding evidence, asking people not to disturb any tape or markings and to respect the barriers placed about.

The paramedics had quickly prepared themselves properly though. The protective gear that they wore protected them from the pool of blood that had settled onto the floor as well as protecting the blood from any outside contamination. They gently but quickly began to roll Travis once they reached him.

"One. Two. Three!" they counted in unison.

"What the fuck?" An older paramedic with a bald head and gray beard jumped up from the position in which he was just crouching. "Hell no. Hell fuckin' no," he rambled on with his hands on his head. Confusion and disbelief erupted from the murmuring crowd of onlookers as Travis began to cough and sputter.

"Sir? Sir? Can you hear me? Sir?" a lady medic basically yelled into Travis's face.

"I can hear you without all that yellin', damn," he answered clear as day. Other than sounding groggy, Travis sounded perfectly fine. Eyes all around the room grew wide. No one could believe they were hearing Travis's voice in that moment. Everyone was under the same impression that Travis was dead. Relief washed over the crowd simultaneously.

"Aaahhh! Nooo!" Kiesha's scream pierced the air.

Only then did the sickening feeling hit Ke'Lasia's gut as the realization set in. The blood. There was so much blood . . . so, so much blood. But Travis was fine, which only meant one thing. Travis stood with assistance from the medical attendants, and Kiesha's cousin, Tavia, was exposed to the crowded room of people for the first time since the gun went off.

"Oh, my goodness." The male staff member who had been one of the only people earlier when Ke'Lasia arrived grabbed his stomach and put one hand to his mouth. It didn't stop the vomit that spewed through his fingers and onto the floor though. The two other girls who were actually models for the photoshoot, who'd been pretty quiet all night as the shit was unfolding, fainted.

"Fuck," left Ke'Lasia's lips at the same time as the expletive left the lips of the young, handsome bald male medic who attended her. Tavia's body was now in full view with Travis off of her and out of the way. The sight of what she looked like shocked everyone who could see her. People threw up. People cried. People screamed. Some people just shook their heads and covered their mouths.

Tavia lay there on the floor in a pool of blood that everyone initially thought belonged to Travis. She looked drained. Like all the blood she had in her whole body was now on the floor where Travis previously lay. Her chin had a hole in it and so did the side of her head. There were clumps of blood and flesh stuck to Travis's back along with a deep stain that ran from the back of his head to the bottom of his pants. Tavia looked like a ghost. Her face was almost white. The side of her head was almost missing. Half of her face was pretty much gone. It was so terrible. No one could stomach the sight. Even the officers and medics turned away. Groans of pain and agony escaped some of them like they knew her personally. Ke'Lasia never knew her but it was still a sad sight to her too. With her mouth gaped open, she turned to see September still behind her, now in tears. September couldn't believe the sight of Tavia either. Her palms were sweaty as fuck while she wrung them together in fear and disbelief.

"Man, take her ass to jail." Travis gestured toward a wailing Kiesha. She was putting on the best show of her life. Only, it wasn't a show. She was heartbroken over her cousin's death. Relieved that Travis was alive but in shambles that her cousin was surely dead. Shit had gone wrong, real fuckin' wrong. She never meant for Tavia to die or Travis. She never even knew Tavia had brought a gun or planned to kill Travis.

They were just supposed to go there, make a scene, embarrass Travis for fuckin' with the fat model bitch, get him for more money so that they could take a trip to Atlanta with some of their homegirls and be out. That was it. The plan to fake a pregnancy and get abortion money from Tavia's hot little boy toy didn't work. She told him she was pregnant, and the dumb-ass young boy was happy, so he wouldn't give up the money for the fake abortion, and they had to come up with something else. The something else was to get the money from Travis. But then things went horribly wrong. They didn't get the money and now Atlanta meant nothing. Her cousin was dead and that hurt her more than not being able to go on some dumb-ass trip with a bunch of girls she barely even knew. Her and Tavia were supposed to go to Atlanta for the first time ever and fuck it up! They were gonna meet some niggas and fuck the city up. The best time of their life ever was supposed to be had in Atlanta together. And now Kiesha was by herself. Tavia was dead and Kiesha had nobody.

Chapter 15

"Aaaahhhhh! Yes!"

The strange man put his hand over Ke'Lasia's mouth to quiet her. "Shut up and bend over more," he growled his whispering voice at her while guiding her lower back with his hand. "Give it to me. Give it to me. Mmmmm," he growled.

He loved coming here to her. He loved fucking her and touching her. He loved the way she sounded. The way she howled in pleasure. The only thing he didn't get to have was her screaming his name to high hell. He wanted to tell her who he was so bad, but he knew he couldn't. He knew that if he did, she'd lose her fucking mind. *Damn, this pussy good.*

"I want you so fuckin' bad," he whispered in her ear over her shoulder. He wanted to make it clear how bad he wanted her. How he wanted to come through the door and not some random window that she left open for him to sneak in and take her by surprise. He wanted her in every way. To be with her in every way. He wanted to be her man. To be with her all the time, out in public and proud. It pissed him off that he couldn't, knowing what the consequences would be. His anger escaped him with each stroke of his manhood that he shoved in her. He listened to her as she cried real tears of passion.

This muthafucka is the shit! she thought as he continued pleasing her. His sex was so fucking amazing that he had her mind gone. She knew better than this. This shit was dangerous. He could be any fucking body. He could have any fucking thing. And she knew this. She knew all of this, but she just couldn't stop. She couldn't let this stop. She loved this shit. She was addicted to the shit. She was addicted to him. A fucking stranger.

How she got into this shit, she didn't know. How he chose her, she didn't know that either. All she knew was that this super hood, gangsta, down and dirty, nasty, slutty-ass loving that he was giving her, she just couldn't escape from.

She loved how he made her kneel with her back to him and then close her eyes while he bent her backward toward him and held her throat as she held her mouth open for him. The most she'd ever seen of him was his bottom half. She could only open her eyes when she was face-to-face with his dick. As it slid in and out of her throat, she looked at it, watched it slide easily in and out. She knew every inch of his dick. All of the veins, what they looked like when they throbbed, the small spasms it looked like they had when he was about to spill his seed deep into her throat. She knew the birthmark he had on his inner left thigh. Sometimes she would even trace it with her fingers while she let him use her mouth as his personal pocket pussy using only her ponytail that he made her put in each time as a joystick.

She knew everything from the waist down. She just wished she could know him. All of him. From his head to his toes she never saw because they were always in his socks or his boots that he made sure to wear every single time. She swore he was attached to the ground when he wore them. No matter how hard and fast she threw her ass back when he bent her over something, he never lost his balance. She loved that shit! He made her feel like she was only a 120 pounds and not what she really weighed. She felt like a little-bitty bitch the way he manhandled her and threw her around. That shit was like Christmas every time he came to her. Especially when he came over and then came.

"Yeeeessssss!" she let out as her mind clouded over again with an orgasm. The nuts she busted when this man arrived were matched by none. He fucked her mind up every time he touched her, and she couldn't help it. Even though she couldn't hear his actual voice, the baritone in his whisper made her stomach drop and her pussy clench tight. She yearned for the sound of his voice, but it would come eventually, she hoped.

The two, still strangers to each other, found the last orgasm they could handle before crashing to the floor like they just finished a hundred-yard dash to the finish line.

"I fuckin' love the way you fuck me," Ke'Lasia breathed. "I'm addicted to that lovin'. That thug-ass, hood lovin'." She smiled up at the ceiling with her eyes closed, careful not to tempt herself with a peek.

"Mmmmm," was his response so as not to have to say anything. *Man, I'm tired of playin' with her. This my girl and she need to know it,* the stranger thought. He just had to figure out what to do. He knew if he exposed himself, all hell would break loose, but he was tired of being a secret. Hell, he was tired of being quiet. Ke'Lasia was the kind of woman he had been searching for all his life and he was tired of not having her all the way. He was pretty damn close to saying fuck all the consequences that would go along with him exposing himself and just doing it. He just had to find the right timing. Timing would be everything in this situation.

"All rise!" the stocky, bald bailiff with the nice-ass full beard called out. Everyone in the courtroom stood to their feet. In his government-issued police-resembling uniform and the black boots to match, the bailiff who addressed the attendants of the court that morning was looking damn good to Ke'Lasia, and she definitely took notice. *Damn, he fine!* her brain screamed at her. She instantly forgot all about why they were there as thoughts of gushing all over his beard played out in her mind all of a sudden. She stood to her feet but never took her eyes off him and the biceps she could see damn near bursting out of his uniform top that looked like the tight hug she wanted to be the one giving him.

Ke'Lasia was lost in her own wild thoughts, and Travis stood tall and adamant while September eased to her feet like nothing special was going on. Super dark sunglasses were on her face like they were just having a picnic on the beach or something regular and chill. Not like they were in a courtroom getting ready to hear what could potentially happen to the person responsible for a death that almost included Travis. To untrained eyes, she may have been blind behind those glasses for all they knew. But Ke'Lasia and Travis did know, and they knew she wasn't blind. What she was, was hungover from the previous night. Anyone could smell the alcohol on her without even being that close. Just a few feet away from her, you could smell the previous night's intoxication reeking from her pores. She was so strong that she smelled like a distillery. Like, she stood right there all night while they mixed, churned, brewed, or whatever they did to the liquor before they bottled it. She smelled like she had to climb in the barrel and swish the liquor with her hands personally. It was a sad sight to behold. Their friend was a complete mess and there was nothing they could do about it. Especially right now in the middle of Hamilton County's Justice Center in Courtroom B. All they could do was shake their heads and try to ignore her and her stench. People sitting near covered their noses or laughed. It burned Ke'Lasia up on the inside that her dear friend was the butt of these people's jokes, but there was absolutely nothing she could do about that.

"Please remove all hats and hoods of any jacket or coat please," the judge required of everyone in the courtroom as they stood waiting for her to take her seat on the bench. "You all can be seated." She sat down. They all followed suit and sat. The judge, Leslie Chambers, cleared her throat about five times before the bailiff finally spoke to her.

"You need something, Your Honor? Water? Anything?"

"No, thank you, Charles. I'm fine."

"Are you sure, ma'am?"

"Yes. I'm sure." She sat up in her seat, leaning forward on her desk with her fingers intertwined with one another. "I was just trying to give the young woman in the fourth row a chance to remove her glasses as instructed."

Every single person in the courtroom turned and started to look all around the small enclosure, trying to find the person who was just put on blast. September still sat there like she was none the wiser. She made absolutely no move to rectify the situation at all. The remaining liquor in her veins had her totally oblivious to the fact that the impatience of the judge grew because of her. The judge cleared her throat once more and waited for September to finally take the hint. When she didn't, Charles was asked to go retrieve the glasses. He approached September and still she sat there as if he was never even standing there with his hand out. Maybe three minutes he stood there with his hand out waiting for September to comply. When it was evident that she wouldn't, the bailiff took it upon himself to remove the glasses from her face for her.

"What the fuck?" She finally snapped to attention in the room.

"Come on, man, you could've just asked her," Travis defended with an arm across September's chest to hold her in place.

"She was asked." He folded the glasses up and placed them in the breast pocket of his uniform. Then he smirked. "You should probably teach her how to hold her liquor since you give so much of a fuck," he mumbled to Travis who heard him clear as day. He turned to walk away but September was having none of that.

"Who the fuck you think you talkin' to, bitch-ass nigga? Fuck you think this is? I'll beat the fuck outta you. I'on give a fuck about a courtroom or that gun or none of that shit, the fuck! I'll smack fire out yo' dumb ass! Say somethin' else, ho-ass nigga!"

Murmurs and mumbles that weren't so quiet took over the attendees. September was giving them a show that they never expected to have when they showed up there that early in the morning. People who looked half asleep when they all filed in were now on high alert and wide awake so as not to miss anything.

"Ma'am, you need to calm down."

"Nigga, fuck you! I'on need to do shit but spit on yo' dumb ass if you say somethin' else to me."

"Sir? You need to—"

"Oh, my God! September!" Ke'Lasia squealed as the courtroom space grew as silent as a library. She stood there with her hand to her mouth as she, along with the sixty other people there, watched spit slide down Charles's face. Everyone was in shock. Including Travis and Ke'Lasia.

Travis immediately grabbed September, putting his body in between her and the bailiff so that neither party could get to each other. He snatched her up out of her seat like she was a toddler and informed the bailiff that he would remove her himself.

"Dammit, September," Ke'Lasia said. Worry racked her soul. She was so scared that September would be shot dead right there in that courtroom that she couldn't do anything but cuss.

"Bitch!" the angered bailiff yelled, reaching for something on his government-issued security belt.

Ke'Lasia panicked. "Travis, just take her out of here before she get herself in more trouble."

"She ain't goin' no fuckin' where!" the bailiff roared.

"She's sorry, sir. We're going to just take her in the hallway and calm her down, okay? It's cool. We got her."

The onlookers mumbled and expressed their views on the situation while the bailiff yelled and cursed September's name. The judge tried to bring order back to the room to no avail. The show was not over yet.

"Fuck you too, bitch. I ain't sorry for shit!" September screeched past Travis while he tried damn near dragging her out of the row seats and toward the door.

"Girl, I'm tryin'a help you! You need to chill out," Ke'Lasia warned. "You outta pocket right now. Just go with Travis and chill."

"I'm not doin' shit and you supposed to have my back. I knew when I heard that you was really fuckin' him that you wasn't my friend."

"September, that is enough," Travis interjected.

"Nah." She pushed away from him. "Fuck that. She gon' hear this. Snake-ass bitch. Talkin' about you lookin' out for me. Nah, you lookin' out for you. You don't give a fuck about me. If you did, you would've punched that nigga after I spit on him." She gestured to a still furious bailiff Charles. "But you didn't. You too busy playin' innocent sweet girl so you can suck this nigga dick that you just left me hangin'. I should've fuckin' known," she scoffed, continuing her rant for all to see. "Yo' ass ain't down. You fake as fuck. I wish yo' ass would've gotten shot the other day when I tried to push you in the way of that gun."

"Wait. Bitch, what?" Ke'Lasia was dumbfounded. She never expected to hear words like that out of September's mouth. She would've bet her last dollar she just tripped because of all the commotion. Not that her longest friend would've tried pushing her in front of a bullet. "You did what?" Tears stung her eyes and threatened to shower her face.

"Yeah, you heard me. I pushed yo' no-good ass and I wish you would've died right there wit' that other bitch. Fuck you, ho." Then she conjured up a whole mouthful of spit and hurled it with all her might toward Ke'Lasia. By the time the wad of spit landed on Ke'Lasia's shoulder, intertwining with her hair, Travis had September to the exit door and Charles the bailiff had Ke'Lasia in a serious death grip. Even he could see the fury in her eyes through the tears that now rolled plump and fast down her face.

"It ain't worth it. Just let it go. You'll just end up in the same cell she's going to. Just let it go," Charles spoke low in her ear from behind her head to soothe her. Ke'Lasia immediately froze in her spot. Charles, feeling Ke'Lasia's body tense up, immediately released her, apologized with his hands up in surrender, and slowly backed away. He didn't want any smoke with her, too. He just wanted to keep her from going crazy in the place and ending up in jail right where her friend was definitely headed.

Charles entered back inside the boxed-off glass squares where the arrestees, guards, lawyers, and judge were all tucked safely from the commotion of the crowd and closed the heavy door behind him. The judge again banged her gavel and called for order of her courtroom. Once everyone was settled, she got her court docket back in full swing. After the first few people were called to the stand and released on their own recognizance, the earlier hellified events were far from everyone's minds. They were too excited about their loved ones being released from custody to even have time to dwell on what had taken place. Travis was back in the room without September, waiting for Kiesha's name to be called. Ke'Lasia only half heard what was going on. Her mind was too busy back on pornographic thoughts of bailiff Charles and how sexy he would be without his uniform. Or even with it on and his little attentive friend sticking out of his zipper. Never taking her eyes off of him the whole time, she wondered how little his friend actually was.

"Those are my fuckin' kids!" Travis yelled into the phone.

"So, act like it, nigga. You raising yo' voice ain't gon' change shit, tah." She laughed. "Like I said, you either bring me some money, or you forget about these kids. I can't do everything by myself. And since you got they mammy locked up, it's on you. Period."

"I got her locked up? How the fuck was any of this my fault? I almost fuckin' died. Then what were you gonna do? If I was dead, she would still be in fuckin' jail and then who was yo' ass gonna extort for money then?"

"Extort? How the fuck can I extort you when, like you said, these yo' damn kids, nigga? Yours. Not mine. Ain't nobody extortin' shit."

"So, what the fuck was you gon' do then, huh? Where was you gon' get all this money that you need so bad if I was in the fuckin' morgue? Huh? What the fuck would you have done then, Sheila?"

"Probably throw a damn party." Sheila rolled her eyes like he could see her, not giving one fuck about his frustration. These were his kids, and since her daughter was locked up like an idiot, she planned to milk this nigga dry like her daughter obviously couldn't. He wouldn't get that smooth shit off on her. Sheila was hip to all of Freight's "charming" ways, but she wasn't Kiesha. He wouldn't just be able to use that shit to get over on her. Although, she wouldn't mind a shot of that dick she'd heard so much about. "Listen, nigga. You got choices. I told you what they were. Get wit' it or stay the fuck off my line talkin' this bullshit. I got kids to take care of."

"Sheila, I'm not fuckin' you and I'm not givin' you no more money. I just sent yo' ass a thousand dollars a few days ago." Travis gripped the bridge of his nose in frustration. He closed his eyes tight, trying to calm down. He couldn't believe this shit. Ever since Kiesha got locked up, her mom had his kids and was on some bullshit. Kiesha had only been locked up for two weeks. She wasn't even fully sentenced yet and her mom was extorting the fuck out of him already.

"With four kids, what the fuck am I supposed to do with a weak-ass thousand dollars? Huh? That shit ain't even gon' cover the rent over here, boy. You sound stupid."

"How the fuck is me givin' you some dick gon' cover yo' rent then?"

"It won't, but it'll change yo' damn life and relieve my stress from takin' care of yo' damn kids since you don't wanna step up like a man."

"Step up? Step up! I been taking care of my kids since each one of 'em popped into this world and you know it! Yo' daughter was on some bullshit, and now here you go. I see where she gets it from. This shit is crazy."

"It can be as crazy as you call it, it ain't gon' change the fact that I need some cash and to bust a nut, pretty boy. Figure yo' shit out." Sheila hung up with nothing more to say.

Travis could only sit there holding the phone in disbelief. What the fuck had he gotten himself into? A couple of his niggas from the block back in the day had warned him that Kiesha and her mama was crazy. If he would've just damn listened instead of being blinded by Kiesha's nice-ass body and fake nice-ass ways.

Kiesha used to be the best thing that happened to Travis. Treating him like the best thing since sliced bread, he was on top of the world for a while. Until she got pregnant with their first child. Then everything was downhill and been downhill since. The things Sheila was trying to get out of him were the same things Kiesha always bitched about. Some money and some dick. He had to come up off of both for Kiesha to let him even talk to his kids, let alone see them. And now her wicked-ass mama was doing the same thing. Wasn't no way in hell he was gonna fuck her, but $1,000 every few days was outrageous. He had already given her $2,000 since Kiesha been in jail these two weeks and Sheila still only let him see his kids once. This shit wasn't gon' work for Travis. He just ain't know what to do about it.

"What's up, Lasia? You heard anything else about September?"

"Fuck September. I told you that."

"Still, Lasia? Come on, man, that's yo' girl."

"That's not my girl. That's yo' girl. That bitch ain't shit to me no more. She tried to get me shot, then she tried to literally spit in my face. Ain't no fixin' that. I don't give a fuck if they put her under the jail. That bitch is dead to me."

"Ke'Lasia, the girl was on pills and liquor. That wasn't her. You know it like I know it. You can't hold that against her."

"I can and I will. Mmm . . . Uh, anyway . . . Uh, Travis, I gotta go."

Ke'Lasia hung up quickly, and again, Travis sat there holding the phone. *Was she just fuckin' in my ear?* Travis was dumbfounded. Life was getting crazier and crazier as the days went by.

He dialed her number back almost as soon as she hung up. Apparently, she didn't know she answered the phone because all Travis heard from the other end was Ke'Lasia sounding like she was having the time of her life. All kinds of oohs and aahs, moans and groans were heard from her end of the phone. Travis took the phone away from his ear and looked at the call display to make sure he had dialed the right number. He had and he was pissed. More hurt than pissed, but still pissed. *I know this girl ain't play me like that just to be fuckin' some random nigga.* The following thoughts were nothing nice, so he decided to get out the house before he let those thoughts get the better of him.

"Yeah, my nigga. What's up wit' it? I'm tryin'a get fucked up. You down? Cool. That's what's up. I'll meet you there." Since his boy decided he was going to meet up with him, Travis threw his clothes on after a quick shower and headed to the bar. It was time to get fucked up and forget all about all the events that had taken place over the last few weeks.

Speeding off in his 2017 midnight blue Chevy Silverado with sky blue racer stripes and twenty-six-inch Contra D644 rims and a gloss milled blue finish that made it look like they glowed in the dark, he was on his big-boy shit. He was ready to take on the world, pulling as many fine women as he could. His baby mama was on some bullshit, her mom was on some bullshit, and Ke'Lasia, the only girl he'd had feelings for since Kiesha, was also on some bullshit. Tonight, none of them would matter anymore. He was gonna hit the bar and anywhere else the party was happening on a Tuesday night. The city was about to be taken by storm and they didn't even know.

Chapter 16

Ke'Lasia got out the shower and lay across her bed in a towel. The dealings of earlier had worn her out. She was happy, content, and satisfied. Her stranger had been visiting more often and she was getting broken off like a nigga fresh off of D block. He was wearing her out so bad that a few times after his visits, she had to sit in her massive tub, turn on the Jacuzzi jets and soak in some vinegar to soothe her noni. Her shit was swollen more than once after he left her place. It was deliciously painful sometimes, and she still loved all of it.

She stretched out, facing up, and watched the steam from the now open bathroom swirl around the ceiling of her room, cascading around aimlessly until it eventually disappeared. Even though it didn't last long, it was pretty to watch anyway. She allowed herself to be lost in her thoughts.

How am I still messing with this man? Everything I grew up believing to be true tells me that this isn't right and neither of us should be doing it, but everything inside of me tells me to enjoy it for as long as it lasts. This shit is wonderful! The best I ever had. Everything I imagined sexually, I have now and it's great. I don't wanna stop fuckin' with him, but this shit is still weird. I just wanna touch his whole body. I wanna hear his real voice. I wanna be able to look him in his face at least just once. I really wanna see what he looks like. I know he's handsome without even looking at him already, but

I wanna be able to close my eyes and think about what he looks like. Man, damn this man got my head fucked up. Being able to be with him and tell people about him would be the norm, but nothing is normal about this. I don't know how to be happy with something that makes me feel so good but is so wrong.

She smiled at some thoughts and frowned at others. Yeah, he had her fucked up, and the situation was fucked up, but she liked it in all its fuckedupness. Every last minute of it. To Ke'Lasia, as crazy as it was, it was the best situationship she had ever had. She ain't have to worry about no nigga lying to her or beating her up. She didn't know nothing about him, so she didn't have to worry about no fake-ass sisters or cousins smiling in her face but dogging her behind her back or covering for him when they knew he was dead wrong. Shit, she ain't have to worry about no old-ass, fake-ass mama who felt like her son could do no wrong either. All she had to worry about was draining his dick of all the semen it possessed, taking every single ounce of energy out of him before he left and enjoying each and every minute of it. Well, and snatching his soul out each and every time. But that was an extra bonus for her.

Ke'Lasia slipped on some powder blue Adidas joggers with a white Adidas sports bra that zipped in the front before looking in the mirror and fixing her Senegalese twists just right. She grabbed her gym bag that was already packed and ready to go, then headed out. She usually put a T-shirt over her sports bra when she went to work out, but today, she was feeling like what the hell. After one last smile at herself in the mirror, she was gone.

Turning into the parking lot of the gym she frequented, she couldn't help but be salty at herself for not stopping to get a quick bite to eat first. She already had a mean-ass workout earlier leaving her hungry as hell, but she wanted to go get in some real cardio and forgot all about eating. She shrugged it off, deciding to just get something light on her way back home. James, the cardio class instructor, had a class that wasn't full yet, so she settled on full instructional cardio today instead of just spin class. She ain't feel like being in that little room with all those hot and sweaty skinny bitches anyway, so James's class seemed like the right choice for her anyway.

Outside of him having room left in his session for today for her and a few other people, and him being almost fine, she saw a couple of thick bitches who matched her weight in there already. She ain't have to worry about them trying to dog her or throw shade at the fact that she was a curvier woman because, hell, they were too. She could enjoy her workout and not feel judged. She smiled to herself, feeling like she was going to fit right in with this class today. Apparently, she was all smiles today. Her smile hadn't stopped yet.

Ke'Lasia waltzed into the cardio class still high on life and smiling it up, ready to bust this two-hour workout down to nothing. She spoke to a couple of women as she passed by, picking an empty spot on the far side of the classroom to set up her stuff. The girls were friendly enough to speak back. The instructor, James, walked into class looking as good as he could. James wasn't ugly by far. He just wasn't the type that Ke'Lasia went for, so she wouldn't get sidetracked by him in his class. He was tall enough at about five foot eight. He had sandy brown curls in his low taper that gave him an extra interesting thing that added to his looks. His hair was so sandy it almost looked like it was supposed to be blond and just didn't make it. He was thin though. Muscle cut to the gods for sure but still thinner than what she usually liked. You could tell the cardio classes he taught really worked for him because there wasn't an ounce of fat anywhere on him. He weighed about 135, maybe forty pounds of pure muscle. When he removed his muscle shirt and revealed his abs, they were so rock hard and cut up that it looked like an actual washboard from back in the day that they ran clothes over when they handwashed outside in a metal basin. He was phenomenal to look at. Ke'Lasia had thoughts from time to time on what it would be like to run her fingers or even her tongue across his sculpted physique, but it never went any further than her own private thoughts. The way he smiled so hard in the skinny white girls' faces who came to class sometimes told her that she probably wasn't his type anyway, even if she was actually interested.

He had both his arms inked in full sleeve tattoos that were intriguing to anyone who saw them. Ke'Lasia felt a twinge of jealousy anytime she saw them because they were lit with color. That was the upside about being as light as James was. While Ke'Lasia could only get hues of black because her skin was so chocolate, people the color of James who were only barely kissed by the sun and almost literally yellow could get whatever color they wanted. You would've thought James favored warm colors because his tattoos showed different shades of red, orange, and yellow in them. He had fire surrounding the images on his right sleeve that just gave you the feeling like the images really meant something real to him. But it was anybody's guess what his actual favorite color was because the left sleeve had ice playing background and was colored with various blues, whites, and grays. Some shades of black and even purple went into the makeup of that scenery, and Ke'Lasia never did get close enough to find out what they were. Instead, she admired his odd, unattractive handsomeness from afar each time she saw him.

When Ke'Lasia first started coming here a year and a half ago, James used to only wear loose-fitted basketball shorts to his classes. But after several stories swirled around about how big everyone thought his penis was, he started wearing tights under them to control any extra movement that may have been had from his counterpart. She believed it was more so to not distract the ladies in the class and so that none of the men would feel uncomfortable. What man was ashamed or embarrassed about having a huge dick? It had to be for the comfort of others. It was nice enough, but Ke'Lasia wouldn't mind an eyeful of big dick swinging around while she sweated. Hell, it may have been an incentive to come to class more often for her.

James started the class with some easy stretches to warm them up. Everybody geared up quickly. Ke'Lasia felt like she had never missed a class. It was a breeze getting through the first half hour. By the time he went into the ab workouts though, Ke'Lasia could've collapsed where she stood but she kept going. She was keeping up with the class, and for that, she was super proud of herself. Matching the instructor step by step had her feeling accomplished. She definitely was happy, but she was also tired as shit! She hadn't done a cardio workout this intense in months! She was drained. Especially after the amazing time she had already had today in a personal one-on-one workout all her own at home. All she wanted to do was sit the hell down while she guzzled down some ice-cold water. Wishful thinking though. She still had thirty minutes to go.

"Let's go class! Let's get working!" James yelled to them, signaling the end of their too short break. Ke'Lasia didn't know how much longer she would last but she gave it her all. "Whew! That was great! Everybody feeling the burn? Everybody feeling accomplished?" Ke'Lasia was one of the few members who shook her head as she drank from her water bottle like she'd never had a drink in her life while others whooped, hollered, and cheered like they'd just won a game in the final minutes of the last quarter.

Everyone high-fived and gave each other words of encouragement and congratulations for being able to finish the class. Some people stood to the side talking and sweating while others just continued to sweat. Ke'Lasia took her time packing her gym bag back up so that she could go. Out the corner of her eye, she'd thought she saw someone pretty close to her. It was just some girls from the class though, so she carried on about her business.

Getting her things together and finishing the rest of the water in her bottle, she packed that up too and picked her bag up to sling back over her shoulder. "Fuck!" Ke'Lasia let out all of a sudden. She grabbed her stomach, going straight to the floor. People from the class, including James, ran to her side to see the problem. She could only hardly breathe and barely move. Pain racked her body. She couldn't do anything but curl up and hold herself. Fighting back tears, she rocked back and forth on the ground.

"Somebody get the medic! Now!" James shouted to the crowd that had formed.

She opened her eyes in search of whomever agreed to the task to try to tell them that she didn't need a medic. That she was fine and just needed a minute to recuperate, but the words never came out. The pain shot up her sides and spine, paralyzing the words on her tongue. All she could do was close her eyes again. But not before she could've sworn she saw September's boyfriend, Slash, standing at the door to the classroom. A confused feeling settled in right behind her pain. She hadn't seen him in class and didn't remember ever seeing him at this gym at all. Maybe she was just tripping and didn't really see him.

The pain eased up and she pried her eyes open to take another look, assuming that if Slash was there, maybe it meant September was nearby. From what she'd heard, they didn't do a lot of moving without each other these days. Only, once she'd gotten her eyes back open, Slash was gone from in front of the door where she swore she saw him, and September was also nowhere in sight. She closed her eyes again and tried to shake off the events and people that were happening around her.

"Shit!" she cried. The pain had brought tears to her eyes, and they were now pouring down her face. The pain was coming back and it was way more excruciating than before.

"Dammit!" she howled out as agony gripped her whole entire body.

"Make a hole! Make a hole, dammit!" James hurled at the crowd of bystanders as he tried as politely as he could to move people to the side. "Make room. They have to get through!" he told them. They parted upon command and let the gym medics through to access Ke'Lasia, still lying on the ground in pain.

"Ma'am? Ma'am? Can you hear me?" Two medics knelt down next to her. One spoke to her and tried to get her to calm down as well as get vitals on her while the other searched through a medical bag they had with them. "Can you speak? Can you tell me where it hurts?"

"Everywhere," Ke'Lasia forced out. "Hurts so bad. Uuuuugggggghhhhh!" More painful groaning forced its way out of her.

"Can you tell me your name?" the bag medic asked as he shined a light in her face, forcing her eyes open to check them out.

"Ke . . ." She was unable to finish even her name because the next thing you knew, she was spewing vomit all over the medic. The sight was horrible. The medic could do nothing but try to shield his face from the wet, sticky, foul-smelling assault. The second medic laughed hysterically as the scene played out, but no one else found it funny. People in the crowd tried their best to hold back their own vomit. Some succeeded, others did not. There was now vomit spewing from multiple people at the same time and no one could do anything about it. James jumped out the way when a male member of his earlier class turned his way to let his insides go. He held back with all he could but ended up in a full run to the nearest toilet to do his emptying in peace and privacy. The last thing he needed or wanted was an image of him in someone's head tossing his guts up.

The paramedics continued to check Ke'Lasia as best they could around the smell and the wet parts that now donned Ke'Lasia's sports bra and her stomach. She continued to spew bile every two of the next eight minutes they took trying to check her out. Finally deciding they'd had enough, they wheeled a stretcher in and strapped her to it. They made a path through the even bigger crowd that had gathered in the last few minutes and loaded her into the back of the ambulance. They never even tried to ask if anyone would be riding with her, and no one dared volunteer.

Ke'Lasia lay in the back of the ambulance under an oxygen mask, fading in and out of consciousness with sirens blaring loud and strong in her background. All she could think about was dying on this stretcher in the back of this ambulance on her way to the hospital without September by her side.

Chapter 17

It had been five long weeks since the day September wiled out in the courtroom and got detained for misconduct and attempted assault on a government official. The odds were finally in her favor, and after court that morning, they let her out on bond.

"Thank you, bitch. I had to get my ass up outta there."

"Yeah, I know. That li'l shit ain't no ho. Just make sure you go back to court 'cause I'on got five grand to just be throwin' away," her friend, Monica, told her, giving her the side-eye.

"Girl, fuck them. You'll get yo' money back. These people better leave me the fuck alone. Ain't nobody done did shit to them."

"Yeah, whatever." Monica shrugged off her comment, knowing one way or another September always came up with the cash she needed. "What were you in there for anyway?"

"Girl . . ." September rolled her eyes thinking about the day she got locked up. "So, me, Travis, and Ke'Lasia go to court for Travis weak-ass baby mama, right? I mean, we wasn't about to testify or nothing. We just went to see what they was gon' do. I mean, Travis ass might've been tryin'a save her, but I was just being nosy. Anyway. So, we up in there and this weak-ass bailiff come over talkin' about take my glasses off 'cause I had on sunglasses in the courtroom. I told his ass to step."

"Right! The fuck. What he mean? Them yo' glasses."

"Girl, right. So, I tell his ass to step and he get to talkin' crazy, talkin' about I can be removed and all this lame shit. So, I tell him I'm not going nowhere 'cause I hadn't done shit. Here Ke'Lasia ass go talkin' about some 'just take the glasses off, September,' so that li'l shit pissed me off. You know I'm zooted as fuck, like why she even talkin'? So, I take the glasses off and this nigga talkin' about 'yeah, I thought so.' So, I cussed his ass out. He gets salty and tried to run up on me, right?"

"The bailiff? Girl, no he didn't!" Monica said, stunned. Trying to drive the car and pay attention to September, too, she was lost in the conversation.

"Girl, yes the fuck he did. So, I crack the nigga like back up. He keep comin' though on some bullshit. So, I get to swinging all on the nigga, crackin' him in his shit, right? Ain't nobody doin' shit. The nigga Travis lettin' him swing on me, and this bitch-ass Ke'Lasia just cryin' like 'September stop, September stop.' I ain't listenin' to none of it. I'm fuckin' this nigga up, he bleeding all over the place, people watchin' and laughin', cheering me on. So finally, the nigga screamin' get me, get me. So, Travis ass jump up and grab me. I started to swing on him too, but I didn't. Ke'Lasia talkin' about I'm ghetto and ratchet and that's why can't nobody take me nowhere and all this. So, I'm arguing over Travis shoulder tellin' her how she supposed to be my girl, but she let a nigga put his hands on me and she talkin' about that's what the fuck I get for being so ignorant and that old girl Keisha cousin should've shot me instead."

"Bitch, that did not happen! Not Ke'Lasia?" Monica's mouth hung open. She was so in shock by the story that she didn't even notice the light had turned green. A car behind her blew at them to keep moving. "Girl, I can't believe this shit. That was yo' girl. How she ain't have yo' back? Talkin' about you should've got shot. That's deep as fuck."

"Girl, tell me about it." September rolled her eyes and continued. "So, I'm like damn, I should've got shot? She like, 'Hell yeah, bitch. That's why I pushed you in the way when she pulled out the gun.' Bitch, I 'bout died when she said that."

"September! Ke'Lasia did not tell you she pushed you in front of a gun!"

"Yes, the fuck she did. Right to my face in the courtroom after lettin' me fight a nigga all by myself. Sure did."

"Girl, I can't believe no shit like that. Not Ke'Lasia. Ke'Lasia? Hell nah."

"That's how the fuck I felt, but I couldn't make this shit up if I tried," September told her friend as she held her hand in the air like she was telling the God's honest truth. "Oh! But then I tell her fuck her 'cause my feelings hurt right now, right? Why she say fuck me, I can die, and then tried to spit in my face?"

"Now I know you the fuck lyin'! That girl did not try and spit on you. You! Her homegirl? Her sister? No, she didn't. I ain't even about to believe that."

"You think I'ma make all this shit up? Girl, I was no mo' good. I couldn't do nothing but just let Travis walk me in the hallway."

"So, what Travis do?" Monica asked, shaking her head at the whole thing.

"Nothing."

"Nothing? What you mean nothing?"

"Just what the fuck I said, bitch. Nothing. He walked me in the hallway and went back in there with her. He left me by myself. You know they fuckin' now, though?"

"They fuckin'? I know you fuckin' lyin'!" Monica burst out. Her eyes were as big as saucers as she looked at September in disbelief. The two girls sat in Monica's two-door purple Lexus in front of September's downtown apartment. Monica couldn't believe her ears. "You mean to tell me the bitch you been callin' yo' sister for umpteen years cussed you out, admitted to pushin' you in front of a gun, wished death on you, spat on you, and fuckin' the nigga you been crushing on for the last two, three years? Is that what the fuck you tellin' me?" She questioned September like she had all the answers to life's biggest questions, ticking them off on her fingers as she went.

"If I'm lyin', I'm flyin'," September confirmed with the straightest face ever and her hand raised again. The two girls sat and looked at each other in silence.

Monica shook her head as September shook hers. "Girl, you fucked up like me. I would've never thought."

"I know you wouldn't have because I wouldn't have. Lasia was always the realest one of us all. Like, we all did shit, but damn, Lasia though." It wasn't a question so much as a realization.

"Anyway, ho." September shrugged finally. "Let me get in here. I know my man been waitin' on this pussy." The girls laughed.

"All right, bitch. Don't hurt that poor man."

"Girl, fuck him. I'm tryin'a knock that nigga dick loose." The girls laughed again and high-fived. September jumped out the car then, still laughing, and walked up to her door. Monica waited until she got in the house safely before pulling off. She waited until she drove the short distance to her own apartment on the other side of downtown in the City West townhome complex before she pulled out her phone and sent a text.

Monica: She wasn't even fuckin' that nigga. Yo' dumb ass just did all this shit for nothin'. I swear you don't listen.

Raheim: How the fuck was I supposed to know that? You the one said she was fuckin' the nigga!

Monica: I said she was trying to fuck the nigga. Damn. How the fuck don't you know the difference?

Raheim: Bitch, you the one was feedin' me this dumb-ass info in the first place. If you ain't gon' do yo' part, how the fuck am I supposed to know what to do on my end? Make that shit make sense. Bitch, get off my line tf. You soundin' stupid. Go be useful.

Monica: Shut yo' dumb ass up. I gotta do every fuckin' thing. Just chill 'til I find out what I need to know. Smmfh. Don't do shit 'til you hear from me, stupid mf. Nothin'. Don't fuck this up either.

Raheim: Fuck you.

Monica: Maybe later. I'm busy.

She dropped her phone back in her purse and hit the steering wheel in frustration. These niggas never listened. How the fuck was a plan supposed to go smoothly and these niggas ain't follow directions? Monica massaged her temples trying to figure out her next move. She had to make sure Raheim's dumb ass ain't fuck shit up this time.

"Incompetent," she muttered aloud to herself as she exited her vehicle.

Monica got in the door and threw her purse and jacket on the couch. After kicking off her shoes in the middle of the floor, she headed into the kitchen to find something to eat.

"So, you just gon' leave yo' shit in the middle of the floor?"

"If it's bothering you, move them," she said without ever turning back around.

"It should bother you. That's how people places get dirty."

"From some shoes? Please leave me alone wit' that shit."

"That's just facts. What the fuck is wrong wit' you? You get into it wit' yo' li'l boyfriend or somethin'?"

"He ain't my damn boyfriend, Vic, I keep sayin' that." Monica slumped toward the kitchen sink and shook her head, not ready to have this same damn conversation with him again. It was getting old and he was getting the fuck on her nerves with it over and over again.

"He seem like yo' boyfriend to me. Shit, he see you more than I do."

"Maybe. But yo' ass ain't my boyfriend either," she shot over her shoulder. Vic walked up behind her still at the kitchen sink and pressed his dick up against her ass.

"Maybe not. But I'm the one fuckin' the shit out of you though." She couldn't argue with that. Between the two of the men, Vic had way better dick game than Raheim, but that didn't mean she was only fucking one of them.

"You right, baby," she purred to him, trying to change the mood of things.

Vic wasn't her man and he was way more irritating than she imagined he would be, but his ugly ass had the best dick she'd ever had. It wasn't that Raheim was bad, he just wasn't as good as Vic. His dick wasn't as big either. Raheim was just way easier to look at. And sometimes, even to talk to. A lot of girls thought Raheim was just average because he wasn't very tall, or he didn't weigh very much. He was black as midnight with a mouthful of gold. A lot of the girls called him Tracey Morgan behind his back even though he didn't resemble him at all. It was just funny for them, so they went with it. To Monica though, his dark chocolate ass was some of the finest shit she'd ever seen and at no time did he act like it either. That humbleness that Raheim had, Vic didn't possess.

Vic was full of himself and felt like everyone should just fold to his will while Raheim was always eager to learn and get this money. Vic was too old and set in his ways. He always thought his way was the best way when in fact it hardly ever was. She'd had to go behind him a million times and fix shit that he wouldn't hear was fucked up. She was so used to it now that she didn't even bother to tell him when he wasn't right. She just listened to him and devised her own plan from what he said. She'd let him take the credit for it. That wasn't a big deal to her. All Monica cared about was getting to the fucking money. She didn't give a fuck who got the credit from it as long as she got her coin.

That was the upside to Raheim. He always, always got his money. No matter what or who was in the way. Anybody standing in his way would be dealt with. Yeah, he fucked up from time to time, but it wasn't big fuckups, so it was cool. Monica always had it anyway. No matter what.

The two dudes were so different in so many ways. It was totally different the way she fucked with them. All the way down to the sex. But if she had to pick just one to keep, it would have to be Raheim. Vic's old ass had his time. Raheim still had some years left to put into this game though, which meant she still had years left of her gravy train flowing. As long as she stayed behind the man of the hour, she would be fine. And right now, that was both of these niggas. Vic was too old to last much longer though. And with Ears on his ass the way he was, his days may be even shorter. She knew that. She just used him for the connects he still had at the moment. She planned to meet everyone she could and play whatever hand she had to before Ears wiped his ass out for good.

I hope the nigga Ears got good dick too, she thought as she bent forward some more, letting Vic pull her panties to the side under her dress. She knew she would have to start fucking Ears soon if she was gonna get in good with him like she wanted and that was absolutely fine with her. She never hesitated to give up some ass. It kept her in good graces with any nigga she was using at the time, but it also worked in her favor when the dick was as good as what this nigga Vic had to offer. It never ceased to amaze her that, at 50, Vic could still fuck like a twenty-something young boy.

Her hands gripped the sides of the sink panel for balance as she stood on one leg and Vic held the other in the air in his hand, giving her back shots that vibrated the whole sink. He sunk into her as hard as he could over and over again, and she was loving every strong-ass thrust.

"Harder, baby! Harder! Yes!" Vic did as he was told and pushed himself into her harder than before. She never even knew he had this amount of strength to put behind a stroke. "Yes! Yes!"

"Give me this pussy, bitch. I told you, I ain't them young niggas you used to."

"You not, baby! You not! This dick good as fuck! Shit!" She moaned loud and carried on because that's what he liked. That's what he needed from her, so she gave it every time. It was her job to make him feel like the best on the planet and she damn sure did. She didn't have to try too hard either.

"Damn, girl, I'm cummin'. Shit! Fuck! Shit!" he growled. Vic leaned forward and bit down on her neck as he let his juices spill inside of her. Monica didn't mind. It just made her cum harder feeling his liquid warm her up and his teeth break her flesh. She liked that rough-ass nasty shit and Vic delivered every time.

Done with their quickie, Vic zipped his pants and slapped her on the ass. "I'm seeing that ass later?"

"Hell yeah, baby." She smiled seductively as she turned to him and let her wet panties drop to the floor.

"You better quit before you fuck around and make me late." He bit his lip looking at her. Monica then slid her two fingers under her dress and inside of herself. Vic could barely see her fingers moving, but he knew what was happening and almost couldn't control himself. She pulled the two fingers out and put them in her mouth, sucking every last hint of their mixed juices from her fingers. Vic's dick visibly grew inside of his joggers. She smiled again to entice him, but he held back. He grabbed his dick and backed up.

"You play too fuckin' much." He smiled, inching toward the door. "You just better be ready for this dick later. You better be just as nasty or yo' ass will be in trouble."

"Yes, sir," Monica purred. She was a little disappointed that her trick to get more dick didn't work, but it was all for the best. She had money to get too. She just had to find out who was gon' get her together first because she was not going around the rest of the day horny seeing as though she had no intentions of seeing Vic later. After making sure that Vic was actually gone, Monica pulled out her phone to make damn certain that she wouldn't be.

Monica: you tied up or nah?
Raheim: not right now. What's up?
Monica: you, shit.
Raheim: say less. I'm in the Lot.
Monica: omw

Monica kicked the panties to the side that Vic had soiled and didn't bother to put any back on. Raheim would just snatch them off anyway, ruining another pair, and she didn't have time for that. Instead, she grabbed her purse and keys and jumped back in her car. She pulled up on the Tot Lot in like ten minutes. She pulled over and rolled the window down, waiting for Raheim to see her. She waited a few minutes before she was spotted, but it wasn't long.

"A'ight, my nigga. Let me go hit this lick before this bitch start blowin' this damn horn." Raheim dapped his boy up before leaving.

"A'ight, my nigga. Be safe. I'm about to make a few moves of my own, feel me?"

"No doubt." Raheim put on a brisk walk over to Monica's waiting car. He couldn't move too fast as to draw attention to what he was doing. He ain't want nobody to think that Monica was more than a lick for him, but he also knew how she was. He didn't want to make her wait too long and she pull off. Monica had some fire-ass pussy and even better head that Raheim wasn't trying to miss out on getting.

He jumped in the car with not so much as a greeting. She didn't mind though. In her mind, there was nothing to say anyway. She pulled the car off and turned a few corners until they were on a side street that not a lot of people traveled down. She made sure she chose a one-way so that they could see anybody coming. She turned the car off and looked at him expectantly. Feeling her eyes on the side of his head, he looked up at her and then out the windows of the car.

"Oh, yeah?" he said. It wasn't really a question. Monica just continued to stare without answering. "Oh, you on yo' big-girl shit today I see."

He got out of the car, dropped his cell phone into his pocket, and walked around to the driver's side door where Monica sat. After opening the door, he pulled her out roughly, but careful as to not hit her head on the roof. Once she was fully standing, with nothing said, Raheim spun Monica around and bent her over. Her hands fell onto the driver's seat where she just sat a few seconds prior. He pulled her dress up and admired her ass from his angle.

"All this ass," he said as he slapped her on it, one cheek, then the other. He had fun playing with her ass. He would slap it and it would bounce right back at him. He got excited every time. "You got a fat ol' ass, I swear," he said, slapping her ass cheek again. "You came ready for this dick, huh?" He asked another rhetorical question.

He just wanted her to know that he appreciated her skipping the panties. He rubbed her ass with one hand as he freed himself with the other. He wasted no time jamming his thick dick into her waiting, wet pussy.

"Ummmm," she moaned for him.

"You like that shit, huh? That's why you keep hittin' me up? I thought you was done with this part, huh? It was only business, I thought." He taunted her as he thrust himself into her hard and quick and she struggled to keep control of her legs and arms. Raheim wasn't much bigger than Monica, but she still had to arch herself up on her tiptoes to be able to meet him ass to pelvis. Every thrust he sent careening into her body threatened to knock her forward. She did everything she could not to fall and fuck up these strokes.

"Shut up and fuck me. Hard. Harder! Harder, muthafucka!" she commanded.

Raheim sent his body hurling into hers as hard as he could. Wrapping his hand in her long weave, he held firm and pulled her back into him. He used his other hand to hold her waist for more leverage. At the angle he was, he was able to give her shorter, but quicker thrusts with more severity than before. She moaned and yelled loud as fuck like they were on the street alone or in a bedroom by themselves. She didn't give not one fuck about the people who lived on the secluded side street who would be able to hear them and, because she didn't care, he had learned not to either.

This wasn't the first time they had rendezvoused here, but usually Monica was nutty and Raheim had to talk her into it. Quick car sex was mostly what he gave to her. Somewhere on a side street inside or on the car in some type of way. It was very seldom that he took her to a house with a bed or a hotel room. He didn't want her thinking that they were more than what they were and all they were was fuck buddies and business partners. Not so much emphasis on the buddy part. Raheim didn't even like Monica. He didn't like her as a person let alone as someone he could be with. He only liked what she had between her legs and her hustler ambition. Her pussy was fire, he couldn't lie. And her head game had the nigga seeing Jesus any time she put him in her mouth, but that still didn't make him want to be with her. He wasn't sure if she felt the same way, but he did what he could to make sure she didn't feel like anything else but a fuck and a person to bust a move with. Monica was an ain't shit bitch and he wasn't going to run the risk of losing his life or no money over fucking with her more than an occasional fuck here and there. Had she been different, maybe. But as far as he could see, this was all he was willing to give her. Monica was a skept-ass bitch with no loyalty to nobody and nothing but God's almighty dollar and Raheim knew better than to get caught in her web. He used her for what he needed: getting these niggas out the way so that he could get this money without the interruption of anyone else. Other than that, he had no use or desire for Monica. None at all. No matter how good her sex was.

September would've been the kind of bitch he would've married though. But now, even she had to go. People with no loyalty meant Raheim no good in his eyes, and both of these bitches was in bed with the ops. Literally.

"Yes, baby! Yes! Keep going!" she yelled. Her screams pulled Raheim back from his treacherous thoughts. Just in time to notice that he honestly didn't even want to be doing this.

"Aw, shit! Fuck, baby!" he moaned, faking a nut. He pushed his dick deep inside of her and used his muscles to bounce it around a little bit as he stood still. This girl would be none the wiser that his climax hadn't actually arrived. All she cared about was thinking that she had a nigga gone, so Raheim used that knowledge.

"Shit, baby. Damn. You be wearing a nigga out. Whew!" he said, backing up and zipping his pants back. She stood and straightened her dress before turning to smile at him.

"I just be tryin'a keep you happy, baby. You know I love that dick." She winked at him sexually. Raheim smiled in return.

"Good. Keep keepin' a nigga right and you won't have no problems." He took his turn to wink at her before leaning in and placing a soft kiss on her face. "You be cool with that for now tho', li'l mama. I got shit to do. I'ma head in here and see what's poppin'."

"Okay, daddy. Talk to you later," she flirted. She got back in her car and pulled off. Raheim watched her go before walking into the building across the street.

"You get all that?"

"Yeah, I got it."

"What the fuck is wrong with you?" Raheim was confused as hell.

"You just be going around faking nuts all the time, huh?"

"Man, what the fuck are you talkin' about now? Damn! It's always somethin' wit' you! You know I gotta keep this bitch around in order for me to do what I gotta do. So if she wants some dick from time to time, I'ma give it to her. Why you trippin' now? I kept it real wit' you, right? Just like you asked me to, right?"

"Yeah, you did. But you sure looked like you was enjoying that shit at first. What you do? Remember I was over here and fake that weak-ass nut so I wouldn't get salty? You real fuckin' funny, bra."

"Cut that shit out. You know what that was. I faked the nut 'cause I ain't wanna be fuckin' her."

"Is that why you fake them same weak-ass nuts with me?"

"I don't fake nuts with you, man, stop. You know that shit ain't true."

"Yeah, whatever, muthafucka."

"Why you on this, for real? Just tell me so we can figure this shit out and move the fuck on."

"You know why I'm mad. I'm tired of havin' to deal with all these different bitches. I told you that and I'm not gon' keep sayin' it, the fuck. This shit dumb as fuck."

"It ain't all no bitches, it's only her. That's it. I got rid of the other bitches like I said I would, but we need her. You and I both need her if we gon' get this money, so just fuckin' chill, okay?" Raheim closed his eyes, shook his head, and took a deep breath. He didn't have time for this today, so his best bet was to not even engage. He kissed the same kiss he always did to the forehead, took the SD card that held the footage of him and Monica, and left.

Monica got back to her apartment and once again kicked her shoes off in the middle of the floor. What Vic had said to her earlier meant nothing to her. The shoes in the middle of the floor didn't bother her at all.

She lay across her bed holding her phone and smiling, thinking about Raheim. Wondering what she should send to him to let him know that she was thinking about him. She didn't know why Raheim did what he did to her. Especially since she knew she should keep it business. And all the shit that dumb-ass September had told her about him didn't make it any better, but she couldn't control it. It was just something he did. His dick wasn't even good enough to be gone off of. He just put a tickle in her spine from time to time and she liked it.

Monica: good seeing you today.

She waited for a text back from Raheim that was taking too long to come through. Instead of getting pissed off, she decided to just take a nap instead and worry about all this bullshit when she woke up.

"Damn! Why the fuck is you trippin'? Fuck, you been gettin' some new pussy or somethin' since I been gone?"

"Really, September? Really? Some new pussy? Are you fuckin' kiddin' me right now?"

"Shit, nigga, you been gettin' somethin'. Yo' ass actin' real fuckin' strange right now. Like, super weird and I ain't feelin' this shit at all."

"Because I ain't wanna fuck soon as you walked through the damn door?" Slash roared, getting angry at the shit September was saying and accusing him of.

"Well, that's for number one. Hell yeah."

"And what you came up with was new pussy? You gotta be out yo' fuckin' mind."

"How? What am I sayin' that's so farfetched? I know you like pussy, nigga. You ain't fuckin' boys."

"Of course I like pussy, September! That's dumb as fuck! Yeah, I like pussy, but what the fuck does that mean? I get new pussy on a daily. Did you forget that shit? Pussy and head don't mean shit to me. I just fucked two different bitches before they released yo' ass this fuckin' morning! One of the bitches had my whole dick down her throat with my balls and stuck her tongue out and licked my asshole. What the fuck you think I'ma be runnin' around out here for some pussy for? If I wanted that shit that bad, I could just take my ass to work. Make sense!"

"So, my pussy don't mean shit to you? I'm just some basic bitch off the street, huh? 'Cause you like gettin' yo' asshole licked?"

"September, I'on like the way you just said that shit, so I'ma ask you to chill out and watch how you talkin' to me before this shit go sideways."

"How did I say it? Like you like yo' ass licked? And played with? And probably—"

"September."

"Shit, you said that shit like it was the shit."

"September, I'm not fuckin' playin' wit' you. Stop now," he said, trying to warn her one last time before shit got out of control.

"And probably fucked, too." She plastered a smirk on her face and posted her hands on her hips. True to her fucking nature, she had pushed the bar too far.

Slash's initial reaction was to choke her ass to death for disrespecting him. But the moment he got in her face, all his anger dissipated. *She ain't even worth it,* he told himself. There was no point in even getting mad or roughing her up. Knowing September, she would just like it. *This girl is something else,* he thought before he told her, "You know what? You right. You got it. You wanted me gone? You could've just said that."

He reached behind her and a smile erupted on her face. She just knew she had pissed him off enough to get him to rough her up. She closed her eyes and waited for the snatch of the back of her neck to moisten her already wet panties. Instead, she felt his jacket whip by her. She opened her eyes in just enough time to see him close the door behind him. Confused and pained suddenly, she ran to the door. Hurling insults at him as he descended the back staircase to his car, her eyes poured over with tears she never dreamed would come.

"Fuck you, nigga! Fuck you! You a soft-ass nigga! Dick in the booty–ass bitch! I knew yo' ass was suspect! I knew it. I should've listened when my homegirls told me not to fuck wit' you! Fuckin' faggot! That's right! Run! Run bitch! You can't even be a fuckin' man, you fuckin' mud slinger! Doo chaser! Fag! You better never come back here, bitch!" Slash was in his car and halfway down the street as she stood on her balcony still crying and cussing into the wind.

September finally pulled herself together and got ahold of her shaking body by the time she watched him turn the corner. Most of her hoped like hell that he would just bend a few corners and come on back. The other part of her knew it was no such chance.

"Dumb-ass, girl. What the fuck is wrong with you?" she quietly scolded herself, watching the corner just in case he did change his mind and come back. She was instantly sorry but there was nothing she could do about it now.

On her way back in the house, she caught her next-door neighbor standing on the ground floor just outside of her patio door trying to act like she wasn't listening. "Fuck you, old nosy-ass bitch. Take yo' ass back in the house, damn. Mind yo' fuckin' business while you at it, too, bitch! Don't nothin' up here concern you." She could see the neighbor close and tighten her robe up around the throat, and then she went back into her apartment as instructed.

September stormed in her apartment and slammed the door so hard that the glass screen door cracked. It didn't break or fall out, but the force left a hideous crack from left to right running through it in a diagonal line. She just shook her head and walked away. Before she got too far, she came back and grabbed a drinking glass out of the cabinet in the kitchen in which she still stood. She tossed it on the counter and then went over to what was supposed to be her wine rack. She grabbed the bottle of Hennessy she had on display there. For a second, she stood there looking at all the bottles. Today was rapidly turning into a "fuck it" day, so she traded her half-drunk bottle of Hennessy in for a fresh bottle of Twenty Grand. The smooth mixture of vodka and cognac in the same bottle would do her the justice she all of a sudden sought.

September had been drinking for a long time by this point, so mixing light and dark liquor no longer bothered her. Having it already mixed in the same bottle was just a treat for her.

Deciding to skip the juice, she dropped a couple of ice cubes in her glass, grabbed it along with her bottle, and made her way to the living room. She plopped down on the couch and turned the TV on. Nothing seemed good so she turned on Netflix to find a movie. Her phone started to buzz and her heart lit up. She just knew it would be Slash calling her to talk things out, which she was going to be happy as hell to do. Only, it wasn't Slash. It was only Travis. Her heart fell all over again.

"Hmm. What's up? What you want?"

"What the fuck you mean what I want? Damn. You cranky as hell."

"Hell yeah, I'm cranky. What's up?"

"What's wrong?"

"What's wrong? What's wrong? Nigga, I went to jail for you and Ke'Lasia punk asses! What the fuck you mean what's wrong? Nigga, you are what's wrong. So like I said, what's up?"

"How the fuck you go to jail for us? You were the one high as fuck, smelling like liquor, and talking crazy all in the courtroom. How the fuck was that anybody fault but yours?"

"Nigga, you let that security guard bitch jump on me!"

"Nobody jumped on you, September." He huffed and she heard it. *This nigga still tryin'a to play me.* She let her thoughts get the better of her, so she decided to be petty. "How is Ke'Lasia anyway? Y'all still fuckin'?"

"Can we be grown here?"

"I'm being grown and so are y'all." She laughed. "Doin' all the fuckin' y'all doin', I would hope that y'all grown."

"September."

"What? It ain't no secret no more. Y'all li'l cat out the bag. Or should I say her cat?" She laughed again. She was getting a kick out of stressing him out. *That's what the fuck he get for tryin'a play me and lettin' my ass sit in jail, so oh, well.*

"Maybe I should call back when you feeling better." He was growing more frustrated by the second at this conversation and her childish antics.

"Nah, I'm good now. What's up? You may as well say that shit now so you ain't gotta call me back. I'on want yo' li'l girlfriend gettin' salty 'cause you on my line on no weak shit."

"Ke'Lasia is not my girlfriend and I called you to see if we could hook up."

"Oh, yeah?"

"Yeah, man, damn. You gon' meet me or not? Damn. Quit playin' wit' me."

"Where you tryin'a meet at then?" She swallowed the last of her fourth drink down her throat as she listened to him give her the details of where he wanted to meet. She agreed and hung the phone up. Tossing the phone aside, she sat there for a few more minutes with her head back and her eyes closed. *Fuck it. She ain't my friend no more.*

September hopped up off the couch and went to find something to wear. Choosing a pink sundress that satisfied her, she checked the time. She had just a little bit under an hour to meet Travis.

"I ain't think you was comin'," Travis said when September sat down.

"I ain't think I was either."

"I'm glad you did though," he warmly told her. His flirting made her smile and get a weird, warm feeling in her chest.

A few months ago, she would've never even dreamt of getting cozy with anybody Ke'Lasia even looked at twice. But now? Now shit was different, and this was Travis. September had been waiting to get with him for damn near as long as she'd known him. It wasn't her fault Ke'Lasia chose to step in between that.

"I got somethin' I need to tell you, I just don't know how. I don't know what you gon' say or how you gon' act."

"First of all, why we out here?" She waved her hand toward the open park where they sat ducked off to the side on a park bench.

"I didn't know how comfortable you would be wit' me at yo' house. Especially after you answered the phone so rude."

"Okay, yeah. I had an attitude. Shit, you would've too had the people that was supposed to be your friends let you go to jail."

"We didn't let you go to jail, September. We never even thought they were gonna actually lock you up. I thought they were gonna talk a lot of bullshit to scare you and us, and at the end, let you go with a warning or something. We didn't know you was gonna end up like that."

"Well, now you know. I did almost two months in that bitch over nothing, so don't expect me not to have some kind of attitude."

"You barely did a month, September." He laughed at her. "You was only in there a few weeks. Why you so dramatic?"

"Boy, ain't nobody dramatic. I almost did six months. Shit. Fuck you talkin' about? Hard time. In the clink."

The two laughed at each other's silliness for the first time in a long time and it felt good for the both of them. Travis just hoped that once he told September what he had to tell her, they would still be this cool. He was about to lay some heavy shit on her without knowing what direction it would take. That was the real reason why he asked her to meet him at the park. That way, if the shit went south, he could get away.

"Anyway, boy, are we goin' to my house or not?" She giggled, hitting him in the arm.

"Girl, watch yo' mouth. I'm a grown-ass man." Travis stood up, smoothed his pants, and began to pose like she was snapping pictures. The two died in more laughter all the way back to the separate parked vehicles.

"Just follow me."

"I got you." They both jumped in their cars. Travis waited while September pulled off first, and then he followed behind her just like she'd asked him to do.

They pulled up at September's house and she waited for him to park behind her before unlocking her door and walking in.

"Welcome to my humble abode," she told him, twisting in a circle to fake showcase the place.

"Wow. I never been in your house before, do you realize that? This crazy."

"Well, you could've been over here had you not been playin' so long." She sauntered back across the room to him, flirting with her eyes and body movements the whole way.

"What? Playin'? Girl, bye. Ain't nobody played with you." He tried laughing off the situation that he saw was about to go straight left. He hadn't come over here for this. *Dammit!* was the only thing that played through his head. His feet were stuck dead in their spot, not willing to move. It was then that he realized that he had fucked up.

"September, I—"

She silenced him with a kiss to his lips. A deep, passionate kiss that he had not wanted, nor expected. "September," he pled, pushing her away and stepping back. "September? I, um, I think you got this all wrong." The look on her face let him know everything.

"Wrong? What's wrong about this?" She slid her sundress down her body, and he watched as it hit the floor.

"September."

"Don't be scared. It's only pussy." She stepped out of the circle her dress made on the floor at her feet and advanced toward him once more. "I know you want some of this. I know you have for a minute now. You fuckin' Ke'Lasia don't mean shit to me. After you get a shot of my shit, you ain't gon' want that ordinary-ass shit no more no way. I know good and well she can't fuck better than I can." September pinned Travis between her body and the door. He could barely move. She smiled sweetly, but it only unnerved Travis more. He couldn't believe she was acting this way. Not because she wanted to fuck him, but because her and Ke'Lasia were friends. Sisters. He never thought it would get to this. Even if he had wanted her, this was a turn-off.

September was his friend. He wasn't disgusted or anything like that. He just didn't want her in that way. Never had. He never looked at September as a potential for anything other than what they were. Friends. He was in a sticky situation and had no clue what to do. All he knew was that he couldn't fuck her. He wouldn't fuck her. That was what she obviously wanted, but it was never going to happen. So, he did the only thing he could do in this moment.

September's hand reached his zipper. "September, I know who tried to kill you. I asked you to meet up with me to see if you knew who he was and why he wanted you dead, but then I got other information that let me know that it was Raheim behind the whole thing." He rushed it out in one breath. All her movements stopped. Travis stood stuck, still looking up at the ceiling. It immediately felt like all the air was sucked out of the room they were in and he was going to suffocate.

"What?"

"I know who did it."

"Tried to kill me? It was an accident," she reasoned.

"No, it wasn't, September. You were supposed to get shot that day. You were supposed to die." He looked down at her when he felt her hand drop from the zipper of his jeans. She slowly turned and walked away. September found her a seat on the couch and slowly sat down. Her lips moved but no words came out. Travis walked over, picked up her dress, and took it to her.

"Here, boo. Cover up, ma." She absentmindedly took the dress but still didn't put it back on her body. She just held it to her frame that now looked small and scared.

"He tried to have me killed? Raheim? Why? By who? What? He what?" She couldn't comprehend. There were so many questions swirling around in her brain that she couldn't catch just one to finish out a full thought or sentence. All she could do was ask questions. "He what? Raheim? What?" Her voice sounded so small as she repeated the same words again and again.

Travis was crushed. He never wanted to have this conversation. He didn't want to have to be the one to tell her that the man she once loved wanted her dead. Especially for something so insignificant.

"It was a robbery gone bad like the police said. But Raheim sent the boys down there. He sent them because they were going to rob and kill him. He knew you were there that day at the barbeque joint with me. He knew because he had been having you watched. He thought you were cheating on him while y'all were together. After y'all broke up, he assumed you left him for another man. Me. So when the guys came to rob him, he took that as an opportunity to get you knocked and the nigga he first thought you were sleeping with robbed."

"The first nigga? I wasn't even sleeping with you! Who else did he think I was fuckin'?"

"A guy named Vic."

"Vic?" Her eyes grew wide. Initially, Travis thought it was out of fear, but soon he realized it was from confusion. "Vic? How did he think I was fuckin' Vic? Vic and I had been over for a while before Raheim and me," she explained.

"That's not what he was told. He was told that you and Vic were still fuckin'. And then, me and you. He assumed that's why we were there that day. Meeting up on some fuckin' date type shit. I guess he didn't know we were just friends."

"He did. I told him when I told him about you. That we'd been friends for a few years and we worked together."

She left out the part where she threatened Raheim about her fucking Travis. That she told him she would start fuckin' Travis if he didn't want to act right and stop fucking with the nasty-ass bitch Kiesha he was cheating on her with. She also left out the part where she told anyone who would listen that he, Travis, had been trying to talk to her for years and she was the one who kept saying no. She just shook her head at the information Travis was feeding her and kept her input to herself.

"I didn't even know you knew Vic."

"Yeah, I know him. We used to fuck around. Like I said though, that was before me and Raheim. Before, before. Like, I don't even see why that would matter. I had to die over that? That's bullshit. It's somethin' else. It gotta be."

"That's all I came up with. Nothing else. Vic owed somebody some money and figured he'd get it from Raheim's spot since they were beefing."

"They been beefin' for a minute, but that shit ain't got shit to do with me."

"Well, apparently it did. A lot of it was you."

"Me? That's crazy as fuck. He never mentioned one time while we were together that any of that shit had shit to do with me."

"I guess he just ain't want you to know."

The two sat there in silence, mulling over what Travis had just revealed. Travis himself didn't even understand how it sounded either, but he never understood a man being ready to lay it down for the rest of his life over no female. It was too many out here to go out like that. September, on the other hand, knew that something else was up. There was no way Raheim wanted to kill her over getting dick. He had fucked a few bitches while they were together, including the Kiesha bitch from downtown she fought and went to jail over. The one who couldn't let go. So there was no way Raheim just flipped on her like that over this weak shit. There was more to it and she had to find out what.

Chapter 18

"Yes! Yes! Yes! Fuck! Hmmmmm. Fuck. Shit, yes! Fuck me! Fuck me! Right there. Hmm. Right there, Justin! Yes!"

"Shut yo' ass up before somebody come in here, damn. You loud as fuck." Justin Sagent worked hard on the nut he expected to get from this rendezvous.

"Just fuck me, damn. Harder. Hmm, yes. Just like that."

"You like that shit, bitch? Like that? Huh? That's the shit you like?"

"Hell yeah, baby. Hell yeah. Give it to me. Hmm. Give it to me. Fuck that pussy, you sick muthafucka. Fuck me."

"Cum on this dick, bitch. Cum on it so I can shove it down your throat. Cum on it!" he demanded as his climax neared. He dared not get there before her, but he needed her to hurry up. He couldn't hold it much longer.

He had his body trained to an internal time clock. His assistant had an hour break, but she always came back fifteen minutes late, so he timed himself for an hour. He needed to fire that wack-ass assistant, but at times like this, her tardiness came in handy. He had five minutes to go if he was going to be able to clean up and get this bitch out of here before his assistant came back.

Just like he planned, his sexual conquest came on command. He stroked her deep and hard as her body shuddered and fell forward to his desk when she couldn't contain herself any longer. He pushed in deep and held it there for a few seconds to make sure her orgasm rode its full wave before he pulled out of her and pulled her to stand by her ponytail.

"Get on your knees. Do it now. I wanna watch you drink all this shit." She slid to her knees, not turning to face him until she reached the floor. "Pick yo' head up. Look at me." She followed every direction she was given, and it turned him on. His dick swelled with pleasure. He needed to release himself bad. It was taking everything in him not to explode too soon. "Open your mouth, you nasty slut. Open it. Wide. Stick your fuckin' tongue out. You know how I like it." She obeyed. He gripped her head to steady her with one hand as he manually pulled at himself to release the build-up inside of him. He watched her eyes, and she watched his.

"You want this shit, don't you, bitch? Unh huh. You want this shit. You need this nasty shit, don't you? Answer."

"Yes, daddy. I need it."

He reached down and tore her blouse open. The buttons went careening around the room. The two heard buttons bouncing off of walls and fixtures around the room, but it didn't stop their flow.

"Uuuuugh! Ugh! Shit! Yeah, bitch. Take that shit." His strokes sped up as his seed started to spill from him. He lathered her face, mouth, and tongue with his seed. Before he was empty, he made sure to pull back and let the remnants of his liquid joy spill down her chin onto her chest and her bra. Happy he reached his peak for her, she closed her mouth around his swollen red with his juices still on her tongue and sucked him hard. He slammed into her face with as much force as she sucked with.

He used his penis to wipe his seed from her face and put it back in her mouth. She sucked it clean for him again. Amusement danced in his eyes as he watched her.

"Yeeeeaaaahhh," he moaned, fully enthused by what he was watching. She used her hands to help her mouth along. She felt him begin to swell again. His veins thumped hard. "Cut that shit out. She'll be back in a minute and I gotta get back to these clients. I can't keep playin' wit' you like this." She kept on sucking him to death like he hadn't said a thing. He made no movement to stop her, so she didn't stop. She just kept looking him in his eyes, calling for his soul through his penis as he watched her. "Mmmmm," he moaned again. "Stop. She'll be here," he said with his mouth but nothing about his actions made her feel like he meant anything he said.

She sucked more and he motioned back. His hands found her hair again and he pulled her from his body. Only, she pulled back. He pulled away and she pulled him back in. Both of her hands were on his penis moving at the same time. Left hand clockwise, right hand counterclockwise. The spit from her mouth gathered thick on his dick. It sloshed everywhere, loud and clear. The only sounds in the room were his moans and her slurps. No more words were spoken. He allowed her to do as she pleased. Her happiness meant his fulfillment.

He snatched her head backward and pulled his dick from her mouth. He circled behind her and leaned against his desk, almost sitting. She looked over her shoulder at his new position and smiled. She knew exactly what she was in for. "I thought you were running out of time."

"Get over here, slut." He pulled her by her neck and pushed her head down into his lap. Her tongue found his dick and she went back to work. He held her head in place in his lap while he controlled the situation by thrusting himself in and out of her mouth as he held her still. Her body lurched forward several times like she would throw up, but she wouldn't dare throw up on him. She didn't care if she couldn't breathe or how far he put his dick down her throat. She had it. She took all of him in her throat like a pro with no hesitation or resistance. She let him control the whole situation.

"Dr. Sagent, I—" His assistant's voice broke the smooth rhythm of saliva being choked from the girl's throat, but he didn't break a stride. He kept thrusting. Only this time, he watched the wide eyes of the female assistant as she watched him in astonishment reach his second peak. He didn't break eye contact as he pulled his lover farther into his lap and released everything he had left into the back of her throat. He smiled at her. She licked her lips and smirked at him as she slowly backed out of his office and closed the door behind her.

"Didn't I hear your assistant come in?" she asked him once he released her throat and she had swallowed down all of his seed.

"Yeah, you did."

"Why didn't you stop me?"

"For what?" She buttoned her new shirt and looked at him like he was crazy. "I'm sure she done sucked some dick before. Probably not as good as you, but she has." He laughed.

"You sick for real." She laughed.

"Oh, Miss Lady, you have no idea." He smiled and winked at her. She just shook her head and laughed some more.

"Let me get out of here before you be tryin' to have a threesome." She grabbed her purse and blew him a kiss before she opened the door.

"Keisha?"

"Yeah?" She stopped and turned around to look at him.

"Make sure you doing what the fuck you need to to keep Freight's ass as far away from them as possible. This shit gon' get ugly and he gon' get caught in the middle. If you love him, you'll protect him from that. I don't wanna have to be the one to tell him and it don't seem like you do either."

"Justin, if anybody fuck with my kids' daddy in any way, I won't be out of jail the next time. By the way, thank you again."

"I don't need a thank you. You know I got you. Kiss my kids for me and remember what I said. Oh, and keep that nigga away from my kids. I'm cool on that shit. He ain't they daddy."

"Stop sayin' that shit out loud. Them is Travis's kids. And speaking of Travis's kids"—she emphasized his name so that he understood what the hell she was saying to him—"I need some money." She waited and looked at him expectantly.

"I know you do. I been told you to tell me what they need, man. That nigga ain't got enough money to take care of y'all. I'ma call the bank. Just stop by there and pick it up. They'll have it waiting for you."

"Well, you should've been there then, and okay. I'll go right now before I pick them up."

"You know what I had to do. Don't act like that. But I'm ready now. We gon' be a family like we should've been before. I just need a few more weeks."

"Whatever. Just make sure you keep our business to yourself." She gave him another air kiss and walked out the door. A half hour later, Justin's assistant came back to the door. She stopped to knock this time.

"Come in, Camella."

"How you feeling?"

"Like a million bucks." He smiled and put his hands behind his head as he sat back in his chair. "What can I do for you?"

"Boy, yo' three o'clock is here." She rolled her eyes and turned toward the door.

"Eh!" She turned back toward him to see what he had to say. "You get that package I sent you?"

"Yeah, I got it."

"You put it up like I asked?"

"Yeah, I always do."

"You ain't put 'em all together, did you?"

"Nah. I never do."

"Good girl." He smiled at her again, this time letting his eyes trail down her body.

"I'm up next?"

"You know you my favorite, baby. Only you know what daddy like."

"Yeah, whatever." She rolled her eyes again.

"Who's daddy's girl?"

"Me." She smiled hard that time.

"That's right. Bring my client in, baby girl."

She nodded at his words. "Yes, daddy." She walked out, leaving the door cracked. He rubbed his dick through his slacks, looking at her ass as she walked away. He had a quick image of her riding his dick in that skintight skirt she had on and he almost canceled his appointment so that he could call her back in there.

Only about three minutes passed before Camella was back at the door with Ke'Lasia in tow.

"How are you today, Ke'Lasia? Thank you, Camella." Justin came around his desk to greet Ke'Lasia and get started. They shook hands and she sat down. Camella shot Ke'Lasia a disgusted look behind her back, rolled her eyes at Justin one last time, and then left out the door, making sure to leave it cracked. Justin walked over to the door and closed it himself.

"I'm pretty cool. Shit, it looks like you're more than okay today though." She smirked smugly in his direction. He stood in front of her as he came back from the door.

"Me? What makes you say that?"

"Um, I guess it ain't no need to be bashful, huh?"

"Not at all. This is a safe space, Ke'Lasia, you know that."

"Well, I just assumed you havin' a good day since yo' dick still hard. You must've had a damn good lunch, huh?" She giggled, trying not to look at his lap anymore. The vibe in the room changed up as soon as she said it. She could tell from the look in his eyes that he was thinking the same thing that she was.

He scooted over to where she sat on his loveseat and leaned in closer to her from his chair. "I would answer that question, but we both know that if I did, neither of us would be able to continue being professional. Let's just act like it never, um, came up. Shall we?"

Ke'Lasia grinned softly at him before shrugging her shoulders. "I won't tell if you won't."

Justin got up out of his chair with his pants bulging from the full erection he now had. He leaned over Ke'Lasia, whispering strongly in her ear, "Baby girl, if this went that way, you'd tell everybody you know. Trust. And if you didn't, that sweet pussy would tell on you first." He straightened himself back up and stood in front of her, his dick eye-level with her. "So, Ke'Lasia, what's new today?" He walked over to his desk and sat on the edge, choosing to give himself and Ke'Lasia some space to cool off. Ke'Lasia took that as an opportunity to entice him even further. Before Justin had a chance to change his mind, she would give him all the more reason to not want to. She no longer gave a fuck that he was her therapist. She wanted him and she would have him. She just had to bide her time. So in the meantime, she would play his game.

"My visitor came over again," she started.

"Oh, yeah?"

"Yeah. He fucked me again."

"You want to tell me about it?"

"Yes, sir," she answered him. Her intent was written all over her face, but Justin couldn't get past her answer. It drove him crazy when women called him sir. It was getting harder to wish away his erection.

"Go ahead then. Tell me as much as you want."

"Details?"

"Every last one." He readjusted himself again as she began. Everything inside of him was going wild. He wanted to fuck her so bad that it almost hurt. Too bad he had to stay away from her.

Ke'Lasia began her story. Her eyes never left his lap and his erection never went away. She felt like she could see it growing harder and harder as she told him every single detail. It excited her to see him stimulated by what she said. She made sure her details were extremely colorful for his benefit. His interest aroused her to no end. Her stranger was cool. She enjoyed his visits, but he wasn't enough. She needed somebody she could have all the time and Justin seemed pretty available, regardless of who had given him that hard-on. Her thoughts faded to Travis, making her eyes drop from Justin. He noticed the change and spoke on it.

"What's wrong, Ke'Lasia? What happened there?"

"Nothing. I was just thinking."

"About what?"

"Travis, honestly."

Dr. Sagent sighed deep. He tried to keep his frustration out of his voice. "Ke'Lasia, we talked about this."

"I know. I know. I remember."

"You do? Are you sure?"

"Yeah. I'm sure."

"Good then. No Travis. He's dangerous and he'll just bring drama to your life."

"I just don't understand how though. Travis has never—"

"Ke'Lasia!" Dr. Sagent reprimanded.

"But..."

He looked at her pointedly. Her eyes lowered again, and she fell into her heart. Travis was a good guy, the kind of guy she could see herself with. But Justin was right, and she knew it. Travis wouldn't be good for her. He did come with a lot of baggage and she had her own to deal with. It was just unfortunate for her that the two guys she could see something with were both off-limits.

"Now what are you thinking?" he asked.

"That it's crazy that the only two guys who are probably worth my while are off-limits."

"Two?"

"Yeah. Travis and you." They looked at each other. The gaze grew deeper as the stare held. Justin started to say something but then the phone on his desk rang, stopping him. He looked up at the clock and saw that it was 4:15. Their session was over fifteen minutes ago. He was saved from the mistake he was about to make.

Chapter 19

"Yeah, Ma. They let me out like an hour ago," Kiesha said, lying to her mom about when she got released from the county jail. She didn't feel like answering all kinds of questions about where she'd been the last few hours. She was going to go pick up her kids. She just needed a little adult time first after being locked up around a bunch of bitches for so long.

"Well, where the fuck you been at then? Why you ain't been to get yo' damn kids?" Sheila asked her, pissed off. She hadn't done a thing that was hard since she had Kiesha and Travis's kids, but you would've thought she had done the absolute most. Kiesha was salty she ain't just say she got out right then. This was what she was trying to avoid. "I'm tired as hell and they won't give me no break."

"Mama, them kids big as hell. Ain't no way they bothering you that much. Come on now." Kiesha rolled her eyes on her end of the phone, knowing her mom couldn't see her.

"Girl, you don't know what the fuck they doin' to me. These muthafuckas is on my damn nerves. Come get they ass before I put them outside," she threatened.

"Maw Maw, can we get some pizza? We hungry." Kiesha heard one of the younger kids ask their grandmother.

"See what I mean? They stay askin' for some shit. All the fuckin' time. They had to eat a few hours ago. I just ran to the store and bought them some fuckin' noodles and now they want pizza. Girl, I can't take this shit no more." Kiesha heard her mama sighing hard into the phone like she was really that stressed because she had to feed some damn kids. It was noodles, for heaven's sake. How full did she think they would be? Kiesha's thoughts were none too pleasant toward Sheila at the moment. Her mama really got the fuck on her nerves for real, but it was her mom, so she dealt with it. Honestly though, she secretly wanted this woman to hurry up and die. She would just never say it out loud.

"Don't worry about it, Ma. I'm finna be on my way to get them now. I'll figure out something for them to eat. You don't have to worry about it, okay?"

"Well, you better hurry up 'cause I ain't spendin' not one more dime of my money on y'all hungry-ass kids. You or they no-good-ass daddy ain't gave me no damn money for them. I'm goin' broke over here fuckin' wit' this stupid shit. Get here and get them." Sheila hung up on her daughter.

Keisha couldn't believe it and knew she had to have heard something wrong. Travis not taking care of his kids just didn't make sense. Unless he was dead, making him physically unable to. That's why she picked him instead of Justin to be her kids' dad in the first place. She always knew he would be a damn good father. Better than even Justin. And she hadn't heard anything about Travis being dead, so her mom had to be lying. It wouldn't be far-fetched if she was either.

Keisha picked up the phone and called back. She decided to lie to see what her mama would say. "Ma, I just talked to Travis. He said he gave you some money when he came to get the kids."

"Girl, that nigga sent me a punk-ass hundred dollars! We not gon' do that lyin' shit! He gave me a weak-ass hundred dollars and he wouldn't even come get these damn kids at all! I kept tryin'a call him to get them and everything, and his ass ain't even answer my damn call. Then when he did, he made up all this bullshit about what he had to do and whatnot. Girl, bye. I'm not finna listen to this bullshit."

"He ain't come get them? That's odd as fuck. I don't usually have that problem with him."

"Well, you weren't here, so that nigga ain't been doin' shit he supposed to. That's why I told you long ago not to fuck wit' that silly-ass nigga. He can't even give up no money for his damn kids and you just wanna keep on though. Hmm. Just keep on then. Fuck it. I tried to help, but yo' hardhead ass don't ever fuckin' listen to me no way. Keep lettin' that nigga play you stupid if you want to. Fuck it. I don't even give a fuck. Just come get these muthafuckas."

"Mama, I do listen. I always listen. That's why my kids' daddy ain't livin' wit' them now. 'Cause I'm listening to you. Always listening to you." Kiesha was on the verge of tears thinking about how stupid she had actually been over the years. Listening to her mom had gotten her into so much dumb-ass shit time and time again, but she just kept listening. Listening to her was what had Travis leave her in the first place. Kiesha hurriedly shook her head to shake the memories away before she was crying for real. Then she'd never hear the end of Sheila's mouth.

"Well, you need to listen good then," Sheila continued, not even noticing the sadness in her daughter's voice. "That nigga ain't shit. Hell, soon as you went to jail, he was tryin'a fuck me." She laughed. She laughed a hard, cackling laugh. One that pissed Keisha clean off. She hated when her mom laughed like that. Like she was better than her and Keisha was just some stupid young girl who didn't know what was going on. But she was hip to her mom by now. She knew for sure now that she was trying to play her. If she didn't know anything else, what she did know was that Travis would never try to fuck Sheila. Ever. So now she knew she had to go get her kids for real before her own mother was able to find a new way to fuck her life up. She already ruined Travis and her once, and she wasn't gonna give her a chance to do it again.

"Ma, I'm on my way. Can you just have my kids ready please?"

"Oh, you ain't like that, huh? You mad yo' mama still got it good enough to pull a young nigga like Travis? Well, I'm here to tell you, Miss Thing, I've been pullin' young niggas." She laughed some more. "That young thing you had last year? Reco or whatever his name was. Yeeeees, honey. He was a good fuck. That dick was goooooood! I had to teach him how to handle this pussy though 'cause you young girls don't know what y'all be doin' wit' these big ol' dicks. Yeah, I taught his ass real good. I still can't get him to stop callin' my phone."

Sheila laughed and bragged until Kiesha just couldn't take it anymore and hung up. She put in her location for her Uber to pick her up and then put her phone on airplane mode so that she wouldn't have to worry about Sheila's phone calls anymore.

About twenty minutes later, a little white lady pulled up in a silver Chevy Cruise looking lost.

"Hi. Are you Shelly?" Kiesha asked her from the curb, careful not to get too close.

"Yeah. That's me!" she happily agreed. Kiesha got in and they took off. She sat back quietly while Shelly drove and softly sung along to the R&B music Kiesha was surprised to hear pouring from the car's stereo speakers.

"Do you like this kind of music?" Shelly asked. "If not, I could turn on something else."

"No, it's fine. I actually like this song," Kiesha confessed.

The soulful sound of Alicia Keys asking how come he didn't call her anymore had her deep in her thoughts of her and Travis. She still hated herself for letting her mother come in between them. But after everything that had happened by this point, she knew there was no way Travis would ever give her another chance. It made her sad realizing that the only man she had ever truly loved would never love her again, but those were the consequences she had to face for the decisions that she chose to make.

Shelly's happy ass pulled up to Sheila's house and cut the engine off. "This is your first stop, honey. I'll be sitting right here when you come out, okay?"

"Okay. Thanks." Kiesha closed the door and walked into the building. She waited for the elevator and then pushed the button for the sixth floor. She didn't feel like being bothered with Sheila at all, so she made the mental plan to get in and get out.

Her son, Amari, opened the door up for her after five minutes of her standing in the hallway. The tears in his eyes immediately sent alarms off in Kiesha's brain.

"What happened, baby? Why you crying?"

The sounds of Sheila yelling at the kids to call an ambulance caused Kiesha to push her son out of the way and run into the small apartment. Seeing her daughter laid out on the hard linoleum floor, she dug her phone out her purse to call 911. Luckily, her phone was still on airplane mode, so the emergency call screen was the only one to pop up. Kiesha pressed the numbers and impatiently waited to be answered.

"Yes! I need an ambulance to the Alms Apartments at 2525 Victory Parkway, apartment 612, right now! My daughter is having a seizure!" Kiesha tried as best as she could to remain calm enough to answer all the questions the lady asked her and follow all the directions. She held her daughter in her arms as she began to violently shake all over again. "She's doing it again! Please help me! Please!" she screamed into the phone that now lay on the same floor as her daughter, on speakerphone. "Please send somebody! Please!" she cried.

"You need to calm down. They gon' get here, damn," Sheila told a hysterical Kiesha as she lit her freshly rolled joint and sat back on the couch. "You doin' all that hollerin' ain't gon' make 'em get here no faster hell." Sheila puffed hard as she looked down at her daughter and grandchildren all huddled around each other on the floor and shook her head. "See, it ain't that damn deep. She done stopped that shakin'. Them people gon' get here for nothin' and be mad. Then you gon' be stuck wit' a big-ass bill for nothin'."

"Ma, you the first one who said to call 'em, so what you mean?"

"I didn't think you were here. I just wanted all these kids outta here. They was crowding me and makin' me nervous, hell. Figured I'd give 'em somethin' to do, hell." Kiesha would've believed her too but her mother's hand shook fiercely as she pressed her joint to her lips and pulled long and hard. She knew Sheila cared way more than she was letting on. She was just as nervous as Kiesha was and that just made it worse.

"Ma'am, we need you to back up." The medics came flooding through Sheila's open apartment door giving instructions. Kiesha did as she was told as Sheila tried hastily to put out her joint and fan the air like she wasn't just smoking. The medics strapped Justina, Kiesha's daughter, to a stretcher and hauled her out of the apartment faster than Kiesha could process what was happening. She followed them down to the ambulance and jumped in the back with her. "Ma, I'll be back to get the kids later," she called out before the doors were shut.

"Like hell you will! We'll meet you there," she told her as she ushered the other three kids toward the parking lot spaces to find her car.

Kiesha watched through the windows of the ambulance as Sheila put her kids in the car and pulled off. Then she turned back to the medics working on her daughter.

"Will she be okay?" she asked, frightened to the core.

"We don't know yet, ma'am, but we need you to have a seat and answer some questions."

Kiesha did as she was told, answering questions for one medic while watching the other do all sorts of things to her daughter's still body. She answered the questions but barely heard any of them. All she could hear were the prayers she prayed over and over again in her head for her daughter's safety.

"Hold on, ma. Let me take this. It's my kids' mama."

"I can't even believe you answering that bitch," September said with disgust.

"It could be about my youth. I gotta take it." He stood up and stepped in the kitchen to have a little more privacy. "What's up, Kiesh? When you get out?" he answered and asked, noticing that the caller display showed her cell number and not the one from the county.

"Travis, you gotta get here now. I'm at Children's with Justina. She had a few seizures and they rushed her here. I don't know what's going on!" she cried into the phone. Travis's heart leapt into his throat, making it hard for him to respond.

"Here I come," he told her, then hung up. "September, I gotta go. My daughter in the hospital."

"What? What happened? I'm going with you." She jumped up, redressed as quick as she could, and threw on her shoes, not waiting for him to deny her. They ran hastily out the door and jumped into Travis's car. Before he knew it, he was doing eighty miles per hour up Reading Road, heading toward the hospital with dread in his heart. He didn't speak a word.

"Everything is going to be okay, Travis. Trust me, she'll be fine." Travis didn't answer but September didn't expect him to. She was just there for support. She reached out in the silence and took his hand. Travis didn't object. They sat that way until finally they pulled up in the emergency department of Children's Hospital Medical Center.

They jumped out of the car almost instantly and rushed inside. September stood by Travis every step.

"Excuse me?" he said to the nurse behind the desk as he cut the line, not caring about the groans of complaints from the people behind him. "I'm sorry, but I need to find my daughter. Her mom called and said she was here." He waited impatiently as the nurse pulled her up in the system from the information he had given her.

After confirming that she was there, the nurse rounded the desk and led Travis and September to where they held his daughter. They walked in, and Travis began to cry. The machines Justina was hooked up to made a quiet humming noise and some irritating beeping. The nurse let them know that the doctor would be in shortly to speak with them. Travis didn't acknowledge her or what she'd said. He just held on to his daughter's unmoving hand with his head down and cried his silent tears. As soon as the door closed behind the nurse, Kiesha acted up.

"Why is she here? I thought you said she wasn't yo' woman."

"And she's not," Travis responded without looking up. "She was with me when you called, so she offered to come for support. That's it. Regardless of why she here, why is my baby here, Kiesha?"

"I don't even know, baby daddy. I honestly don't even know what happened," she spoke to Travis, but her eyes never left September, who was standing over in the corner looking afraid to walk farther in.

"How could you not know?"

"I had just got there to pick yo' kids up and when Mar Mar let me in, Ma was yellin' and Justina was on the floor shakin' and shit." She walked over to Travis. She rubbed his shoulders as she stood behind him while they went over the situation. Travis looked like he got more stressed when Kiesha touched him instead of less. She also didn't take her eyes off of September. It was like she was trying to make her feel some type of way or something. September wasn't affected by her actions at all. All she worried about was getting out of that room.

"Eh, T, I'ma go sit in the waiting room, all right? I hope y'all daughter good though."

Travis finally looked up and he realized, looking at a visibly shaking September, that this probably wasn't the best situation for her to be in. A hospital room was probably the last place she needed to be. "Oh, yeah, damn. My fault, September. You probably shouldn't be in here no way. That's my bad. I'll be out there to take you home in a minute."

"Nah, I'm good. I can wait on you. Take care of yo' daughter."

"His family," Kiesha added with a nasty-ass attitude.

"Yo' family." September rolled her eyes and shook her head, not having time to give a fuck about Kiesha's attitude. She bowed out of the confrontation Kiesha wanted before it ever got started. "Take care of your family. I'll be out there waiting on you and praying for y'all baby. And family," she added for extra measure, then she exited the room quickly and quietly. That way, no one else could say anything to her and hold her there longer. Especially

Kiesha's bitch ass. September wouldn't be above kicking her ass. And if it weren't for Travis's daughter being laid up, hooked up to all those machines beeping and making noises in that hospital room, she would've kicked her ass as soon as the first fly shit left her lips.

Lost in her own thoughts, not paying attention, and trying to get as far away from that room with that little girl laid out like that, September literally bumped into a man walking down the hallway.

"Oh, excuse me," she offered.

"No, no. You're fine." He smiled his apology back. "I should've been paying attention to where I was going. As clumsy as I am, you'd never think I've been walking for thirty-some-odd years, right?" He laughed but waited patiently for a response.

"It's cool. I wasn't lookin' either."

"Well, where you headed to? Miss . . ."

"September."

"Miss September. Well, nice to meet you. If you're not in a big rush, you wanna grab a bite to eat in the cafeteria with me?"

"Aren't you here to see somebody?" September threw attitude at him. She wasn't understanding how he could stop himself from visiting a loved one just to chill with her. It didn't sit right with her at all.

"Actually, I'm here to visit with my family and really just need to clear my head. I didn't think tryin'a spend that time getting to know a pretty lady like you would be a sin." He chuckled. September could see the hope in his eyes and decided that maybe he wasn't so bad after all.

"I guess I could use some coffee." She shrugged, giving in.

"Good. Coffee is good. It's a start." The two headed toward the elevators to find their way to the cafeteria.

"I'm sorry. What you say yo' name was again?"

"I didn't, but I'm Justin. Justin Sagent. Nice to officially meet you, Miss September." They shook hands as he smiled. "You know, my birthday is in September."

"Is it?" September rolled her eyes. Hearing this dry-ass line all her life didn't even impress her anymore.

"No, really, it is September fifteenth."

"Mines is the sixteenth."

"No shit?" he asked with wide eyes.

"No shit," she confirmed with a small smirk, warming up to him.

"I guess it was kismet then, huh?" He looked at her and winked. The elevator sound dinged, letting them know the elevator they waited on had arrived. The two looked at each other and stepped on. Justin let September get on first and admired her ass as she walked. He licked his lips at the thoughts he had before stepping on and letting the doors close behind him.

"Justin? What are you doing here?" Kiesha jumped up from the chair she sat in, seeing it was Justin walking through the hospital room doors and not another doctor or nurse.

"What you mean what am I doing here? Didn't you say Justina was here?" He looked from Kiesha to the sleeping man behind her. "Why the fuck would you tell me if you were gonna have him here?" he growled in her face.

"Shhhhh, Justin, damn!" she whispered angrily to him while putting her finger to his lips and backing him up toward the door.

"Fuck that. Ain't no fuckin' shh. You tryin'a be funny or what?" he asked her with his voice louder than needed. All the professionalism he possessed at his office had seeped away and Kiesha could see the real him showing through. The street-ass hood nigga she'd known way before he decided to start his therapy business to cover up the drug money he needed to wash. Way before he started putting on ties and suits and being nice to white people. The real Justin, the top drug dealer in all of Cincinnati, was standing before her now and she was scared as shit.

"You're going to wake him up. What the fuck are you doing?" The panic was written all over her face, but Justin didn't care. "Can't you just come back later?"

"Come back later? My daughter laid up in the hospital because of God knows what and you want me to come back later? Fuck no! I'm not going anywhere."

"Justin, please?" Kiesha begged.

"Nah, he ain't gotta leave. He may as well stay right here 'cause it sounds like I got some questions I need answers to."

Had Kiesha been any darker, no one would have noticed how pale she turned in that moment. Hearing Travis's voice come from behind her made her heart leap into her throat and hit the pit of her stomach at the same time. She turned to him with a look on her face that let him know he'd heard exactly what he thought he did.

"Travis, listen," she started.

"Oh, I'm listening. I'm listening real good. I'm listening hard as fuck, matter of fact. 'Cause I'ma need somebody to tell me what the fuck is up, quick. This shit ain't sounding right to me. Maybe I'm still asleep or somethin'."

Travis sat up on the small hospital couch he had been lying on. He hadn't been asleep for a minute now, but he lay there with his eyes closed anyway, listening to the beeping of the machines Justina was still hooked up to. He didn't feel like being bothered by conversation with Kiesha seeing as though she couldn't fill him in on what had actually happened to his baby. To him, there was nothing that needed to be said. So, he lay there with his eyes closed, allowing her to think he was asleep instead. He never thought that he would happen upon any of this.

"Travis, I—"

"Did I just hear this man say 'his daughter'?" Travis asked his question to Kiesha, but his eyes never left Justin's face. It was taking everything in him not to act a plum fool in this hospital room and wipe the smirk this nigga Justin wore on his face right the fuck off.

"Just let me explain, Travis."

"Nah. I'll explain." Justin moved Kiesha out the way to step up to Travis and have the conversation himself. Travis stood up from his seated position to face Justin man-to-man.

"Well, then you tell me." Travis followed the challenge he felt like Justin issued to him. He needed to hear the words although he already knew what it was.

"I guess Kiesha hadn't got a chance to tell you yet but, yeah, Justina is my daughter."

Travis looked between the two of them, his anger threatening to get the best of him. "Your daughter? And you knew about me?"

"I did," Justin admitted nonchalantly.

"And you just stood to the side and let me take care of your daughter for eight years?"

"Well, actually..."

"Actually?" Travis prompted after Justin trailed off.

"Actually—"

"Justin, please," Kiesha interrupted, cutting his sentence short.

"No, My'Kiesha. Let him finish what he was about to say. I'm interested to know. Actually what?" His gaze had grown so intense on Justin that it almost made Justin uncomfortable. Nobody ever had challenged Justin this way before, face-to-face. He almost didn't know how to react.

Travis could see some of the cockiness that Justin just had fade. He saw his eyes change and that made him smile. He knew that Justin would do his best to repair what he'd done with his next words, but it was too late. Travis already knew what he would say and although he was crushed on the inside, he would never let either of them see the pain that they had just brought upon him. Travis's heart was breaking in two as the seconds ticked past, but he masked it with his own smart-mouthed retorts and smile. He refused to let them see what he was going through internally.

"Actually what, Mister Justin? Let's hear it. What is it that you have to tell me that My'Kiesha couldn't find the time to? Huh? What's the rest of the terrible news that you want to personally deliver to me? I'm listening. I'm a big boy. I can take it." He smiled menacingly at Justin again. Travis braced himself for the words he knew were coming.

"Actually. You've been taking care of my kids, not just my daughter. All of her kids are mine."

"Is that right?"

"Justin, no," Kiesha breathed more than said. All of the life was being sucked out of her in this moment. She knew she would have to tell Travis one day, but she didn't think that that day would be anytime soon. She damn sure didn't think it would be like this either. Her world was spiraling out of control as she stood there watching the two men she loved face off. She knew there would be nothing she could say to Travis to make this right. Especially not after hearing her government given name fall from his lips. He hadn't called her that since she was 16 years old. She was always Kiesha, baby, or even love. But now, he used the name her mom had given her at birth, and she knew all hope was gone. All she could do was stand there and let the tears roll down her face.

Travis looked at Kiesha. His eyes pleading for it all to be a lie or even a dream, but it wasn't. The truth was evident on Kiesha's face. She dropped her head in shame. Travis let out a loud, hearty laugh, scaring the both of them. You would've thought he had just heard the funniest joke in his whole life. And he kind of did. *This whole thing has to be a joke,* he thought. No way Kiesha could be doing him like this. He knew Kiesha wasn't shit. Hell, her mom wasn't shit. His boys told him years ago that Kiesha wasn't shit. He heard all the stories, but this was a whole new low for her. No way this could've been true. Almost eleven years of being a father and twelve of dealing with Kiesha couldn't just be wiped away in this instant. It couldn't be. Travis couldn't believe it.

"So, you tellin' me"—he looked from Justin to Kiesha again—"that for damn near eleven years, I've raised these kids, paid for these kids, loved these kids with everything in me and not one of 'em are mine? Not one?" He looked at Justin who shook his head. Then at Kiesha who shook hers before repeating himself. "Not one? Nobody? None of these kids are mine?" His voice shook as he asked the same question over and over, getting the same answer time and again. The kids weren't his. They never were. His life had been a lie and it took one minute to take it all away from him. Everything he was and everything he'd known was gone now.

Travis fought hard as fuck every day to get to where he was in life and most of it was because of his kids. And now, in a five-minute conversation, all of it was for nothing. The anger and pain swirled inside Travis and collided. Without another word, he walked to Justina's bedside, placed a kiss on her forehead, and left. Justin and Kiesha looked at each other, and finally, Kiesha let the tears spill out.

Chapter 20

Monica: So, you really not gon' answer me for real? Really, Raheim?

She sent Raheim another message and after ten minutes of waiting and a message from him still didn't come through, she was done.

Monica decided she was done playing with all these men for once and for all. She had to go for what should be rightfully hers and it had to be today. She didn't have time to sit around and waste any more time than what she already had.

Raheim had been dodging her calls and messages for days, and she was sick of it. She needed him to pull this whole plan off, but fuck it. It was time for plan B. She couldn't wait anymore. She planned to wait until after she told Raheim that she was pregnant but that was just going to have to wait now. Now, more than ever, she had to make sure her bag was secure and the only way she was going to be able to do it was to go ahead and bag Ears. He was the man on top and the one with the most money. Fuck Raheim and fuck Vic. It no longer mattered how she felt about either of them. The only thing that mattered now was her and her baby. Regardless of who she'd have to pin this baby on, her plan was going to have to go into motion, and quickly. This was a whole new ball game now. No more Little League.

Monica made up her mind. She would go to Celebrities Nightclub tonight and convince Ears to leave with her.

Once she got him to fuck her, she could wait a few weeks and then put the baby on him. Fuck it, she had to do what she had to do. All of his other children were taken care of, them and their moms. All she had to do was insert herself in the lineup. Ears already had ten kids and seven baby mothers. He wouldn't trip about one more of each. He was paid and he was cocky. To him, the more the merrier. That would only mean to him that he would forever be able to fuck with her, but for Monica, that was just fine. That only meant that them dollars would never stop rolling in and her and her baby would be set just like she'd planned.

The plan Monica had with Raheim to set Vic up and take him out was just going to have to go another way. She did all the work and got the September bitch out of the picture already so that she could make Raheim the head nigga in charge and her man, but Raheim still wasn't trying to act right. The Kiesha bitch he couldn't leave alone, and who he had September fighting with all the time was also out of the picture. She was in jail still from having someone hit Raheim with her car, so she wouldn't be a problem at all either. Monica had heard she was in jail getting turned the fuck out on some lesbian shit, so it was really over for her. By this point, she had driven all of Raheim hoes out of the way to have him all to herself for the time it would take for her and Vic to milk that muthafucka dry, but now he was tripping. She even had a small thought to keep him around for real as her real live man, saying fuck Vic and cutting him out, but that didn't look like it was going to work so fuck it.

Her and Vic had gotten as much money as they could out of Raheim thus far anyway and she couldn't see them being able to get any more, so he was now obsolete. The dick Raheim gave (no matter how good), could be replaced too, just like him. That wouldn't be a problem for

Monica at all, but she knew ahead of time that he would be.

At first, she had no thoughts that Raheim would just vanish, but now that he was pretty much doing it himself, he was helping her out. Well, and himself. *Now, he may not even have to die after all.* That made it much easier for Monica anyway because she wouldn't have to worry about the cleanup. Less risk. Raheim was known deep in the streets so she knew that someone would come looking to find out who killed him. It was better for her if she didn't have to worry about doing it. He could just go on thinking he ghosted her, and it would all be the same to her.

Vic was getting more and more strange by the day and Raheim's ass was just flat-out tripping, so the only thing she could count on now was pulling off her backup plan to get with Ears and live off his money. Then she wouldn't have to worry about neither one of them gym shoe–hustling niggas no more. It was her time and she was ready to shine. Vic and Raheim weren't doing anything but holding her back anyway. Especially since she was usually the one that would have to fix their fuckups.

Monica called up her girl Tamika to see if she had any openings to do her hair within the next hour, and then she called up Amber to see if she wanted to go to the club with her that night. *This broke-ass bitch always down to ride,* she thought, rolling her eyes as she listened to Amber get hype on the other end of her phone about going out with her that night. Tamika only got that excited because everything would be on Monica as always. Monica was forever a broke bitch's dream.

Monica got up and changed into a cute little red one-piece Vic bought her a few weeks back that had a plunging neckline that stopped at her waist. She thanked God for the blessing of the double-C-cup titties He had given her because they filled her one-piece out real nice. She threw on some white pumps and grabbed a white clutch. After she transferred all her belongings from one purse to another, she grabbed her car keys and headed out the door.

"What's the hold up, boss? Why you ain't lettin' us move on this shit yet?" Ant, a young nigga from the hood who worked for Vic, complained. "We tired of sitting around here not doin' nothin'."

"Be cool, young buck. I got y'all. Just give me another week or so and then y'all can bust that move. I'm just tryin'a make sure I secure the bag first, feel me?" He laughed a little bit at himself. No one else would understand, but that's because only he knew what was on his mind.

"And then what?" Ant asked.

"And then y'all kill her." Ant and his boy looked at each other and nodded in agreement that they both understood.

"Just let me make this li'l money and we good. I've been falling back to give her enough room to do what she need to do, so hopefully she'll have his money soon and then y'all can kill her." Vic almost thought he saw saliva build up in the young boy's mouth. They were so ready for some action that they could taste it.

It came in handy to have young niggas like this on his side. If he needed someone hit, they were on it and it only ever cost him a few thousand dollars. The young goons he had running around for him only wanted quick money to live off of and maybe help their strung-out moms or pops. Sometimes they just wanted the clout in the hood. Either way, it worked for him. He couldn't rob or kill Raheim himself, so he would let that dumb-ass bitch Monica think she was playing him and bide his time while she was getting him for everything he had. Then he would take it from her and have the young hittas kill Monica and Raheim, making him the head nigga in charge. It would all work itself out and that would be that.

Vic: What's up? You fuckin' wit me today?

Vic sent Monica a quick text like he actually gave a fuck and waited for her response as he cruised the streets. He knew exactly where he wanted to be, and he headed there. The text to Monica was just to make it seem like he was still checking for her when honestly he was just waiting for the whole thing to be over. Then he would be able to fuck with who he really wanted. He was tired of waiting. He wanted to be done with this bitch already, but Raheim was worth a lot. He couldn't miss out on getting his hands on that money. No matter how much love he had in his heart for the one he really wanted, that shit would just have to wait. This money had to come first.

Chapter 21

"Fuck me, baby! Yeeeeeesssssss!" Ke'Lasia yelled at the top of her lungs as she hung over the loveseat from the back. The top of her head touched the seat cushions as her ass sat high enough for her to feel every stroke her assailant gave to her.

The blindfold she wore kept her from being able to see for the millionth time, but by this point, she ain't even care anymore. Her eyes were closed anyway. All she cared about was getting the lovin' that he gave to her every time. When he showed up, she was never disappointed.

She took her back shots like a champ. Her handcuffed hands reached for salvation or anything to steady herself with. The blackout curtains were closed tight, but it was daytime outside still and the neighbors would hear her scream if he let it continue. He raised her head by her ponytail like always, placed a rubber ball with a leather strap attached to it in her mouth, and then strapped it behind her head. It kept her from being able to scream too loud. Now her screams were muffled. She could scream as loud and as much as she wanted to now and the neighbors would never hear her.

He took that as his opportunity to show out. He rolled her over roughly. Her ass now sat propped up on the headrest of the loveseat as her legs struggled to help her keep her balance. Her handcuffed wrists made her hands no help. Her strange assailant took this as an opportunity to devour her whole. He sucked, slurped, and kissed all over her wet love box until the wall behind him and all down the front of him was saturated. Ke'Lasia had come and squirted until she could do nothing but allow him to control her body parts and cry. Her body continued to shudder as he lowered her to the loveseat and uncuffed her wrists. He released the ball gag that he had placed in her mouth and Ke'Lasia breathed deep. All of her emotions came seeping from her as she finally descended from her sex high. Her stranger, knowing just how to treat her body, eased his way up her body, placing kisses all the way up, starting at her feet.

   He kissed from the soles of her feet, past her ankles, all around her calf muscles, to her knees, her thighs, her still dripping pussy, her stomach and hips, her breast and neck and then finally her face to her lips. He took her bottom lip into his mouth and sucked it gently. Then he eased her mouth open with his tongue and let it explore inside. Her heartbeat sped up thinking he was ready for another round. Her pussy throbbed at the thought. He kissed her deeply and passionately before lying on her chest and listening to her heartbeat.

   When Ke'Lasia woke up, her eyes burned. She thought it was the next day. The blackout curtains that hung from the rod covering her huge windows in her living room were providing enough blockage to shroud the room in darkness so that Ke'Lasia was confused. She blinked a few times and rubbed her eyes some more, feeling like she hadn't been able to see in quite some time or almost like she couldn't see at all at one point. Then she smiled as her memory came back to her. The blindfold her stranger made from the piece of cloth he tore from the nightgown she was wearing came back to her mind. She touched her face, gently removing the blindfold with care.

"What the . . ." She trailed off, not understanding what was happening. As her vision became clearer, she sat up.

"What the fuck?" she said, this time startled. "What the fuck? What you doin' here? What you doing in my room? In my bed? What the fuck?" Ke'Lasia started to lose it slowly but surely. She had no understanding of what was really going on. Her eyes had to be playing tricks on her.

"Listen, I know you're not gonna understand what I'm doin', but I'm doin' it. I love you, Ke'Lasia. I love you and I know you don't love me back, but I love you and I'm tired of hiding it."

"Hiding it? Who the fuck are you? What the fuck are you talking about you love me? What the fuck?" Ke'Lasia started trying to reach for anything close to her to cover up with, realizing all of a sudden that she was sitting here stark naked as the day she was born in front of a man she didn't know. "Who are you? How the hell did you even get in here?" She scrambled around, panicked. Ke'Lasia was on the verge of hysteria. She didn't understand what was happening. All she could think was that she had fucked around and set herself up for failure. All the times she'd left a door or a window open for her stranger to come visit her at any odd time he wanted to, had to lead to anybody thinking they could just come in whenever they wanted to. She started to get scared and lightheaded.

Sitting back down, she spoke to herself. "What the fuck did I do?" Now wondering if the man she so freely let have her body at his whim, whenever and however he wanted, could have very well not even been the same man. She could've been allowing herself to be ravaged and had by several different men. She'd never seen any face or heard any voice. How could she know if it was even the same person? How did she even know that he wasn't setting her up for any man to come in and have her? She scrambled around, feeling dumb as fuck all of a sudden. She couldn't even be mad at anybody but herself. As bad as she wanted to blame this stranger, or her stranger, she couldn't. This was her fault alone.

Ke'Lasia felt herself falling further and further into the shambles she now felt. She was spiraling inward now, only concerned with if she was infected with anything from any of these men she'd let have her.

"Ke'Lasia?"

"Don't fuckin' say my name! Who the fuck are you?" she choked out through her tears. "Explain this. Explain something! Tell me something. Oh, my God, what the fuck is going on?"

"Don't cry, baby. It's just—"

"Don't fuckin' baby me!" Ke'Lasia exploded, jumping up from her place on the loveseat where she'd been ever since her encounter with her stranger. She looked around while trying to keep herself covered with a small pillow from the loveseat at the same time. She didn't even know what she was looking for or what she needed to do. All she knew was that this situation had gone to shit quick. "Don't fuckin' call me baby. I'm not your baby. I don't even know you. I don't even fuckin' know you." She cried harder, not being able to believe what was happening.

"You do though, it's me. The same man I've always been. You can just see me now. See me, Ke'Lasia. Look at me," he pleaded with her. She kept her eyes diverted from months of making sure she didn't see him, and now that that's what he wanted from her, she was scared to give in. She couldn't bring herself to do it. She couldn't even understand what was happening here. "Ke'Lasia, please," he begged more.

She stood with her back to him for a tad bit longer, asking herself if this was really happening. While she listened to him explain why this happened this way and how long he had been wanting to reveal himself to her, she went over everything in her brain, every single little piece. She had so many answers now but still felt like she had so many questions to ask. She didn't know what to do or think.

With her back still turned to him, she asked him, "Why me? Why did you pick me?"

"I didn't pick you, Ke'Lasia. The first time I saw you, I knew then that I wanted you. I knew I had to have you. But I also knew that it would be dangerous tryin'a fuck with you. Given the situation, I couldn't just step to you like I wanted."

"So, you figured you'd just break into my house and fuck me, getting what you want, and leave me like that? You figured, fuck it? That you'd just take and use my body however you wanted without even fuckin' askin' me, just because of what? You must be some kind of dope boy or somethin'," she snarled at him, whirling around to get in his face, approaching this thing and this man head-on. Until her eyes actually fell on him. This time, she was able to see just who her stranger was and see that he wasn't really a stranger at all. Her eyes widened with disbelief and her mouth fell open with no words being able to escape.

"It's not like that at all. It wasn't just that simple, all cut-and-dried like that. I never knew what the situation would be when I first saw you at the gym. I knew right then I wanted you, but I couldn't talk to you because you were in your class, and I was leaving. I waited around for you for what seemed like forever, but you finished one class and started another. I had a move to go bust and I was putting a lot at risk waiting for you. So, I told myself that I would say something as soon as I saw you again and I left. But the next time I saw you, you were with her and I knew it was a wrap." Ke'Lasia realized in that moment, looking at him fully for the first time, that it wasn't that simple like he'd said. It wasn't simple at all. This shit had hit a whole new level of crazy.

"Why the fuck are you here?" she asked, finally finding her voice again.

"Because I can't leave you alone, Ke'Lasia. I tried, but I can't. I love you, and it ain't shit I can do about it."

"You can't love me," she told him, barely above a whisper, letting it sink in that she also loved him. "This can't be fuckin' life."

"It is though. And I need to know if you fuckin' wit' me. I need to know if we gon' be in this together."

"How can I fuck with you, Slash? You're September's boyfriend!"

"No. I'm not. Not anymore. I broke it off with her and I ain't been fuckin' her in months."

"Because she was in jail, duh. Nigga, who you think you runnin' game on? Did this bitch send you over here to do this sick-ass shit? She must really want beef, huh? Well, you tell that stupid bitch—"

"She didn't send me, Ke'Lasia. She don't even know I'm here or that I've ever even been here. She don't know shit about this."

"Yeah? Well, the bitch will." She walked over to the end table next to the loveseat that she decided now had to be burned and grabbed her phone out of her purse.

"Ke'Lasia, please."

"Please what? Please let y'all continue to make me look like a fuckin' fool? Fuck outta here." Tears collected in Ke'Lasia's eyes. Looking at him made her feel like an even bigger idiot than letting a strange man fuck her in the first place.

"Ke'Lasia, she doesn't know and if you tell her, you know she just gon' get worse. You know she been hitting them pills hard as fuck and tellin' her this ain't gon' make it no better. Just let me explain."

"What? What you mean you—" Ke'Lasia's whole sentence was cut off when she heard the way September answered the phone. Here she was, trying to be a stand-up person and friend, and this bitch was tripping!

"Girl, what the fuck do you want? What is you callin' me for? We not cool, so what's up?"

"How the fuck you answer the phone like that? Like I did some shit to you. You got yo' fuckin' nerves," Ke'Lasia growled into the phone, abandoning all thoughts of the reason she was calling in the first place once she heard September pick up.

"Bitch, fuck you. I ain't do shit to you that you ain't do to me."

"So, I pushed you in front of a bitch with a gun. September? I would've laid down my life for you, bitch, and you tried to get me killed!"

"Girl, bye." September laughed in her face. "Yo' fake ass wouldn't' have done shit for me but try to keep me in yo' shadow like a lame. Oh, well. Had she shot you, at least something would've been original about yo' fake ass." Ke'Lasia's eyes fell back to where Slash sat with his head down. She decided to say fuck the dead-ass conversation with September. It wasn't going to go anywhere, not now.

"I tried to call you and give you a heads-up about what was goin' on right now, but you fuckin' ignorant. I don't even know why I wasted my time. Fuck you." Ke'Lasia spat into the phone in pure disgust at the voice on the other end of the phone that used to be that of a friend.

"I don't know why you did either, stupid. I'm cool on you. You ain't got no reason to be calling me, bitch." September laughed in her ear, pissing Ke'Lasia off. She no longer even cared how September would feel about this, or what she had to say. She was fucking done with her. Whatever happened from here would just have to happen.

Ke'Lasia hung up on September in the middle of whatever the fuck the girl was saying. She didn't care anymore. Her and September was no longer friends, and she would just have to get used to that. But now, it was time to figure out what Slash had up his sleeve.

"Start talking," she told him, looking down on him.

Monica woke up with a major headache. She instantly knew she was going to suffer a hangover from hell. But looking around and remembering she was at Ears's house made it all better. He wasn't in the bed and she heard the shower running. Slipping out the bed and into one of his discarded T-shirts on the floor, she decided she would ease downstairs to find something to cook him for breakfast. Her plan was to surprise him when he got out of the shower. It would be more incentive to keep her around. She felt like being a good cook and a porn star in the bedroom would earn her brownie points in his eyes.

Nearing the bottom of the steps, she heard voices coming from the kitchen that were on the other side of the wall and stopped to listen.

"You stay swearing I'on fuck wit' you, but here you go actin' funny. That's what I be talkin' about. All this double standard shit some female shit that I don't be on at all."

"Nigga, who you talkin' to like that?"

"You!" the angry man roared. "I'm talkin' to you! You stay cryin' like a bitch about every fuckin' thing I do, but then I come over here to kick it and spend time with you, and you actin' funny. But had I gone about my business, you would've been on my phone complaining about not seeing me. But it's good. I'm outta here. Fuck it."

"Wait, Raheim! Just wait."

"Raheim?" Monica repeated, coming around the corner. She knew that voice was familiar as hell. Her presence now known to both men had them shook. "What you mean spend time with him? Spend time with him like what? What does that even mean?" Monica felt herself getting hysterical. She tried her best to remain calm, but she was quickly losing that battle. She couldn't understand what she was hearing. Although she knew exactly what was happening, it just didn't want to register. She didn't want to understand. Monica shook her head back and forth rather quickly. Her hands shook and she had to hold herself to feel as though she kept her body from shaking. "Somebody better tell me somethin'! What the fuck is going on?" She stepped farther into the kitchen where the two men stood with total shock on their faces like they had just seen an apparition.

"Hold up, Monica. This ain't what you think it is," Raheim rushed to say. He found his way over to her in what seemed like three steps.

"Don't fuckin' touch me!" she screamed at him, snatching away from his grasp. "Don't fuckin' touch me! Y'all must think I'm stupid or some shit."

"Monica, baby, just let me explain."

"Don't fuckin' baby me, nigga! Is you fuckin' him? Are you really fuckin' him, Raheim? Tell me you niggas not fuckin'. Tell me!" Monica doubled over at the waist, and her hand flew to her mouth. She tried turning away.

"Monica, baby, don't be crazy. You know it's me and you. We were just talking business. It wasn't nothing else. Come on, baby. You trust me, right?" Raheim stepped in toward her again to try to soothe her, but it wasn't happening.

"Raheim, I swear to God you better not put yo' fuckin' hands on me if you been fuckin' that man! If yo' ass is gay . . ." Monica grabbed her stomach again and ran to the kitchen sink. Her words were cut short by the bile she felt rising up into her throat.

"Man, just chill," Raheim told her. "You doin' a lot. Ain't nobody fuckin' gay. Fuckin' a nigga? What kinda shit you think I'm on? You foolin', just know, homie. We was rappin' about some business." Monica straightened herself up from spewing her guts all in Ears's kitchen sink and turned toward Raheim. She looked from him to Ears, noticing that Ears hadn't yet said a thing. "You good? You throwin' up for no reason and shit. Grossin' yo'self out bein' fuckin' extra. You know me. You know I ain't finna be fuckin' wit' no nigga. Come on. This me." Raheim opened his arms for Monica to walk into, advancing toward her once more, but she stopped him once again. With her hand up to halt him in his tracks, Monica dropped a bomb in Raheim's lap.

"I'm pregnant," she told him. Even though she said her statement to Raheim, she stared Ears dead in his face, waiting for any sign of anything in his face that would confirm what she felt like she already knew to be true.

"By who?" both men blurted out together.

"By you, nigga." Monica folded her arms across her chest, rolled her eyes at Ears, and looked at Raheim, waiting for the bullshit to happen. She waited with attitude for this nigga to fix his lips and say her baby wasn't his.

"I, uh, but I—"

"You what? 'Cause we both know you can have babies, so what? You what? You about to deny my baby in front of this nigga?"

"I'm not denying my baby, Monica."

"Yo' baby? How you know that's yo' seed, nigga?" Ears finally piped up from the back. Just like Monica knew he would.

"'Cause he been shooting the club up like a nigga that just lost a fight! That's how, nigga. So I'ma ask you niggas again. Are. Y'all. Fuckin'?" She looked from one man to the other, arms still across her chest, waiting for one of them to tell her the truth that she knew she didn't wanna hear.

"Wait a minute." Ears stood up off the stool he was sitting on with a look of confusion on his face. Monica was sure he was finally speaking up. "So, you mean to tell me you knew you had that seed in your stomach last night while you were getting drunk as fuck, drinking all my babies? You had a nigga baby in you, and you got down like that?"

"Don't forget you had a couple bullets to let loose in the club too, nigga, so don't act all shocked and innocent. This could've been yo' baby. Shit."

"Bitch, that would've never been my fuckin' baby."

"Bitch? I got yo' bitch." Monica advanced toward Ears with hell in her eyes but Raheim interceded.

"Hold up, y'all. Y'all trippin'. Ears, don't call her out her name. That shit ain't cool. That's my baby mama."

"Oh, yeah?" Ears replied, not really asking a question.

"Yeah, man. Chill."

"Are you niggas fuckin' or what?" Monica asked again, calming herself for the time being.

"Why the fuck you keep askin' me that? What the fuck I gotta do? What you want me to say? I'm not fuckin' him or no other nigga, damn! Now you say that gay shit again and we gon' have a problem, a'ight?"

"Yeah, a'ight. If you say so. I know I heard some bullshit but it's cool. I know bitches in these streets that know everything about every fuckin' body. I'll get to the bottom of this shit. And when I find out what you niggas got goin' on is some fuck shit, I'ma tell anybody listening what's up wit' y'all. Y'all got me fucked up."

Raheim wasted no time getting pissed. He turned all the way up on her right there still in the kitchen. They started to argue like two people who absolutely hated each other. They were so mad that they never saw Ears leave his seat on the barstool the second time.

"You heard what the fuck I said, Heim!" Monica yelled over her shoulder to him as she walked toward the archway of the kitchen, leaving him to argue with himself.

"Yeah. You heard what the fuck I said, Monica. I'll break your fuckin' neck if you play wit' me girl. This man ain't shit to me."

"Oh, yeah?" Ears said again. "That's yo' word, huh?"

"What the fuck are you doing?" Raheim yelled. Monica turned around just in time to see Ears raise the gun. The gun went off and Raheim screamed. So did Monica.

Raheim ran to Monica's side as she slid down the wall toward the floor. Blood covered the front of her shirt. Her eyes were wide with fear.

"Monica!" Raheim yelled. "Monica! Monica! Hold on. I'ma get you outta here, okay? Just hold on." Raheim watched the tears roll down her face and it broke his heart. "Man, what the fuck did you do? What the fuck is wrong with you?" Raheim spat at Ears, who stood there still holding the gun, unbothered by what was happening.

"You think you just 'bout to stand in my face and treat me like I ain't shit? Nah. Fuck you and her, nigga." Ears let off another shot into Monica's head. Brain matter splattered onto the kitchen wall behind her. Blood sprayed across Raheim's face.

"Oh, my God! Somethin' is wrong with you!" he belted.

"Nah, nigga. Somethin' wrong with you if you thought I was about to stand here and let you and this bitch disrespect me in my house. You went too far. Gettin' that bitch pregnant? What? You thought you was gon' love that bitch and shit was gon' be sweet? Nah. Fuck that. Yo' ass belongs to me. I played that game long enough."

"What you think we gon' do now, huh? How the fuck is we gon' clean this up?"

"I got people for that. I ain't worried about that at all." Ears pulled out his phone and made a quick call. Hanging up, he asked Raheim, "So what you gon' do? You got choices to make here. You said it was me and you, but you obviously loved her. Is this some shit I gotta worry about?" Raheim looked at Ears, unsure of what to say. "Hello? Time ticking, nigga. Speak up. Do you love me or not?"

"Love you?" Raheim stood and Ears turned toward the other side of the kitchen that led to the front of his house. Vic stood there with a look of confusion.

"Vic, listen. This ain't what you think," Ears started explaining.

"What I think is that the nigga I been fuckin' wit' for five years just said he love somebody and got me out here lookin' dumb as fuck. That's what I think. I just came all the way over here to tell you I was all in and this what I find?"

"Vic, listen," Ears tried again. He wasn't even finished before Vic's eyes bulged and he fell to the ground in front of him. Raheim stood there with a bloody knife, staring Ears in the face. "What the fuck was that about?" Ears yelled.

"It was fuck her, so it's fuck this nigga." He gestured to a now fallen Vic who lay bleeding at their feet. "If it's you and me, that's what the fuck it is. You and me. Nobody else." Raheim glared at Ears, daring him to object. Ears just pulled him in and kissed him.

"It's you and me," he told him.

Ninety days later, shit got more real.

Chapter 22

"You know I love that shit."

"Or do you love me?"

Ke'Lasia thought about it for a minute even though she already knew the answer. Hell no she didn't, but she wouldn't say that and fuck up what they had going. He was the therapist, but she knew good and well his ego couldn't take the truth. So instead, she just smiled and kissed his lips.

"You gon' give me some more of this dick before you go to work or nah?" she asked. Justin rolled over on top of her. He kissed her forehead, nose, and both cheeks before planting a deep kiss on her lips. His manhood started to grow, and she moaned at the feeling pressing against her opening. She silently thanked God that neither of them had slept with any clothes on.

"Nah." He laughed. "I gotta go and so do you," he reminded her. Ke'Lasia rolled her eyes and let out a deep sigh. He was right. She had a photoshoot that day for the Victoria's Secret plus-size catalog.

Her and Justin had been seeing each other since the session they had when she caught him with his after-rendezvous erection. The story she told him about her own encounter did exactly what she expected it to do. Later that night, he was calling her phone for a "follow-up session." Since then, they'd been meeting two or three times a week. Their time together was bomb. Ke'Lasia loved every single moment of it. He was just as nasty as she imagined he would be. Whatever she didn't encounter fucking with Slash, she got it from Justin. Because yes, she was still fucking with Slash.

Justin had asked her did she love him, and she didn't want to hurt his feelings by saying no. The fact of the matter was, she didn't. What she actually discovered was that she little more than liked Slash. She hadn't planned on it. It just happened to them. Luckily, she wasn't alone in her feelings. Slash had already told her he loved her that day he revealed himself to her and had been telling her ever since. She just hadn't said it back yet. She couldn't bring herself to let those feelings be true. The time she spent with him was phenomenal to say the least, but she still couldn't shake the fact that he was September's ex-man. She didn't like feeling like they were doing anything behind her ex-friend's back, but by this point in life, fuck her. Their friendship was over by her own choice, so what September felt like no longer meant anything to Ke'Lasia. She was happy and if no one could understand that, then that was on them. She knew her heart belonged to Slash and whether he knew it or not, it would stay there.

Ke'Lasia tried to keep loving September, even after all the bullshit. But anytime she tried to call, September either hung up in her face or tried to make her feel stupid for calling in the first place. So by this point, she was done. She would do what she wanted for herself and that was it. Fuck September and anyone else who didn't like it.

Ke'Lasia was keeping Justin pretty much a secret from everyone because what she wanted right now was Justin and Slash. They both gave her something she didn't want to lose. Which was why she never mentioned to Justin that she now knew who her stranger was. Especially since he had asked her to stop what she had going with him. He promised her that it was over with whomever he was dealing with too, but she knew better. Which was another reason why she wouldn't cut off Slash.

Ke'Lasia's photoshoot went off without a hitch. It was a breeze and so much fun. She enjoyed the whole thing and the people she worked with. Even the photographers had her cracking up laughing the whole time. It was just an extra bonus that the gigs she had been getting lately were for big-ass money. Bringing in this kind of money, she could work one gig every six months and still be fine if that's all she wanted to do.

"See y'all. Everybody have a good day." She waved to everyone she passed on the way out the door. She got to the parking lot and pushed the alarm for her car. She threw her bag in the trunk.

"What the fuck?" she screeched, grabbing her chest. "What the fuck are you doing out here lurking?" she asked Justin when she saw that it was just him behind her and not some crazy person.

"I came to make sure you got home safe."

"You could've just called me. You scared the shit out of me, Justin, damn."

"That wasn't my intention. I just wanted to check on you."

"And what else?" she asked him, noticing his demeanor. He wasn't acting like he usually did, casual and collected. He was acting paranoid and out of it. She didn't know what his problem was, but it was scaring her.

"And to ask you when was the last time you saw Freight."

"Freight? Who the fuck is that?" she asked, relieved that it wasn't Slash he was asking about.

He paused and she was back on alert. She didn't know who the fuck Freight was, but whoever he was, he was someone who had Justin worried. She could see the panic all over his face even though he was trying to hide it. It just unnerved Ke'Lasia even further, making her feel like she wasn't necessarily safe out here with him. He never touched her but the look in his eyes told her a whole story. He was crazed and on a mission. She knew lying to him would be dangerous in this moment, so luckily for her, she wasn't lying.

"Ke'Lasia, I'm not in the mood to play right now. I need to know. When was the last time you saw him?"

"Saw who? I don't know who that is. Justin, I have to go. Call me later." Ke'Lasia opened her driver's side door, but Justin forced it back shut. He grabbed her by her neck, turning her toward him, growling his words in her face.

"Stop fuckin' playin' wit' me. You know exactly who I'm talking about. You think I'm stupid? Huh, bitch? Stay away from him or I'll kill you and him." He looked her deep in her eyes as they started to bulge before he let her go.

Ke'Lasia fell against her car door gasping for air. She didn't know who the hell Justin was talking about, and now, she didn't even care. All she wanted to do was get home. She made sure she couldn't see him anymore before she opened her door and climbed in.

Ever since Travis had walked out of that hospital room, he hadn't heard from or seen his children. He felt bad as fuck, but the anger toward Kiesha he still had wouldn't allow him to bring himself to call her phone for them. He also couldn't fight off the recurring thoughts of what that Justin nigga had said to him. Travis was essentially missing kids who weren't even his, which only angered him more.

Travis got up from his chair. Dropping his towel in front of the closet, he found something to wear. The bar called After Werk on the west side of the city right past Werk Road and Queen City Avenue had become Travis's new favorite spot. With cheap beer and liquor and always a seat at the bar, Travis frequented this place almost every day since the devastating blow he was given at Justina's hospital bedside.

"The usual?" the nice female bartender asked him as he sat down in almost the same exact spot he sat in every day. Travis shook his head in agreement. The bartender was back rather quickly with his double shot of VSQ and a bottle of Heineken. No sports were on the TV, so Travis was left to drown himself in liquor to quell his thoughts. By drink number five, it hadn't worked. He was more frustrated than ever. He figured someone owed him some answers and he was going to get them.

Travis threw back his sixth double shot of the smooth brandy, drained the bottle of beer, slammed the price of his tab along with a generous $20 tip down on the bar, and headed out. He pulled up to Kiesha's apartment building in no time. He hadn't been there in what seemed like forever, but it was still as piss poor as it was the last time he was here.

Climbing the steps two at a time, he banged on the door.

"Open this door, Kiesha! Open it! Don't play wit' me! Open this fuckin' door!" he demanded between bangs.

Kiesha flung the door open. Wide-eyed and confused, she snapped on him. "What the fuck are you doing here bangin' on my door like a fuckin' lunatic? What the hell is wrong with you? Are you fuckin' stupid?" Travis bumped past her and into her apartment like he lived there, not even worrying about what she was saying to him.

"Yeah, I'm stupid, Kiesh. Stupid enough to believe that those kids were mine," he slurred. "Everybody told me not to believe you, that you was a ho. But nah, I ain't listen. I fell in love with yo' simple ass anyway. Tried to give you the world, too," he slurred on almost incoherently. "And ya know what I got back? Hmm?" he drunkenly asked her, reaching out for her to pull her closer to him. "You know what I got?"

"Travis, please. You're drunk."

"I got another nigga's kids. That's what I got."

"Travis."

"Travis, what? Huh? Travis, what?" He staggered backward, throwing his hands up. "What? You gon' tell me to calm down? You gon' tell me to relax? Hmm? Travis what?"

"Travis, just—" Kiesha's sentence was cut short by a gun suddenly put into her face.

"Travis, what? Be okay that you been thinking four whole-ass kids was yours for damn near fifteen years? Travis what? It's gon' be okay? What, huh? Travis what?" he yelled and swayed, barely able to hold the gun on her properly.

Kiesha didn't argue back for fear that in his drunken state he would shoot her dead right there. She could tell from this whole situation how much Justin had hurt Travis with this information. She knew he would be hurt, just not like this. She almost thought he would be relieved to find out that he no longer had to deal with her or the kids seeing as how hard he tried staying away from her no matter how hard she tried to trick him into getting back together. No matter what lengths she went through to make him hers again, he didn't budge. She figured the news would somehow alleviate the burden he felt. Without having to deal with the kids, he wouldn't have to deal with her anymore either.

Now standing there with a gun in her face and an angry-ass drunk ex-boyfriend on the other end of it, she could see how extremely wrong she was.

"Travis? What are you doing, baby? You don't wanna do this."

"Don't tell me what the fuck I wanna do! Don't fuckin' say shit!"

"Travis, please."

"Now you wanna be nice. Now you wanna care? After everything I've been through with you? You do me like this and now you give a fuck?" Travis let off a shot that rang through the room. In his drunken state, he had forgotten to attach the silencer to the gun that was in his pocket. It was too late now. The shot had let off loud and clear. He was sure the neighbors had heard it and would call the police soon. He just prayed that they would hold off seeing as though she did live in the hood.

"Travis!" Kiesha screamed out. Shock that the bullet had missed her sat on her face.

"I should fuckin' kill you," he scowled at her.

"I'm sorry," she cried.

Travis watched as she melted to the floor with tears seeping from her eyes big as raindrops. He was unmoved. Kiesha no longer affected him the way she used to, and although he wanted to kill her right there, right then, he didn't. He put his gun back into his jacket, shook his head, and walked away.

Before he reached his last steps to the door, he heard her whisper through her tears, "Thank you, Travis. I really am so, so sorry. I hope you can forgive me one day and understand what choices I had to make for my babies." Before he could stop himself, Travis summoned up a wad of spit from the pit of his soul and spat it right into her crying face.

"Fuck you, My'Kiesha!" he growled at her angrily. Then he slammed the door shut behind him.

Chapter 23

Ke'Lasia and Slash were having the time of their lives. They had just gotten back in town from their trip to Cabo a few days before and were already packing to leave for Venice in two more days. It seemed like all they did was leave. Slash was taking a hiatus from his porn career and Ke'Lasia had chosen to take a break from her career as a model, and the sexual habit she had formed, to focus on her new relationship. She was now all the way into Slash. No one else mattered. He was treating her so good that she didn't even think about being with another man anymore. Life had been nothing but up since her and Slash were getting more serious. She hadn't even thought of Justin in the whole time that her and Slash had been together. He was now a thing of the past, and Slash was her future. Her happiness. He was all that she needed now.

"I love you, baby." He leaned over his open suitcase and kissed her lips, distracting her from what she was doing.

"Boy, quit playing and pack." She laughed, deflecting him and the hints she knew he was throwing her way.

"I'm for real this time," he told her, smirking. He had that look in his eyes that she wasn't going to fall for.

"Well, I love you too. Now pack." These nine months had gone past so fast that it felt like a dream to Ke'Lasia. She never knew that she could possibly be this happy, but she was. And she loved it. Every single minute of it. The nasty-ass sex they shared was particularly exciting for her. Slash kept the spark in the bedroom at every turn. She expected way less from a porn star, but she was pleasantly surprised. Ke'Lasia actually did love Slash and she believed him when he said he loved her. Everything in life was perfect. Ke'Lasia was living her dream.

They finished packing and headed to the patio for their nightcap. Every night they started with the same routine. A nightcap on the patio. Whether they were in town or out, they started the same way every night. Ke'Lasia usually sipped on something sexy like red wine while Slash sipped on something more manly. His favorite choice right now was brandy. Korbel to be exact. The liquor cabinet stayed stocked at his place and hers now, so every night they went out to the patio with their pick of whatever they wanted and sat under the stars. Now that the seasons were changing yet again, Ke'Lasia kept a blanket somewhere on the patio so that she could cover up with it if, and probably when, she got cold.

The two sipped their drinks dry while looking at the stars in a comfortable silence. They held hands and relished their own thoughts until their glasses were empty. Ke'Lasia took the initiative to get up and pour them new drinks. Slash never had to get up while he was with her. She loved getting things for him and serving him. She always wanted a man she felt the need to do domestic things like that for, and now she had one. She went to get their drinks with a huge smile, lost in her own thoughts.

She was so happy with her new life and even happier that she let it happen to her. Letting go of Justin and all the other indiscretions she participated in showed to have paid off for her after all. Especially after she caught Justin in his office with his pants down for who she now knew was Travis's nasty-ass baby mama, Kiesha. She always knew that bitch wasn't no good and seeing her with Justin just made everything so much clearer for her. Justin had been begging her to stay away from Slash and

Travis. Now she saw why. He didn't want her up to the same things that he was.

That day, she decided to hell with it. She threw all caution to the wind and went all in with Slash. That decision was the best one she'd made in a long time and she was proud of herself for it. Life couldn't have gotten any better.

Ke'Lasia walked back out to the patio with the replenished drinks in hands. "For you, my love," she damn near sang as she reached out to hand her man his drink. But the glasses she held for her and Slash careened to the ground. The sound of them hitting the concrete flooring was drowned out only by the sounds of her screams. She arrived back out to the patio only to find Slash covered in blood. Someone had slit his throat, leaving him dead in the chair where she'd left him a few minutes earlier.

"Girl, I ain't been worried about his ass in I don't know how long. His ass is old-ass news. Super old," September told Amber, who was on the other end of her phone. "Girl, after that shit with that Kiesha bitch from downtown happened and he let me go to jail behind that shit, I ain't been fuckin' wit' that lame-ass nigga." She rolled her eyes like Amber could actually see her as she lied through her teeth. But her friend knew her well enough to know exactly what she had done.

"Girl, don't roll yo' eyes like you wasn't gone off that nigga." Amber laughed, hearing the eyeroll all in her voice.

"I ain't think you was ever gon' leave that nigga alone. Even after all them bitches he fucked with, you still just hung on in there. Girl, I thought y'all would be married or something by now, going through hell and high water, together forever." Amber got dead weak at herself as well as by herself. September wasn't feeling the little joke at all, so she didn't join in on the laughter.

Amber and Monica both always thought the shit she went through with Raheim was just one big joke for everyone to laugh at. And although September thought some of the shit was funny too, hell, some of the shit she caused intentionally, it didn't mean she thought all of it was funny. A lot of that shit she brought on herself she did because she knew it was only a matter of time before Raheim brought it on her anyway. It was better if she just beat him to the punch.

"Girl . . ." September trailed off, trying to decide if she should cuss Amber out for that smart-ass remark she made about Raheim cheating. Or for any of the fucking shade she had just thrown. She knew good and well that that shit was gon' set her off. Yeah, Ke'Lasia was the only one to know exactly how deep it got with Raheim and her, but Amber still knew how toxic that shit was for her and yet, she still continuously found it funny anyway.

"Anyway," she continued like Amber hadn't said anything, deciding not to even waste energy on her at all.

"Girl, are we going out tonight or not?" September muted the phone as Amber talked so that she could get herself together. She didn't want Amber to hear the hard-ass drag she just took from her homemade pipe. What she did or didn't do was none of anyone's business. Espccially Amber's.

The two girls acted real cool around each other, but September knew that Amber really wasn't shit. She knew that if Amber found out she was sitting there free basing while she was on the phone with her that by the end of the day, everyone everywhere would know. No matter how cool they acted, September and Amber were frenemies at best. September didn't trust Amber any further than she could throw her, and Amber felt the same way.

They had been "friends" for years, but they were never really on that level. They were more acquaintances than anything. Just two people who hung around two people they knew. September knew Ke'Lasia and Monica first. Monica and Amber were friends to begin with like September and Ke'Lasia were. Since their friends were friends, it was only right that they befriended one another as well. And it worked out, too. For a long time. But once you put females together, it's always some mess. Especially when they meet each other because of other friends. It always ends up with fuck shit in the game.

Because Ke'Lasia was cool with Monica, September figured being at least cordial with Amber wouldn't hurt, but she saw early on that Monica and Amber both were full of shit. Amber was the type of bitch who liked to high cap. She just wanted to fit in with everybody, so she normally said anything that sounded good. Which was another reason why September didn't need Amber too far in her business. She would gossip with her, but that was about it. Amber told everybody's business as soon as she found someone who would listen. September couldn't have that. She was already taking enough heat from people she used to be cool with for popping pills. If they found out she was now snorting dope and free basing, they would be trying to rush her to a rehab center for sure. She laughed a little to herself thinking about the song by Amy Winehouse about her peoples trying to make her go to rehab.

"No, no, no!" Just thinking of the song was hilarious to her.

September wrapped the conversation with Amber up because now, her high was kicking it and she didn't feel like pretending she didn't know the girl was lying anymore. "Yeah, 'cause the last time I was up at the Ritz, that nigga Bo was trickin' big. Bitch, he was in there payin' for everything. Soon as he saw me and my bitches step up in there he was on dick. I couldn't get the nigga to leave me the fuck alone. But shit, it was cool 'cause our whole night was free since that nigga thought he was gettin' some pussy." September knew she had already fucked Bo several times. Why she was lying about it like it was more than that, September didn't know, but that solidified what September already thought in the first place. That Amber was still not to be trusted and she wasn't going to fall for her bullshit.

Cutting off the rest of her lies about Bo, September set up the details on where they would meet and when before hanging up on a still talking Amber. Then she put her phone on silent and lay back on the couch, letting her high take control. She couldn't do nothing but smile at the feeling she felt. This high was a good one and she wanted to enjoy every piece of it. Getting high was the only part of life left that September enjoyed. Well, getting high and going out. The high kept her spirits up and gave her energy while the club gave her a reason to come out the house. She needed those little reasons ever since she got out the hospital almost a year ago with the news she had to live with forever. Mu'fuckas would never get why she turned to drugs, but as long as she kept people like Amber out her business, they'd never have to.

September: Going out tonight. Hope to see you later.

She sent Justin a quick text to let him know her plans for the night and that she was hoping to see him. She had enjoyed herself with Justin for the last few weeks. Besides the drugs and the clubs, he was the only thing keeping her smiling. She hated that she had to keep a secret so big from him, but she also didn't want to ruin anything. After all the crazy shit that went down with Slash, and him being the only one who knew the whole story behind who she was now, she decided that she would keep her business and her true feelings to herself. Wasn't no point in getting too caught up with someone else who would just leave anyway. Justin was great and all, but she had already fallen for a pipe dream with Slash. She wasn't hardly about to do the same thing again.

Getting dressed for another night of bullshit and shenanigans that had become the norm for Travis, he loaded his chrome Glock .19 with hollow-point rounds and headed toward the door.

"Yeah, foo, I'm finna pull up in a second," he told his guy as he finally approached the club. Jumping out of his car after parking, Travis spoke to almost everyone still hanging freely around the parking lot. A lot of people from his former life he saw were still hanging out doing the same bullshit that he could no longer judge since he was now doing it too. He silently shook his head, more so at himself than them because he had other options. He had chosen this path for himself when he knew he could be doing something different. He didn't blame anybody for what he was on like they did though. Even though this all stemmed from Kiesha's bitch ass, it was still his choice.

"Hey, Freight." A group of old thots from the old neighborhood he once knew greeted him as he walked past. He had already smashed three of the five back in the day, so nothing interested him in stopping to speak. He just smiled and nodded his head as he continued his journey inside the club.

Reaching the line that led up to the door, Travis dapped up the two bouncers who stood guard before proceeding in, ignoring the moans and groans of disappointment he heard fill the crowd that he walked in ahead of. He smiled and nodded at the disapproving people.

The music was loud enough in the place. His favorite rapper, Jay-Z, poured out of the thunderous speakers, reminding people that it was a hard-knock life. This was why Travis loved coming here on Thursday nights. It was old-school night, so they played all the hits from his days of running the streets. He didn't have to be surrounded by a bunch of young people barely reciting the lyrics to a whole bunch of new, young, slow-sounding dudes who didn't make sense. He could easily follow along with the lyrics and understand the song, allowing him to enjoy it.

The night picked up. Hands were in the air all over the place to Young Jeezy's "Trap or Die." All the guys shouted lyrics at the top of their lungs and even the women were having a good time and singing a few of the words. Travis was on chill mode in the cut with his third drink of Patrón in hand, his head bobbing to the familiar tunes. A smile had stayed plastered on his face the whole time he had been there. Him and his niggas were fresh as fuck, chilling, and catching all the action from the ladies. The night was turnt. Travis enjoyed every minute of the laid-back ease that the night had brought him. He didn't think of My'Kiesha or her dumb-ass bullshit once. His mind was free and clear, and he was loving every single piece of it.

Pow! Pow! Pow! The club erupted in screams as the loud gunshots rang out. People started ducking and running from every angle, only worried about themselves and their own safety. Travis, playing it smart, dropped his cup and backed up through the short crowd of niggas behind him. He put his back to the wall and watched his surroundings as numerous people tried to fight their way out of the death trap that was once the club. No one knew where the shots had come from. All they knew was that they needed to get out.

Travis watched as people were pushed to the ground and some even stepped on by others who were trying to find their way through their panicked emotions to get out the club. He didn't move. Even though he had his gun on him, he knew that stepping out into the chaos wouldn't be wise. Until the crowd thinned out, Travis stayed pressed against the wall, watching as much as he could. The DJ never got around to turning the lights on, so there wasn't too much light in the club for him to see too far ahead. Once most of the people seemed to be out, Travis left his spot against the wall to help the nearby people still on the ground from the stampede to their feet.

"You good, shorty?" he asked as he picked up a fallen woman.

"Yeah, I think so," the younger girl who was pushed down in the middle of all the happenings confirmed for him when he helped her up.

He found the people he could on his way out the door and helped them up too. Even men if they needed it. One guy Travis happened upon almost to the door of the club had a broken leg as a result of the earlier stampede. Travis held him up and helped him limp his way out of the club and to the sidewalk outside. The police officers usually on duty at the club at night of course weren't there.

"I'ma sit you right here so I can call the boys, a'ight?" Travis informed rather than asked the victim. "You good with that, right?"

"Man, yeah. I'm good," he said before actually sitting down. "I mean, except . . ." He trailed off as he reached in his jacket and pulled out a pistol.

"I'ma get rid of this, my man. Don't worry about it. I got you." Travis took the pistol and disappeared. After ditching the dirty weapon, he came back to the injured man, informing him that he was now in the clear.

"That's cool, man. Just get me some help. Damn this shit hurt like a muthafucka." The guy eased to the ground holding his leg.

After the call was placed to 911 and Travis had successfully answered all of what he felt like was unnecessary-ass questions that the dispatcher asked him, he informed the injured man that help was on the way. He stayed long enough for the ambulance to arrive before he shook hands with homie and parted ways.

"Shit got crazy out, foo. You good?"

"I'm good, boa," Travis's boy confirmed for him. They said what they had to say, then wrapped their conversation up. Travis placed his phone in the cup holder, lit his joint, and put his car in drive.

As soon as he pulled out the parking lot to leave the club and the madness behind, a black SUV cut him off. Spinning out in front of him, causing him to slam on his brakes, all four doors on the truck popped open and four men got out. The size of the guns should've scared Travis, but they didn't. Four guys with Mac 10s pointing at him should've had him fearing for his life, but that wasn't the case here. The shit that threw Travis for a loop and had him at a loss for words, trying to quickly plan his way out, was seeing September's ex-boyfriend, Raheim, standing at the driver's door leading the pack.

"Get the fuck out the car!" he screamed.

Travis sat there like he had suddenly gone deaf. He didn't make a move. The two men stared each other down through the windshield of the all-black Charger that Travis remained seated in. He felt the sweat start to gather on his mustache. Raheim watched him and waited for his orders to be carried out. Seeing Travis not move only made him angrier.

"Get! The! Fuck! Out! The! Car!" Bullets from his gun rang out. Shots flew up into the air warning Travis that his demands were real. "The next ones will turn yo' whip to Swiss cheese, nigga!" he threatened through the deadened air.

Travis almost regretted waiting so long to leave the parking lot. This wouldn't even be an issue had he left on time. He hated being any fucking steps behind the enemy and yet, that's where he found himself. He was on the other side of ahead and he didn't like it. But he wasn't going out like a sucka. If Raheim wanted to see him, he was gonna have to come face him like a man.

Chapter 24

Ke'Lasia called Travis about a million times in the last two hours and he still hadn't answered or called back. She was pissed. Mad, lonely, confused, and scared, Ke'Lasia sat alone in her apartment looking for a reason to not finish off the bottle of Cîroc Peach that sat in front of her, already half empty.

Since she'd found the body of her lover bleeding to death, she hadn't spent a minute without tears in her eyes. Her and Slash hadn't had a long time together, but the time they had was everything to her. He ended up meaning more to her than she ever thought would be possible. His untimely demise was harder on her than she expected and the only close friend she had left wouldn't answer the phone. She was so fucked up behind the event that she contemplated calling September. Of course she didn't, but she'd thought about it.

"Travis, pick up the damn phone!" she screamed into the deadly silence of her apartment while she listened to Travis's phone ring unanswered again. "What the fuck!" she yelled out as she threw her phone into the couch pillows. Frustration consumed her. She hadn't felt so alone since she lived with her mom all those years ago. The pain from this and having no one to turn to was consuming her. She called the only person left she could.

"Can you come over please? I need you."

"I'm in the middle of something, but I'll be there as soon as I can, okay? No longer than an hour." She hung up the phone and let the tears slide quietly down her face, feeling only a slight bit of relief knowing someone was on their way to comfort her.

Justin hung up the phone and sat there for a few more minutes. He knew with everything in him that if he didn't do something, these niggas were going to kill Travis. He just couldn't figure out if he cared or not. Justin found out where the men were taking Travis earlier and got there in time to sit and wait for them niggas to show up, not knowing what he would do when they got there. All he knew was that he had to do something. Them killing Travis would permanently get him out the way of what Justin was trying to accomplish, but he also didn't want these bum-ass niggas to have the satisfaction. He hated the two of them way more than he despised the fact that Travis owned the heart of his kids' mother. To him, the nigga Travis was just a nuisance. Not really even anything important. Since he had left his days of being Freight behind and was actually cool on fucking with Keisha for good now, he really didn't even need to die.

The choice weighed heavily on him while he watched the goons escort Travis through the path and up to the door of the barn. The light glowed from within, turning Ears and Raheim to only a silhouette. He couldn't make out what they were saying, but he knew it was just bullshit. No matter what Travis agreed to do or not to do, they were only biding their time before they killed him. Nothing in him led him to believe that Travis would make it out of here alive. He told Ke'Lasia to give him an hour but now, he was thinking that it might take a little longer.

He looked at the time with the muted light that his phone screen exuded. He had forty-five minutes to get to Ke'Lasia and keep his word. He swiped September's number off the screen, ignoring her for the fourth time tonight, then put his phone back in his pocket, choosing to go ahead and end this now.

Justin emerged from behind the bale of hay where he hid and made his way up to the crowd undetected.

"This nigga is a problem for all involved," Ears was saying. "We've already lost two of our best men behind this nigga. Vic and Slash." Justin's eyes grew wide at the lie he'd just heard Ears tell. "That's a problem for us. Without them, there is money that we are not making! I called you all here tonight to witness what happens to a nigga that fucks with our pockets and takes food off our plates." Ears cocked his gun, but let his arm drop back to his side. "I spent fifteen long years locked behind bars. I'm here now to straighten out what you niggas obviously couldn't. Luckily, Raheim was out here with you niggas, watchin' my back and holdin' shit down since you niggas are clearly in-fucking-competent."

"These niggas might not know," Justin spoke up, emerging from the shadows so that he could now be seen. "But, I do."

"Know what? Who the fuck is that?" Raheim and Ears both shielded their eyes from the headlight beams coming from behind their seven-foot soldiers as they parted and let a figure walk through straight at them. They trained their guns toward the shadow, waiting to pop off if they didn't like whatever the fuck was about to go down here.

Justin stepped into the middle of the circle and let the men behind him block the light from Ears and Raheim once more. Realizing who had spoken up, the two men's eyes grew wide with fear. Travis stood there confused. He looked from Raheim and Ears to the fuck nigga Justin he now hated.

"What the fuck is this?" Travis asked.

"This, my nigga, is me saving your life."

"I'm not yo' nigga, and you not savin' me from shit. Do I look scared of these bitch-ass niggas?" Travis spit at Justin's feet. "These niggas don't scare me, just like you don't scare me," he told Justin matter-of-factly. Justin smirked in response and turned his attention away from Travis and back to Ears and Raheim.

"I'll be handlin' shit from here, fellas. Thanks for holding it down so long, but I'm here now. I got it." Justin nodded his head to the two men in a sarcastic bow before crossing his arms in front of him, showing off the gold-plated, triangle-barreled Desert Eagle he held firmly in his hand. Finger already resting close to the trigger. He signaled that what he said was not a request. Travis's face screwed up in confusion. He had been out the game a few years, but from the way it sounded, Justin was the man in charge, and he knew good and well that that could not be.

The head nigga on the streets for years, even when he was in the game, was the nigga Ears. There were a few other niggas (himself included), who did their thing on the streets and made a nice little amount of money. But everyone knew Ears was really the man in charge of anybody eating. If he wanted to, with one phone call, he could've shut down the whole city of Cincinnati and not one drop of product would've been able to come in or out without his word. So, Travis was a bit confused on why this lame nigga Justin thought he could walk up in a meeting he wasn't even invited to and call shots. He knew with everything in him that the shit wasn't gon' work like that and he wished like hell that he hadn't actually left his gun in the car like they'd said to do. He didn't even fuck with Ears or Raheim, but killing this Justin would've brought him pure, unadulterated joy.

"We, uh . . . listen, man, we . . ." Raheim stuttered.

"We? We? We what, nigga? We what? We thought y'all was just gon' take over all this and move how y'all wanted to with no permission? Is that what we thought? Huh?" Justin taunted Raheim for the stumble and stutter in his speech. "Come on, nigga. Let's hear it. We what?"

Justin scratched his temple with the gun he held, feigning confusion. You could see the fear that rose up in both Raheim and Ears. Travis was lost and almost scared. The events taking place in his face were so far outside of his understanding that he felt once again like he was in middle school and his super smart teacher Mr. Coleman was still trying to teach him algebra. He couldn't process what was happening here at all.

"We what? Huh? Say somethin'. Tell me what we. I don't even know the we you mean 'cause I wasn't even invited to this li'l shindig y'all have here." He gestured around with his gun hand. "So, since we're on the subject, why didn't I get an invite? Huh? Raheim? Tony?" he asked each of the niggas separately and actually waited for them to answer.

Travis waited too because now he wanted to know who the hell Tony was and why Ears hadn't shut this shit down yet instead of standing there looking like a bitch-ass nigga. And to think, he was really gon' do what these niggas said if it meant saving his life. He was going to give in to these bitch-ass niggas. His anger swelled. He looked around through the crowd to see who the Tony nigga was who Justin wanted to speak up, but every last one of them niggas looked shook. He was starting to really get pissed. This shit never went down like this when he was running the streets. Somebody would've already been dead. Starting with this nigga Justin.

"Look, Ears, man, we—"

"Nah, nigga," Justin cut him off. "I'm not tryin'a hear this 'we' shit again. I gave you niggas time to explain we and y'all didn't. So now, fuck 'we,' nigga." Justin raised his gun and shot Ears through the eyes. He fell dead where he stood. Raheim damn near jumped out his skin when the gun went off. It looked to Travis like the bitch-ass nigga was going to pee on himself.

"Wait a minute," Travis spoke up, stepping out from behind two of the men who took him captive. One of them stuck a big, beefy arm out to stop him. "Nigga, pull yo' arm up off me before I take it with me," Travis threatened.

The huge guy looked to Justin with unmasked terror in his eyes. Travis shook his head and flung the man's arm out of his way, now knowing that the nigga was soft as cake. He proceeded into the inner circle where Justin stood.

"How the fuck you beefin' with me over nothin' but let this lame-ass nigga up in here to call shots and kill yo' homeboy? And what kind of niggas is y'all to let y'all employer go out like this? Y'all should've popped this nigga soon as he came through the crowd like he was runnin' shit. I don't know what the fuck y'all niggas got goin' on, but back in the day, this shit would've never went down with my crew. Me and him would've been dead on arrival. Fuck the small talk. You niggas is pussy. Get me the fuck up outta here. Tell ya bitch-made-ass driver to take me back to my car before I really get mad. I don't have time for this." Travis had flown off the hook, but by this point, he didn't even care. They were either going to let him go or kill him where he stood, and from the looks of things, he was pretty sure he'd stay alive. "What the fuck do you even want from me?"

"I, uh, we figured—"

"Nigga, fuck you. Bitch-ass nigga." Travis turned and pushed through the crowd of men, heading back to the SUV he had been brought here in after spitting on the ground in front of Raheim and mean mugging him and Justin both.

He stopped at the guy in the back of the crowd and asked for the keys to the car he pulled up in. When the guy took too long handing them over, he hit him square dead in the nose and took them from his pocket once he fell to the ground, screaming and holding his nose as he gushed blood all over himself.

Shots rang out over his head and stopped him in his tracks. Slowly, he turned around. "So what is it that we need to do?" Travis asked when he turned around toward Justin with outstretched arms. "I don't fuck wit' you and you don't fuck wit' me. So, what's up? What the fuck is this weird shit? What is up wit' you niggas?" He faced Justin, ready for the smoke he assumed he was ready to deliver. Either they was gon' fight with hands up like men, or Justin was going to shoot him. Either way, he was done playing this game with these niggas.

"It's funny you should ask." Justin smiled at Travis like he knew something that Travis didn't. "I've recently had a job opening and I'd like to offer the job to you." He smiled.

"A job opening? Nigga!" Travis burst out into one of the hardest laughs he'd ever laughed. "Nigga, what? You want me to sell goofy-ass suits and ties or some cufflinks or some shit? What the fuck could you possibly hire me to do?" Travis laughed some more at Justin's expense. "A job? Nigga, you corny as fuck."

"I'm glad you think so. Everyone has always thought so. Which is why I stay in business and bum-ass niggas like him"—he gestured toward a dead Ears who still lay on the ground at Raheim's feet—"don't. Being corny suits me. It gets me to where I need to go. And because of that, it's put me in a position where I help niggas eat and I'm ready for you to be one of those niggas."

"Man, y'all zoning me out. Say what the fuck is going on here so I can get gone. I don't fuck wit' yo' corny ass.

I don't fuck with that lame-ass nigga." He pointed to Raheim. "And I didn't even know that nigga Ears for real, so fuck him. I don't know these weak-ass niggas." He gestured to the crowd of thugs who still stood around them watching and listening but not moving on anyone.

"So, I don't even know why I'm here. What the fuck do you niggas want? I got shit I can be doing. Either kill me or leave me the fuck alone."

"Well, first, nigga, you not doing shit but tryin'a find someone to go home with so you don't have to live life alone with yo' miserable ass. And second, that bum-ass nigga is not Ears." Justin didn't laugh as should be expected, but he did display a wide-mouthed, pearly white smile. Travis would've bet that he still had all his teeth and paid good money to get them cleaned.

"He ain't Ears?"

"No, he's not."

"So then who the fuck is he?"

"Was he. Who the fuck was he, 'cause he's no one anymore."

"Nigga, cut the games," Travis urged, getting frustrated.

"He wasn't Ears."

"So who the fuck is then?"

"Me. Why you think these niggas ain't shoot me when I walked out? These are my niggas. They work for me. As does Raheim and what used to be his partner."

Travis's eyes dropped once again to the dead man on the ground. He was confused. Justin couldn't be Ears. Ears was one of the most ruthless niggas in the game and in the city. He had also just done mass years in the joint. There was no way the clean-cut, corny dude standing in front of him was the same man who had a whole city shook by just saying his name. Travis never gave enough of a fuck to find out exactly who Ears was. When he was in the streets, he handled his business and then got out when the time presented itself. He and Ears never had a reason to run into each other, giving him no reason to ever be scared or even worried about who the mysterious dude was. Hearing Justin now say that he was Ears wasn't sitting right with him, but Justin's points made sense. The niggas hadn't shot him when he popped up on what he assumed was a secret meeting, and Raheim did seem scared to death of the man who stood before him. But now he needed to know why he wanted anything to do with him.

"So, you telling me this to say what?"

"To say what I've been saying. That I want you to work for me. Get back in these streets and make us some money." Justin went over how Vic, Raheim, and the dead nigga, whose name he found out was Tony, had been his main men the whole time. Tony pretended to be him and took the fall for him when Cincinnati's Finest thought they had finally got him and was bringing his reign to an end. The police never found out that Tony was never the man behind the madness, Justin was. And when they "caught him," Tony took his place and Ears devised a different plan and switched up his whole operation. Because he always stayed out the limelight, no one was the wiser. Except a very small group of people. Justin had found out that they had not only been fucking up his money, but also trying to put together a master plan to get him out the way and take over themselves. He took now as the opportunity to get rid of the problem as a whole and bring in new talent to carry on business as usual. That's why he was there. To take the spot as his top dog and run the streets while he stayed hidden from the world, handling things legitimately.

"If all this is the case," Travis interrupted, "why is that nigga still alive?" He motioned toward Raheim and watched his face go sheet white.

"I have bigger plans for him." Justin threw a smirk Raheim's way and Travis just knew he was going to faint.

"So, you expect me to forget everything that's between us and just work for you like some bottom-feeding bitch?"

"Absolutely not. Not entirely. I don't expect you to be a bottom-feeding bitch at all. I expect you to be my right-hand man." The two men looked each other in the eye. Justin continued, "I apologize that you had to live the lie that you did, but it was the only way to keep Kiesha and my kids safe. Once I saw that she was falling too hard for you, I tried to keep her away from you too, but as you can see, she insisted on living out this lie and you never finding out the truth. My kids would get the father they deserved and you thinking you had a bigger reason to live would get you out the game and out of a lot of people's way. I would've never agreed to you leaving the streets, but when Sheila decided to go turn yo' ass in back in the day and the heat was gonna come down on you and my baby mama, I did what I had to do to keep you out here. My baby mama stayed safe and her mom was able to stay alive. It was never the plan to have four kids with her. It just happened that way. I'm sorry that you had to go through that, but the cards are played how they're dealt."

"What the fuck did any of that have to do with me? Why not just let me get bagged?"

"Because you made more money than any nigga on the streets. Besides me that is." He smiled and it rubbed Travis the wrong way, but he understood. Everything and everybody was part of the game when it came to the streets. "My plan was to eventually put you on my team. But then Kiesha got pregnant. When you found out and started working to go legit, it was the smartest move I ever saw from a street nigga. I admired that and followed in your steps. With niggas like us out here, we can't be stopped."

Travis mulled it over silently in his brain. Justin was right about that. The way Justin was able to avoid even being known in these streets could be an asset to him. They were both legit now and no one would ever expect Justin to be a part of anything illegal. It was actually perfect.

"But what about these people that know who you are?" Travis questioned.

"They've all been . . . taken care of." Everyone's eyes traveled to Tony who lay on the ground with no signs of life left in him.

"And him?" Travis questioned. Justin turned to look at Raheim. He shrugged.

"He's no longer my problem." Travis took the gun from the hand of the man standing closest to him and without hesitation, put a bullet in Raheim's head. Raheim never even had the time to protest. Justin looked at Travis with the smile he'd been carrying for most of the night. "I take that as a yes?"

"I run shit my way, you run your shit yours. I don't work for you. We work together. We get this money and stay out of each other's way. Don't ever fuckin' cross me," Travis threatened.

"All I ask is the same. Oh, and for Kiesha's safety." Travis thought it over in a few quick seconds. He stepped to Justin eye to eye. The two men understood in that moment what wasn't being said, then shook hands. Travis handed Justin the dirty gun, zipped his jacket back up, and turned to walk away. Justin signaled for one of the guys to follow Travis. The two men got back into the black SUV and pulled off. Both men, Travis and Justin, held eye contact until they were out of each other's sight.

Chapter 25

"I'm sorry, baby. I got here as quick as I could," Justin apologized to Ke'Lasia after she let him into her place.

"What's wrong?" Ke'Lasia, not being able to hold it in anymore, poured out the whole story to Justin as tears ran down her face. Justin listened quietly and held her as she cried. He didn't interrupt. He listened carefully to everything she said, masking his rage at the clear love she had for another man. "It's going to be fine, love. Just fine. You'll be fine. It'll hurt, but you'll be fine." He rocked and coddled her through her tears.

He never thought that when he slipped in that night and killed that fool Slash that Ke'Lasia would be this torn up about it. He thought they were just fucking. Never did he think that she would be devastated behind it or he would've planned it differently. Slash was going to die either way, he just would've made sure it didn't affect Ke'Lasia. Especially not like this. If anything, he would've thought it would've been September who reacted this way. But he'd spoken to and seen her several times in the few days since Slash's death and she hadn't even mentioned it. Not since she first admitted to knowing he was dead. He didn't know if it was the drugs clouding September or the obvious love ruining Ke'Lasia. All he knew was that the two women reacted very differently, and he hadn't planned on it. It was September who was supposed to be devastated behind this, not Ke'Lasia.

Justin sat and held his woman until she finally let the tears diminish and fell asleep in his arms. He laid her down, tucked her in, and went to take a shower. He grabbed the bag he walked in with and closed the bathroom door behind him.

The constant beeping and vibrating woke Ke'Lasia from her restless sleep. She searched around, confused as to where the noise was coming from. Fumbling around in the dark, her fingers found the vibrating phone under the covers. With half-sleepy eyes, she answered for September.

"What?"

"What? Who is this?" she yelled into the phone.

"Bitch, who'd you call? Chill out. Stop screaming. My head already hurts."

"Ke'Lasia?" September asked, her voice calming down some but sounding confused at the same time.

"Duh. Who else would be answering my phone? What do you want, September?"

"Yeah? Well, I didn't call your phone. I called Justin."

"Justin?" Ke'Lasia took the phone away from her ear confused. She clicked on the nightstand lamp and sat up. Now seeing the phone in the light, she saw that the phone she'd answered was in fact not hers. Even though September's picture was displayed happily on the screen, it was not the screen of Ke'Lasia's Galaxy S9 Plus. This was Justin's phone with September on it.

Ke'Lasia put the phone back to her ear. "Why would you be calling Justin?" she asked her ex-friend.

"Because I can. Why the fuck are you answering his phone?" she shouted back, her attitude becoming hostile all over again.

"Because I can. Justin is my man."

"Your man?" September repeated in disbelief. "Girl, Justin is not yo' fuckin' man. I swear you so thirsty for attention."

"September, it's three a.m. If Justin isn't my man, why is he here? Why is he in my shower washing his nuts? And why was I able to answer his phone? Not that I did it on purpose, but the fact that I was able to should let you know something. I don't have to lie to you, girl. Not now, and never have I," Ke'Lasia reasoned with her.

"I'm on my way."

September hung the phone up, leaving Ke'Lasia sitting there dazed and confused. She didn't understand what just happened or what was about to happen, but she prepared for the worst. She knew shit between her and September would eventually hit the fan. She just didn't know Justin would be involved when it did.

"I thought you were asleep." Justin looked confused when his eyes fell on Ke'Lasia sitting up in the bed. "What's wrong?" Justin wasn't the smartest man in the world, but he was no fool either. He knew that anytime a man walked into a room with a quiet black woman who had her hair tied up and an attitude, it wasn't a good situation.

"You tell me what's wrong, Justin, 'cause I'm pretty confused." He looked at her with one eyebrow raised. He hadn't the slightest clue as to what she was talking about. He didn't say anything. He just stood there in his towel, still drying off his hair. "You just got a phone call."

"Okay?"

"It woke me up out my sleep. Actually, the four before it woke me up. The last one just pissed me off."

"Why? It's not like it was another female, so what you mad for?"

Ke'Lasia pinched the bridge of her nose with her eyes closed. She could already see that this nigga was just like the rest of them. She thought she was prepared to hear him lie, but now that it was really happening, she was more irritated than before this started.

"Justin, I reeeeally don't feel like playin' games wit' you. The bitch called and I answered. I thought it was my phone in the bed, so I didn't even pay attention to the fact that it wasn't."

"Ke'Lasia, what the hell are you talking about? No woman is calling me. I'm not messing with no woman outside of you."

"You can drop the professional voice. You're busted. I'm not mad. I knew what you were before we fucked. I knew you got around. I just didn't care. Shit, you know my business, all of it. So, you fuckin' somebody else ain't shit. I'm just tryin'a figure out why you chose to do whatever the fuck you're doing with September."

"September?" Justin echoed. He was stuck. He didn't know what to say. He knew he'd heard her correctly, he was just lost on how they got there. How the fuck did she figure he was fucking with September? No one knew about him even knowing that girl. But the better question to him was, why was September even calling this late?

"Yeah, September," Ke'Lasia repeated with mass attitude attached to the words. "Why is September callin' you?" She looked him square dead in the eyes. He figured that it wasn't gon' be no getting out of this, but he honestly didn't know what to say.

"Hello? Speak up, nigga. What the fuck is September doin' callin' yo' phone at damn near four o'clock in the morning?" The attitude coming from Ke'Lasia reminded Justin of Kiesha. The same neck and hand movements that Kiesha did, Ke'Lasia was now doing them. They made him want to slap the shit out of her too. He hated being accused of anything, especially inadvertently.

"I don't know why she's calling me," he finally answered with what he deemed as the truth. He didn't know why September was calling because he hadn't been the one to answer the phone. He also knew that wasn't what she asked, so her angry outburst was expected.

"You think I'm some kinda fool? Huh? You think I don't know what it looks like when a nigga fuckin' around? What? You think you the only nigga that's had a side bitch before?" She rolled her eyes getting up off the bed. "I'm not trippin'. Fuck it," she said, calming down. "You wanna fuck these hoes? Go ahead. I don't give a fuck. Just know ain't either one of us no virgin nigga." She rolled her eyes and brushed past him, mugging him in the side of his head. Justin grabbed Ke'Lasia by the arm to stop her from leaving.

"What are you talkin' about, bay? I'm not gonna play these games with you. Just tell me what it is you're talking about so we can be done with this."

"I told you what it was. September called your phone. I answered. Now you tell me what the fuck is up 'cause, nigga, regardless, we done."

"Done?"

"You heard me, fool."

"Ke'Lasia, quit playing with me. This shit is lame as fuck." Ke'Lasia turned to walk out the room once she heard the knock at the door. "Just call her back so we can clear this up, man, damn," he challenged her while thrusting his phone in her direction.

"Don't trip." She halfway smiled at him. "We're definitely gonna clean this shit up."

She turned and walked out the room. Justin took that time to throw on some sweats before he followed her downstairs to see who in the world could be at the door at this hour.

Chapter 26

"September?"

"Yeah, nigga, September." Ke'Lasia had that evil, half grin back on her face again.

"What are you doing here?" Ke'Lasia could've sworn she heard nervousness bubbling in Justin's throat. She couldn't do nothing but shake her head. The only thing in her life that hadn't been too good to be true was Slash, and he was gone. Justin reminded her of that. He reminded her that he wasn't nothing but an option she should've left at that.

"Justin, what you doing here? She talkin' about you her man and shit. What the fuck is goin' on?" September asked as she pushed her way through Ke'Lasia's front door.

"Calm down. We can figure all this out." Justin had that condescending-ass tone again that pissed Ke'Lasia off every time.

"Ain't shit to figure out. You can go grab yo' shit and be out wit' yo' bitch." Ke'Lasia stepped to the side of the still open door, signaling for them both to get the fuck out.

"His bitch?" September spun around on her, confused. Ke'Lasia stood firm with her arms crossed. Her head gestured toward the door. "Wait a minute. Who is his bitch?" September asked.

"Bitch, you! You came to get him, so take his ass with you."

"No, I came to see for myself if he was actually here."

"Okay. Well now you see. And now you can get him and actually get the fuck out."

"Nobody's going anywhere," Justin interrupted. "Ke'Lasia, close the door and come sit down. We can all talk about this. It has been long overdue anyway."

"Nigga, nobody's sitting down nowhere," September told him.

"Shut yo' ass up and have a seat." He pointed to the couch like he was really running something. Both females rolled their eyes in disregard of his commands.

"I'm ready to lie down. Can y'all please get the fuck outta here? I don't need to sit down or hear none of this bullshit. Just please, get the fuck out. I don't care about y'all fuckin' around. It is what it is by this point. Right back ain't cheatin'."

"Ke'Lasia, I told you already, I'm not fuckin' her. I'm not, and I never would." Justin rubbed his face in frustration and asked again for the ladies to sit down. Ke'Lasia couldn't believe her ears.

"Nigga, don't ever disrespect her in my face. We ain't gotta be friends no more, but right is right and wrong is wrong. Don't do that for some pussy. That's some bitch-ass nigga shit."

"Ke'Lasia," Justin simply said, asking her again with his tone. Ke'Lasia turned to September who now sat on the couch as Justin had asked her to do.

"Nah, September. Fuck that. This nigga got us fucked up. He really gon' stand here and lie to be able to fuck with both of us, knowin' we were cool? Fuck that. And you just gon' sit there and let the shit happen, huh? Both you mu'fuckas sick as fuck."

Ke'Lasia flung the door closed and stormed toward the kitchen with an attitude. She grabbed a juice from the fridge even though she wasn't thirsty. She just needed something to do to get the fuck out of there with them. This shit was too much. She just wanted them to leave. She honestly just wished she could lie under Slash and fall asleep. She was over this shit already and ready to go to bed, forgetting about all this shit as best as she could as soon as possible.

Justin rounded the corner to see Ke'Lasia standing at the refrigerator with tears pouring down her face. His heart fell into his stomach. As much as he wanted to, he couldn't tell her what she needed to know. That was going to have to come from September and September only.

"Come on, baby, please. Just hear me out." He reached for her, wanting nothing more than to just hold her. Only, she pulled away from him again. His heart hurt more. "Ke'Lasia, please just come in here. You want answers, but you not listening. How that's fair? If you gon' accuse me of some shit, at least give me the chance to explain." She looked at him with her tear-filled eyes and shook her head. There was nothing left that would make her feel worse than she already did. She conceded and headed toward the couch.

Ke'Lasia passed by Justin without so much as brushing against him. She did everything she could to not touch him. The thought of him fucking September and her made her stomach turn. She knew what she was doing with Slash, but that was different. They weren't even together anymore when she started fucking with him. She never knew Justin was fucking with them both at the same time. This shit was just entirely too much for her. Ke'Lasia sat on the couch with September, but on the other end. She continued to let the tears fall from her face, unashamed of her feelings.

"September, we gotta talk to her," Justin coaxed.

"Ain't nothing to say to her. This bitch don't listen to nothin', and I ain't got shit to say. I'm tryin'a figure out what you doin' here. You still ain't answered that."

"First of all, watch your mouth. Second, that's my woman. She told you that."

"I don't give a fuck what she told me. Why you ain't tell me?"

"It wasn't a secret. We just hadn't talked about it."

"How the fuck would we talk about some shit like that? Justin, you should've told me this shit." September wiped her face. Her eyes stung from being up for hours and her high was starting to come down. She could only regret not getting high first before she flew out the door to come here and confront them.

"What difference would it have made?"

"I wouldn't have been telling you my fuckin' business if I knew you was over here pillow talkin' wit' this bitch."

"I asked you to watch your fuckin' mouth," Justin said through gritted teeth.

"Fuck what you asked me and fuck you. Fuck this bitch too. What did you tell her?"

"I didn't tell her anything."

"Don't lie, Justin."

"What was he supposed to not tell me?" Ke'Lasia interrupted. Both of them got quiet. No one said a word. They both remained quiet. Justin looked at September expectantly while September looked at him with clamped lips.

"September, say something."

"I'm not sayin' shit. I'm sure she already knows too much of my fuckin' business already. This shit crazy. I can't even fuckin' believe I'm here." She stood up.

"September, this shit is serious. You can't leave without tellin' her what's up."

"Fuck you. Did you tell her your side?" Justin looked at her hard, almost deadly. Warning her with his eyes to not say anything else except what he needed her to say. She didn't take heed. "Oh! Now you quiet and shit? What's up? You just wanted her to know soooo much, but now the cat got your tongue, huh?" She laughed in his face, pissing Justin smooth off. "That's what the fuck I thought, nigga." She winked at him teasingly as she tried to evade the request he had given her.

"September, don't play with me. Tell her."

"I'm not tellin' her shit. You want me to tell her some shit, you start. You tell her yo' shit and I'll tell her mine. Other than that, I'm not sayin' shit." Tears welled up in Justin's eyes that he tried vehemently to blink away before either of the ladies could see. He never wanted Ke'Lasia to have to know the truth, but now, he had no choice. September had him backed into a corner by his balls. He could see no way out of this one. He broke a sweat watching her sit there with her arms folded, silently trying to force her to speak up.

"Right. That's what the fuck I thought," September gloated when Justin remained silent. "This some weird-ass creep shit going on here. I'm finna head out. Whatever the fuck you told her, I hope it was worth it," September said, standing up from her seated position on the couch, opposite Ke'Lasia.

"September used to fuck with Slash!" Justin blurted out.

"No shit," they heard from Ke'Lasia. September's head spun toward her.

"What you mean no shit?" she queried.

"September, I was at your house. I met him. How was I not supposed to know?"

"So you saying that to say what?"

"He's telling you that I was fuckin' with him too."

"Ke'Lasia," Justin urged.

"He was my man, September." Ke'Lasia rolled her eyes.

The room fell silent for a while. Ke'Lasia looked from Justin to September as they held their own stare between the two of them. September's eyes bore holes into Justin, silently pleading with him to keep quiet.

This whole ordeal had taken a turn September didn't plan for. She had only come over to go the fuck off on Justin because she assumed he had already spilled her beans all over. She never dreamed that she would be the one who had to tell. This was not going right. She had to go.

"Fuck this. This some bullshit that I ain't for." September started toward the door again.

"September." Justin's voice stopped her in her tracks. She knew what was coming next. She willed herself to finish her journey toward the door, but her feet wouldn't move. Her body was frozen in place. Her mind was going wild. Her brain screamed at Justin to just shut the fuck up. She couldn't understand why he was doing this to her.

This was never what they discussed. "Isn't there something you want to say to Ke'Lasia?"

"Hell no. And nothin' you wanna say either if you wanna keep your license," she threatened him, now up in his face. She was breathing so hard that he almost thought she would start foaming at the mouth. Justin knew he was playing with fire here, but what was about to happen had to be done.

"If that's what you feel like is necessary, then you do what you have to. But you told me that you wished you and Ke'Lasia could repair y'all relationship. You're here now. In the middle of the night. You didn't come over here for nothing."

"I came to make sure you were keeping your mouth shut about me to this bitch. You said you'd never say anything! You promised! You took a fuckin' oath! What the fuck kinda shit is this?" She unfurled. Anger seeped through her every word. Justin knew she was only minutes away from breaking down.

September walked over to the breakfast nook at the entrance of the kitchen. Mumbling fast and furiously to herself, she slammed her purse down and began to rummage through it.

"September, not now. You're so close. This is what you need," encouraged Justin.

"Fuck you!" she spat, pulling out items that weren't so foreign to any of them.

"What the fuck is that?" Ke'Lasia asked, descending upon September. "What are you doing? I know good and well that's not what I think it is." Ke'Lasia got close enough to September to peer over her shoulder despite the fact that she was trying to keep her vision blocked.

"Mind yo' fuckin' business."

"You got that shit up in my house, it is my business. Girl, have you lost yo' muthafuckin' mind?" September turned to look at Ke'Lasia. Tears were now in her eyes. Her bottom lip trembled. To Ke'Lasia, September looked just like that frightened little girl who got left at her house all those years ago. Her heart broke for her old friend. "September, what are you doing to yourself, girl?" Ke'Lasia spoke soothingly as she reached out for September's hand. September snatched away.

"Fuck you! Don't come over here with that 'aw, poor baby' bullshit you always tryin'a pull on me! Fuck you, Miss Perfect!" she spat, disgusted. "Miss I'm better than you. Miss my fuckin' life always goes in my favor. Everybody ain't fuckin' like you! Some of us have demons to fight. I know yo' ass wouldn't know shit about that, but some of us aren't as good as you. Some of us fail."

"You haven't failed yet. You're still here. You're still fighting and you don't need that shit. You just need to want to, September. Remember? We talked about this. When you get down, you come to me or find you a therapist. Not this. September, never this." Ke'Lasia gestured toward the drugs September grasped tightly in her palm.

"You don't get to fuckin' tell me what to do! You don't get to tell me how to fight! You don't get to judge me!"

"I'm not judging you. I'm trying to help. We'll find you a therapist. We'll get you help. I'll help you, September, but please, not this."

Ke'Lasia's tears fell anew down her cheeks. Her heart broke for her friend. She hadn't realized in all this time how much September actually meant to her. She hadn't remembered how much they needed each other until she saw what was once like a sister to her, standing there, giving her problems to the same drugs her own mom had. She couldn't freeze September out now. She couldn't not give a fuck. She had to step in in some way, no matter if September liked it or not. Ke'Lasia refused to see someone else she loved lost, especially to drugs. She wouldn't do it.

"I did find somebody. Him." She flung her arm in Justin's direction as she let the tears finally pour out.

"He was supposed to help me. But after he found out I knew you and I was the friend that you weren't cool with anymore, all he cared about was fixing us. All he cared about was you."

"Me?" Ke'Lasia turned to look at a quiet Justin.

"Yeah, you. Just you. You were everything. You are everything. All anyone ever cares about is you, never me. I'm always lost on the outside looking in at all the people that want to break their necks to help Miss Perfect-ass Ke'Lasia. Well, what the fuck about me? September needs attention, help, and love too gotdammit! What the fuck about me? Huh, Justin? What the fuck about September, Ke'Lasia? What the fuck about me?" September broke then, right before their very eyes. She crumbled to the ground, symbolic of a piece of notebook paper being balled up and thrown to the side.

"I love you, September. I always have. It's always been about you," Ke'Lasia reasoned, bending down to cradle her friend in her arms. Her heart going out to the pain she never knew her friend felt.

"No, it hasn't! That's a lie!" she screamed, pulling away from Ke'Lasia's embrace again. "That's a fuckin' lie and you know it! Everybody cares about Ke'Lasia!" She sobbed.

"Everybody. But who's left to care about me? Who's left to give even one fuck about me? You get everything and everybody. You got a mom. Two of them! Even though your mom was fucked up and mine left me, they both cared more about you. You got a dad and a family. You got every friend and every nigga I ever wanted had to be gone off me before they even met you. Even Travis wanted you and not me," she pouted.

"September, I—"

"You what? You knew. You always knew it and you never cared. You always got the best end of everything in life while I struggled for anything. Slash was the only thing I ever had to myself. And Justin. Until you that is. All it took was one look at you and they both lost their fuckin' minds."

Ke'Lasia's eyes trailed to Justin. Guilt began to eat her alive. He knew all of this and never said anything. As much as she wanted to be angry with him, she knew that it wasn't his fault. She had years to give a fuck about her friend and she never even paid enough attention to notice that anything was wrong. When she helped September kick alcohol in high school, she just thought she was trying to look cool to the guys. She never knew it was deeper, but she never asked either. The realization that her friend had been hurting right in her face the whole time only made her feel worse.

"You just had to have them too, didn't you? Just like everything the fuck else. Nothing can just be for me, can it? You just gotta have every fuckin' thing." She glared at Ke'Lasia with a look of death.

"What? Me?" Ke'Lasia stood up and backed away. "I didn't go looking for either one of them! Slash's ass came to me. He said y'all had been done fuckin' around. He came to me. And Justin was my therapist. How the fuck was I supposed to know you were seeing him too?"

"I wasn't until after I was seeing you. I met September on the humble and tried to get on. You and I weren't serious yet. You were still worried about that lame-ass nigga. Once I heard her speak, the sadness in her voice let me know that she needed help. I found out she was your friend our second session. But after she confessed to me that she was diagnosed with HIV after she got shot, I couldn't stop seeing her."

"HIV? September! Why wouldn't you tell me?" Ke'Lasia reacted, astonished.

"Same reason he didn't tell you he killed Slash." All sorts of things went through Ke'Lasia's mind in that moment. She couldn't figure out what the words meant that September had just said.

"You killed Slash?" Ke'Lasia asked Justin.

"He's also Ears." The word swirled around Ke'Lasia. It felt like the ground had just literally shifted.

"Is this the reason why you wanted to fuck with me? To get close? To find out what happened?" Justin just looked at her, lost for words. "Why didn't you just ask me?" Justin still just looked on. Still not saying anything. Finally, he spoke.

"You both sent me to jail."

"You killed my mom," was Ke'Lasia's rebuttal. "I didn't give a fuck what happened to you." Justin shrugged like it was no big deal.

"So now we're here."

"And now what?" Ke'Lasia asked.

"Now we all know what's up."

"So now what?" she repeated.

"We either call a truce and stay out of each other's way, or we end it here," Justin decided.

"Fuck that. I'm on yo' ass, nigga. From this day forward, I'm on yo' ass. You killed my mom wit' them dumb-ass drugs, and now my best friend is addicted to the same shit. Ain't nothin' about this gon' be over until yo' ass is dead or in jail. Period." Ke'Lasia looked Justin in the eye. She needed him to know that she meant exactly what she had said.

"Your best friend?" September asked, confused.

"Yes, my best friend. I never stopped loving you and now I see you need me more than ever. I get it now, and I'm here for you. We'll get through this together," Ke'Lasia promised. But it was too late for September.

"Nah. I'm cool. You done turned your back on me too many times. I don't need you. I spared you, but I don't need you."

"Spared me?"

"Yeah, I spared yo' ass. Justin was going to kill you a long time ago, but I stopped him. Then he chose to get close to you instead. I couldn't keep him from doing that. You must got magic pussy or some shit, but I don't care about none of that no more. This shit ends here." September pulled out a gun and a box. "You have a choice."

"What the fuck, September? We didn't talk about this," Justin started. September held her hand up to stop him.

"I'm tired of savin' this bitch 'cause you niggas wanna keep fuckin' her. You heard her say she would never let you go on free. Why would she stay alive? Why do you want her alive so bad?"

"Because I love her, September. I told you that," Justin admitted for the first time in front of Ke'Lasia. She was taken aback.

"I don't give a fuck about that! Didn't you just hear what she said? What the fuck is wrong with you?" September yelled at Justin.

"I don't care about that. It's not that serious. I'll be okay. We'll stay out of each other's way, and eventually, she'll heal." They spoke like Ke'Lasia didn't share the room they conversed in.

"I—" Ke'Lasia started.

"Fuck this," September interrupted. She let off a shot that rang out through the house.

"Are you fuckin' serious?" Ke'Lasia yelled.

"Shit!" Justin hollered.

"I fuckin' told you I was tired of sparing you and that's what I meant," she growled at Ke'Lasia, who now understood, in this moment, that her and September would never be friends ever again.

"September."

"No. I'm tired of you winning. I'm tired of you getting everything you want and fuckin' over anybody around you, oblivious to what you're doing and other people's feelings. I said fuck you and I meant it. Fuck you. If I can't be happy, yo' ass can't either." And with that, September let off another shot to seal the deal. Then she tucked the gun away and headed for the door with no sign of remorse whatsoever. "I can't ever heal my hurt, and now, you can't either," she threw over her shoulder as she walked out the door.

"911. What is your emergency?"

"Someone has been shot. I need an ambulance right now." Ke'Lasia answered the questions that the dispatcher asked her as she watched Justin bleed to death on her floor. She calmly took a seat at her breakfast nook to be sure that she didn't disturb the crime scene and waited on the emergency vehicles to arrive. She smiled when she finally heard the sirens, letting her know that they were approaching.

September had thought she'd won, but she was never too bright. What Ke'Lasia and Travis planned all along had come to pass. Travis, aka Freight, was now, once again, the biggest fuckin' drug dealer in Cincinnati with no one to stand in his way while Ke'Lasia got revenge on the man who killed her mother. And now, she would finally be able to rid herself of that hatin'-ass bitch September while she rotted away in prison for the rest of her life. Shit couldn't get any sweeter than that. September thought Ke'Lasia would be devastated about the death of Justin, but she was wrong. That's exactly what she wanted. She was honestly sad about Slash. His death hit harder than she imagined, but she knew it all came with the territory. It was what it was.

"It's done," Ke'Lasia said into the phone.

"Damn, that was fast. What happened?" Travis asked.

"I'll tell you tomorrow. I'm tired."

"All right. See you soon."